RAVEN MOON

A HOWARD MOON DEER MYSTERY

Books by Robert Westbrook

Howard Moon Deer Mysteries
Ghost Dancer
Warrior Circle
Red Moon
Ancient Enemy
Turquoise Lady
Blue Moon
Hungry Ghost
Walking Rain
Eagle Falls
Raven Moon

Coming Soon!
Floating Moon
A Howard Moon Deer Mystery

The Torch Singer *series*
An Overnight Sensation
An Almost Perfect Ending

Left-Handed Policeman *series*
The Left-Handed Policeman
Nostalgia Kills
Lady Left

Other Books
Intimate Lies:
F. Scott Fitzgerald and Sheilah Graham – Her Son's Story
Journey Behind the Iron Curtain
The Magic Garden of Stanley Sweetheart
Rich Kids

For more information
visit: www.SpeakingVolumes.us

RAVEN MOON

A HOWARD MOON DEER MYSTERY

Robert Westbrook

SPEAKING VOLUMES, LLC
NAPLES, FLORIDA
2024

Raven Moon

Copyright © 2024 by Robert Westbrook

All rights reserved. No part of this book may be reproduced or transmitted in any form or by any means without written permission.

ISBN 979-8-89022-207-7

This is for my ski buddy and good friend, David Dawson—in memory of countless philosophical discussions on chairlifts, five minutes long, no dawdling, because when you reach the top you have to get off.

Author's Note

This is a work of fiction. A few elements in this story are true. Billionaires are indeed buying up the American West, as well as Congress, our democracy, and pretty much everything in sight. Some of the very rich have huge egos and behave like 2-year-olds, that's a fact. However, the billionaires in this story are entirely creatures of my imagination. Likewise, there is no ski area in New Mexico called San Geronimo Peak, there is no town of San Geronimo, no San Geronimo Pueblo. I have played freely with geography to suit my narrative needs. My goal is to entertain and perhaps suggest a broader truth than the factual one. Any similarity to real people and real events is entirely coincidental.

Chapter One

At 3:17 pm on the afternoon of Thursday, January 7th, the Wolf Lift at San Geronimo Peak stopped running—abruptly, with a jolt—leaving sixty-seven skiers and boarders dangling over the steep, snow covered mountain terrain below.

The marooned riders were the remains of the holiday crowd that had come for New Years and Christmas. They had been taking their last runs of the day before the chairlifts closed at 4 o'clock. The temperature was 19 degrees Fahrenheit and the barometer was falling, the wind rising. A winter storm was predicted, diving down into New Mexico from the Gulf of Alaska.

Chairlifts stop all the time, most often when low-level skiers fall either getting onto a chair or getting off, so at first it didn't seem like a big deal. But after five minutes, it was apparent that something was wrong.

The first responders were lift operators. The Wolf Lift was a high-speed quad that began halfway up the mountain and rose to the top, an elevation of 11,289 feet. There were two huts for the lifties, one at the base and one at the top of the lift. Working as a liftie was the easiest way to get employment at a winter resort. You didn't make much money but you got a pass and on your days off you could ski or snowboard as much as you liked. Generally, the life of a liftie was pleasant, a nice blend of fresh tracks and easy-going hedonism.

But not this afternoon.

Terry Holcombe, the senior liftie at the bottom, checked the dials of the humming console in the lift shack. Terry was 20 years-old, taking a year off from Bennington College, a nice guy but not an engineer. Everything looked good to him. There didn't seem to be any reason for the lift to stop.

Terry picked up the phone to Bubba McKinley, the senior liftie on the top and they discussed the situation. There was a backup diesel engine that could run the chairlift if the main engine died. But the problem wasn't the big turbine that ran the mother wheel at the bottom. They went through a number of checks, they climbed up into the overhead engine room, but they could find nothing wrong.

Terry radioed to Ski Patrol. "It's not the engine," he said. "It has to be the cable."

It was now 3:27. More than ten minutes had passed since the lift had stopped and the riders dangling in the air were beginning to get cold.

Seriously cold.

The head of lift operations, Tomás Julio Romero, was already on his way, riding a snowmobile up the lift line with two other mo's following close behind. Tomás was in his mid-70s, and he had been riding up and down these trails since childhood. His father and his grandfather had helped build the ski resort in the 1950s, cutting down trees, making trails, building the lifts—starting with a primitive T-bar that often pulled riders three feet off the ground. It had been a family operation at first, but from its humble beginning, more lifts had been built, trails were hacked out of the forest, and over the years San Geronimo Peak had become a major destination for high-end skiers and snowboarders in search of steep slopes, dry powder, and blue New Mexico skies.

Riding up the lift line in the convoy of three snowmobiles, Tomás and his team stopped at every tower to examine the cable overhead. On two occasions, he climbed the towers to a small work area on top, a platform from where he was able to see the cable as it passed through the rows of steel runners that guided the direction of the chairs to the next tower. Everything depended on the cable moving seamlessly past the towers. The cable was made of steel fibers woven together and was nearly an inch thick. It now held the lives of sixty-seven riders hanging helplessly in the air.

By 3:47 the temperature had fallen to 16 degrees. The riders on the lift had begun phoning and shouting chair to chair and to the trail below for help. This was an expensive sport and those who could afford it were accustomed to privilege, outraged at the inconvenience. Several were already writing savage reviews on Trip Advisor.

Ski Patrol was now fully involved in what had become a dangerous situation. Sean Basset, the head of Patrol, made the decision to begin the lift evacuation procedure in another fifteen minutes if the problem with the cable wasn't solved. One way or the other, the riders had to be brought down. They couldn't spend the night dangling in a storm. It was predicted to go below zero by morning.

As Tomás continued to inspect the line, there was something on Tower 7 that didn't look right to his practiced eye. Tomás was a small man, spidery and fit. He had spent a lifetime climbing towers and working on cables and chairs. Using a safety harness, he scampered up the narrow steel rungs on Tower 7 to the top. With a last pull on the handrails, he came out onto the platform.

The view from the top of Tower 7 was incredible. He had always loved it up here, from the time he was 7 years old when his father had taught him how to climb these towers. Now an old man, Tomás took a second to pay homage to the huge panorama of snow-covered mountains and sky, the Sangre de Cristo mountain range that marched mile after mile north into Colorado. There seemed no end to these mountains. The sky that defined them was cold with winter, a faded aquamarine color. Ahead of the storm, small clouds were rushing in from the northwest.

This was his land, the land of his people who had lived in these northern mountains and valleys of New Mexico for more than five hundred years. It wasn't simply that he loved these mountains. They were at the core of his being.

Tomás took a deep breath and returned his attention to the problem of why the lift had stopped running. People's lives were at stake.

He climbed higher, using the rough rebar footholds until the steel wheels that guided the cable over Tower 7 were directly above him. There was a row of upper wheels and a row of lower wheels through which the thick steel-woven cable passed. Tomás could see that there was something obstructing the cable on the uphill side of the tower, but he couldn't tell what it was. There was a black bulge about the size of a softball wedged against the cable at the place where it came to the two lines of wheels that guided the cable over the tower.

His radio burped to life. "Bill Friedman to Tomás on Yellow," said an anxious voice. "What the hell is going on up there?"

"I'm looking," Tomás answered, annoyed that he needed to stop and deal with management at a time like this. Bill Friedman was one of the numerous new vice-presidents of the resort. Yellow was the designated radio channel on the mountain reserved for heads of departments.

"Well, get the damn lift going! I thought you said those lifts were in perfect order! We trusted you. Didn't you do an inspection last fall?"

"Yes, and every lift passed the inspection," Tomás said in his calm, northern New Mexico lilt.

"Listen to me. There are people out there who are going to get frost bite if we don't get them down fast," said Friedman. His voice had risen half an octave. "We'll have lawsuits! So how long will it be?"

Tomás shook his head. Lawsuits!

Four years ago, a Wall Street billionaire had bought the ski resort and Tomás was well aware that the new management from back East were uncomfortable leaving multi-million dollar chairlifts in the hands of someone who hadn't gone to college. His credentials were very basic.

He had spent a lifetime taking these lifts apart and putting them back together again. He knew their every secret. But the new corporate people didn't like him. It was very simple, really. He was not their kind.

"I just arrived at the tower, Mr. Friedman. Why don't you give me a few minutes to figure out what's going on."

"Call me as soon as you know anything! And goddammit, get this problem fixed and do it fast!"

"Yes, yes, of course," said Tomás, thinking that perhaps he wouldn't mind getting fired. Recently he had been seeing bad things on the mountain, things he didn't like. He was old, the world had changed. He had turned his attention back to the cable when the riders in the nearby chairs began shouting at him.

"Hey, how much longer is this going to be?" shouted a skier in Chair 30.

"We're cold!" bellowed a snowboarder in Chair 32.

Down the fall line, Tomás could see twelve chairs dangling on the cable that fell sharply to Tower 6. Four of the twelve chairs between Tower 7 and Tower 6 had riders. Chair 32 had four riders, all snowboarders, filling up the quad. Teenagers. Two chairs behind them, in Chair 30, sat a middle-aged couple, skiers. On Chair 29 was a single man. On Chair 27, a woman sat by herself. She was moving her skis up and down, keeping her legs moving to stay warm.

Tomás made a vague gesture with his left arm that was meant to be reassuring. Beneath him three ski Patrollers in red jackets had appeared. A number of guests had stopped as well, curious to see the emergency. There were at least a dozen skiers now on the snow watching. Once again, his radio barked.

"Tomás, I gotta know if I should start the lift evac. What do you think?" asked Sean Basset, the head of Patrol.

"There's something on the cable," Tomás answered on his radio. "I don't know what it is. Let me climb up there and I'll get right back to you."

He reset his safety harness and climbed upward to the very top of the tower. As he got closer, he saw that the steel runners were mangled slightly so that they gripped the cable rather than allowing it to pass through. The metal here was blackened as though there had been a small explosion. With a sharp intake of breath, Tomás realized this was not a mechanical malfunction. Someone had done this deliberately. And unfortunately, he had a strong suspicion of who that somebody might be.

He was stretching upward to get a better look when he felt a sharp jab in the small of his back. It was like a mosquito sting, only the pain was worse, radiating from a small point into every part of his body.

With his free hand, he reached behind to the small of his back and was astonished to feel a small plastic projectile with fins protruding from the back of his parka.

It was a dart! Someone had shot him with a dart!

Tomás felt the sky fade and grow dark. The Earth trembled. He tried to hold on to the tower, but his body had lost its strength. His hands slipped and he fell backward into the air.

The safety harness stopped his fall with a hard jerk, leaving him hanging inert and unconscious twenty feet from the ground.

A woman screamed from Chair 30. "Oh, my God!" she cried. "Did you see that? He *fell*!"

"I don't believe this!" said her grumpy husband. "You pay $200 a day for a ticket and they can't even keep the lifts running! Next year, Doris, we're going to Vail!"

Chapter Two

Howard Moon Deer was skiing that January afternoon on the back side of the mountain, far from the Wolf Lift on the front, happily unaware of the growing emergency.

He was skiing by himself, unrecognizable beneath his helmet, goggles, neck warmer, sweater, and parka, in his own world of rhythm and turns, disconnected from the rest of the planet. He liked skiing alone, just himself and the snow. When you were in a group, you always ended up waiting for someone who wanted to stop for a bathroom break or a cup of coffee. In a large group there was usually an awkward social moment getting on a lift, deciding who would ride together, and who would be left to ride alone.

Howie was always happy to be the odd man out. "I'll meet you at the top," he would say, grateful for the silence, the time to breathe the glory of the mountains, no need to talk.

Today, Howie had driven up to the Peak in the early afternoon in a bad mood, worried about Claire, his longtime girlfriend. Claire was in Berlin at the moment, thousands of miles away, recording the complete Beethoven cello sonatas with a Japanese piano prodigy, Yoshi Haragami, who was 30 years-old and absurdly handsome. Yoshi was more than a decade younger than Claire, but already a huge star and Howie was just slightly jealous.

Not really jealous, of course. He and Claire were tight. But it nagged at him. Yoshi was one of those dramatic musicians who threw his hair around and groaned with bursts of ecstasy as he played. Women adored him. As for Claire, she had become more glamorous with age as she dressed better and became more sure of herself. She was considered by the musical world to be a beauty, a member of a select coterie of women who happened to look sexy while sawing away at Beethoven.

Claire and Yoshi had played recently for free at a fundraiser to support women in Afghanistan. They were both so good-looking and talented, it made Howie feel like an uninteresting dullard by comparison. While she was off playing packed concert halls, he was working sleazy insurance cases sent his way by even sleazier attorneys. He knew his occupation was barely respectable. Whenever he was introduced to Claire's classy colleagues, they gave him a strange look when he told them he was a private eye.

What is our Claire doing with this guy, they clearly wondered.

He and Claire had been lovers now on and off for nearly 20 years, from before she became so successful. It was part of what kept them together, the memory of how hot they'd been when they were young. But perhaps the world she moved in now—the cultured moneyed elite—was stealing her away . . .

For the past two hours, Howie had been skiing fast and hard trying to rid himself of his dark mood, working short radius turns down Valhalla, a steep intermediate slope. There was a line he liked on the skier's right and he did it again and again, racing against himself, until the hollow feeling was gone and there was only the white relief of speed and snow.

He kept at it, daring himself to go faster, more edge, more angle, until he was exhausted and ready to quit. He decided to take the lift up to the top of the mountain and from there ski one long final cruiser down the front side all the way to the base area and parking lot.

The Rabbit Lift took him from the backside and climbed high above the tree line, ascending a jagged basalt cliff to the top where there was a vast panoramic view of mountains, desert, and snow. Howie was tired but he felt good. Skiing had cleared his mind and done its magic.

Ski Patrol had their headquarters at the top of the mountain in an aging wooden building with windows in every direction and an American flag flying outside. As he came off the lift, he saw a gathering of Patrollers in red jackets stepping into their skis outside the building, most of them with heavy coils of rope over their shoulders.

"Moon Deer!" called one of the Patrollers. It was Emily Calder, a friend of his daughter. "We need volunteers!"

Howie gave his poles a light shove and coasted her way.

"The Wolf Lift is down," she told him. Her voice was stressed. The other Patrollers were already heading down the mountain, disappearing over the edge, skiing fast.

Emily had to take a breath before she could continue. "We're going to do a lift evacuation. There are 67 riders who have been stuck for over forty minutes and we need to get them down as quickly as we can. Can you help?"

"Well, sure."

"Good! Follow me," she said, leading the way over a steep lip down into Lift Line, a difficult black diamond run that had nasty bumps the size of Volkswagen bugs.

***

Though Lift Line was a black diamond run, low level skiers often gave it a try for bragging rights. Which was why it was badly cut, the snow shaped by skiers who chopped and floundered rather than float and dance. As a result, the bumps had no rhythm to them which made them difficult. Howie's legs were tired and he needed to focus on where he was going.

He followed Emily without much grace a dozen feet back, hoping not to fall. He was aware of people above him hanging in the chairs calling down, but he didn't dare look up. Many of the bumps had deep valleys between them that swooped down into roller coaster dives that gave you no room to maneuver. You didn't want to get on the back of your skis here. You had to control your speed.

Emily stopped at the base of Tower 11 to join two other Patrollers. Howie pulled up beside her and nearly fell as he came to a stop. He managed to save himself with an awkward move, a sort of cha-cha shuffle. This was embarrassing. You didn't want to look like a beginner when you were hanging out with Patrol.

"Howie, thanks for your help," said Dave Brown, the assistant head of Patrol. "Look, we have a problem. Tomás climbed Tower 7 to see what was wrong with the cable but somehow he fell. Don't ask me how. We're dealing with Tomás separately. Two of my crew are getting him down the mountain. Meanwhile, we can't figure out why we can't get the lift running. They're still working on it but it's not looking good. The bottom line is we absolutely must get these people down before dark. You've done evacuation training, haven't you?"

"I have," Howie answered.

At the start of every season, Ski Patrol was required to do a chairlift evacuation drill, though this was the first time in his knowledge that it was being done for real. Howie had volunteered twice to be one of the skiers in a chair who needed to be lowered to the ground. It was a daunting experience if you didn't like heights.

"Okay, this is what we're doing," said Dave. "Once we have everyone assembled, we'll have three crews. The first will work their way down from the top to Tower 11. The second will go from Tower 11 to Tower 6. The last will handle Tower 6 to the base. Howie, you're in the third crew. I want you to go to Tower 6. You'll be the talker. This is the steepest part of the mountain, from there to the bottom, so some of those people are going to be frightened. Do you think you can handle it?"

"I'll try," he said.

"You'll be great. Be calm but persuasive. Either they trust you or they freeze to death if they don't do what you say. You need to make them understand those are the only alternatives."

Howie hoped he was up for it. It took a lot of nerve to slip off a chairlift into the void, trusting your fate to a small wooden seat that was nothing more than a short two-by-four plank with a hole drilled in it for the rope to pass through. Once they were on the seat, gripping hold of the rope between their legs, a single Patroller would lower the rider to the ground, giving out rope from around his waist, using a carabiner to control the speed. The "talker" was the person on the ground who told the rider in the chair what to do, and when to do it. It was a vital part of the operation. Sometimes it took a good deal of coaxing.

"Are there any children in the chairs?" Howie asked, hoping there weren't.

"Not in your sector," Dave told him. "Now, get down to Tower 6 as quickly as you can. I'll try to send you more help if we can get it."

One of the problems with a ski lift evacuation was that many of the people you needed were trapped at the base, only able to get uphill by snowmobile, which was a slow process.

Howie had a bad feeling that the next few hours were going to be difficult. With 67 people dangling in the air, cold and frightened, he didn't see how they were going to get everyone down before dark. He looked at his watch. It was after 4 o'clock and sunset this time of year was only a few minutes after 5. Already there were deep shadows creeping across the mountain. The visibility was going fast.

"We're trying to get a few choppers here to give you some light from the air," Dave said, reading his expression. "But I can't promise that. Good luck, Moon Deer."

"Right!" said Howie, taking a deep breath.

***

Howie was bombarded by cries from above as he skied down the trail.

"Hey, do you know what's going on? . . . when are they going to get this damn thing running? . . . we're freezing! How long do we have to sit here?"

He looked up one time to give an encouraging high-sign, but this was a mistake. The tips of his skis came down into a gully and he nearly crashed into the next bump over.

Teenage skiers and Olympians fly over moguls, barely touching down, catapulting from one bump to another. But Howie was 42 years old, his legs were not as fast as they had once been. The only way he could manage bumps was by controlling his speed, going slow, evaluating every centimeter of the snow ahead. He saved himself just in time, but he didn't look up again. Compassion would have to wait.

He continued to Tower 7 where Sean Basset, the head of Patrol, was standing with two other Patrollers.

Howie came to a stop, glad to catch his breath. "Is this where Tomás fell from the tower?" he asked.

Sean frowned. "Howie, don't ask. Let's deal with one disaster at a time. Right now, we have some very cold people who are trapped on a lift. Here are complimentary cards you can give out once you get them onto the snow. It's our way of saying we're sorry for the inconvenience."

Howie looked at the small stack of cards Sean put into his hand. On the front of each card was written: ONE FREE MARGARITA OR SOFT DRINK AT THE BIG HORN BAR AND RESTAURANT.

Howie was incredulous. "That's all they get after being stuck on a lift for an hour with the temperature in the teens? One margarita or a soft drink?"

"Howie, it's totally screwed, but that's all I could wheedle out of management. They're anxious not to admit any legal culpability. Now, please—I heard on the radio they're waiting for you at the base of Tower 6 so you'd better get down there. And look, once this is over I'm personally going to buy you all the margaritas you can hold. I'm really grateful for your help."

Howie took off his right glove long enough to put the cards in the zippered pocket of his ski pants, then he continued down Lift Line to Tower 6. He was glad when he saw two Patrollers standing out of their skis at the base of the tower. He had seen them before on the mountain but didn't remember their names. One of the Patrollers was holding a coil of rope, swinging it back and forth to get some momentum to throw the weighted end up and over the cable just below the tower, which was at least thirty feet above where he was standing. It looked like he had already been trying several times. Without success.

Howie came to a stop next to the Patroller who was getting ready to catch the rope on the other side.

"I'll be your talker," he said, introducing himself.

"You've done this before?"

"Twice. But only in drill. Never for real."

"Hey, what's real?" the Patroller asked, shaking his head. In New Mexico, Ski Patrollers were often advanced thinkers.

On the next try, the rope flew over the cable and the Patroller on the other side pulled it to the ground. The small evacuation seat was attached to the end with an extra loop of rope a few feet up from the seat. The riders would slip the loop over their heads and beneath their armpits. This would be their only protection from a bad fall.

The sky was getting darker but there was still enough light to see. The two Patrollers jiggled the rope over an empty chair and down to chair 7 which had two men on it, early twenties, snowboarders. They looked fit, which made for a good start.

Howie stood uphill from the chair about twenty feet and began his spiel.

"Hello up there! How are you doing?"

"What do you think? We're fucking cold!"

"Right. Well, look, we're about to get you down. My job is to talk you through it, okay?"

After a few false starts, Howie and the two Patrollers got into a rhythm lowering one rider after another from the sky. Howie never got to know either of the Patrollers' names. They were too busy.

He was the one who prepared the riders for what was going to happen. "Don't do anything until I tell you," he warned again and again. Howie would give the word when the Patroller on the ground was set in his harness, the carabiner and the brake ready to belay someone to the ground. Only then, when he said so, was the rider to push himself off the chair onto the wooden seat. He left it unsaid that failure to follow instructions might result in severe injury.

The first evacuation went quickly. The two twenty-something snowboarders were military—the Peak gave them a special lift price—and they let themselves be lowered onto the snow easily. They appeared genuinely grateful to get two tickets for margaritas.

But the others were various shades of difficult. Some were frightened, one didn't listen to instructions and was only saved at the last second when the rope was racing through the brake. Nobody liked being evacuated from a chairlift by a rope dangling across the cable. Not when the temperature was 15 degrees Fahrenheit and falling. One middle-aged man seemed to hold Howie personally responsible, saying some fairly unpleasant things when he was finally safe on the ground.

All in all, Howie's crew lowered eighteen people onto the snow. After each chair was evacuated, one person at a time, the two Patrollers had to whip up a wave along the rope in order to get it over the empty chair to the other side, then slide it down the cable to the next chair below.

With the first ten chairs, there was easy access from Lift Line through the woods to a gentle intermediate trail on the other side. Everyone who got down was encouraged to ski or board off that way, the easiest route to the base.

At 4:55, there was only one rider left to evacuate, a small figure in a silver one-piece snow suit, a skier who sat alone on the chair. A woman, Howie assumed, noting the fake white fur around the collar and sleeves of her ski outfit.

Unfortunately, she was dangling over the steepest section of the lift, just above Tower 3, one of the tallest towers on the mountain. He hoped she was a good skier because once she was down, she was going to need to make her way across steep bumps in the half-light and then traverse through the forest in order to get to the intermediate run on the other side.

He called up to her.

"Hey! How are you doing? I bet you're cold! We're going to get you down and I'm here to talk you through it. It's not difficult," he assured her. He ticked off the first talking point. "My name is Howie. What's yours?"

There was no answer from the figure above. Her silver helmet, that matched her silver ski suit, had a plastic visor pulled down over her face. From where he was standing on the snow, he couldn't tell anything about her. He hoped she was alive.

"Hello!" he called again. "Are you okay up there?"

She stirred slightly. She spoke but too softly for him to hear.

"Can you talk louder? Can you say that again?"

"Help!" she said faintly. It was more a muffled sob than a word. "Help me, please!"

"Yes, yes, that's what I'm here for!" he said with forced enthusiasm. "We're going to lower you to the ground—it's a very simple procedure. But you're going to have to do everything I tell you. You're going to be all right."

In fact, Howie wasn't at all certain that she was going to be all right. Hoping for assistance, he looked uphill to the Patrollers. They were two chairs up, working their way down to him, trying to get the rope unstuck from the runners that held the cable.

"I'm so frightened! I've never been so cold!" she cried.

"Okay, here's what we're going to do," he said with make-believe calm. "First, I want you to throw down your ski poles onto the ground. That's right, throw them down. I'll give them to you later."

Two ski poles flew down from the sky and landed in the gully of a particularly ferocious bump. It wasn't going to be fun getting them.

"Great!" he said cheerfully. "Now I want you to open your arms big and wide and slap yourself on the chest. Do it again and again. Hug yourself. Let's warm you up and get your circulation moving. Okay? Now I want you to wiggle your legs and toes. That's right, don't be afraid to wiggle. The safety bar will keep you from falling."

She was trying to do what he was telling her, but her movements were slight.

"I'm terrified of heights!" she cried.

"I am too," he agreed. Which was true. "But this is going to be really easy. You'll be on a chair with a harness around you. Believe me, I've been lowered several times in practice drills, so I know just what it's like. I'll guide you through it."

"I can't!" she said. "I can't move!"

Howie looked uphill again and waved to the Patrollers to hurry up. This was starting to look bad. He turned back to the chair with as much calm as he could summon.

"So let's concentrate on one thing at a time," he told her. "Right now, I want you to keep slapping yourself with your arms, get your blood moving. Yes, even more than that. Good! Now your legs. Swing them back and forth. I bet you're getting warmer already!"

She didn't answer. He sensed she wasn't getting warmer already.

Howie was running out of optimism. There was only so much cheer you could offer to someone stuck on a chairlift in freezing weather with night coming on. He kept trying anyway, telling her to keep flapping her arms—pretend she was a bird—until the two Patrollers finally arrived. They worked with the rope to get it in place over the cable and raise the evacuation seat up to the woman in the chair. When they were ready, the one with the belay harness nodded to Howie to proceed.

"Okay, the Patrollers have the seat in place. Now you're going to need to do exactly what I tell you. Most of all, don't do anything until I give you the word. Did you get that?"

"Yes," she said weakly.

"Okay. Here's the first thing. I want you to raise the safety bar. You can do that now." When she didn't move, he repeated the instruction slowly. "Raise the safety bar."

"I can't."

"Yes, you can. You must. You can't get out of the chair otherwise. Just lift the bar up."

"I can't raise the safety bar, I can't . . . then I'll be . . . there won't be anything . . ."

"As soon as the bar is up, you'll take hold of the rope, slide yourself onto the chair, slip the safety loop over your shoulders, and we'll lower you down. But before we can do that, you need to raise the safety bar."

"I can't . . . I can't!"

Howie looked to the Patrollers for help. The belayer gestured for Howie to come closer so that they could talk.

"What did you say your name was?" he asked.

"Howie."

"So what we'll do, Howie, is this. We'll lower the seat, put you on it, and winch you up to her. Then *you* will raise the bar for her. You'll need to get your arms around her, pull her onto the seat with you, and we'll bring you both down together. Do you get that? All you gotta do is keep hold of her. What do you say?"

"Well, I don't know . . ."

"Otherwise she's going to die up there. Yeah? So here's what you got to ask yourself. Are you going to do it to save this woman's life?"

***

This wasn't what Howie bargained for when he came skiing this afternoon, but there was no way he could say no.

He stepped out of his skis and slipped the small plank with the rope through it between his legs.

"Ready?" asked the Patroller with the harness.

"Ready," he lied.

He was raised in jerks. The first lurch would have thrown him off if he hadn't had the loop under his armpits. The journey got smoother as the Patroller got a better feel. Howie jerked and stuttered upward to the chair where the frightened woman in the silver fur-lined ski suit sat.

"Here I am!" he told her. "I've come up to help you. Now all we have to do is get you down."

Dangling a few inches from her, he had a better idea of who he was dealing with. He could see her eyes through the plastic shield of her visor. They were beautiful eyes, large, and full of astonishment. From the little he could see of her, he realized she was a very attractive young woman. Asian, he thought. Though he wasn't sure of that.

"You're an Indian!" she said.

"I am," he admitted. "Does that matter?"

"Oh, no . . . I mean, no, of course not!"

"Okay, let's get going. I'm here to get you to safety, that's what's important. But we're going to need to work together. What's your name?"

"Leilani."

She said it so softly, he wasn't sure he heard it right.

"Leilani . . . you're Hawaiian!" He saw it now, her delicate Hawaiian features. This was a young woman who belonged on a sunny beach beneath a palm tree, not a chairlift in the Southern Rockies on a bitter January day.

"Great! We're both Natives. That means we can trust each other? A brother and sister, right?"

She nodded dubiously.

"Okay, I'm going to raise the safety bar now, are you ready?"

"Oh, no, please, don't!"

"Leilani, I can't get you down unless we raise the bar. Just look at me, don't look down. Here we go. Look at me, look at *me* . . ."

He reached out and raised the safety bar, pushing it to its upright position.

"Oh!" she cried.

He saw they weren't situated quite right. "Lower me about a foot!" Howie called urgently to the Patrollers below. With a sickening lurch, he was lowered so that he was seated slightly beneath Leilani's chair. That's what he wanted. He wanted her to slide down onto his lap with her legs around his waist. It was a position he had seen described in the Kama Sutra but that couldn't be helped.

"We're going to do this quickly," he told her. "No time for thoughts. No hesitations! I'm going to pull your chair closer and you're going to slide into my lap, your legs around my waist, and your arms around my shoulders. I'm going to hold you very tightly while Patrol lowers us to the snow."

"No, I can't . . ."

"Yes, you can. On three. One, two, three!"

She let out a small cry as he pulled her from the chairlift onto his lap. They were facing each other, her helmet flush against his face. It was an intimate position for two strangers.

He pushed their seat free from the chair. "Down!" he cried to the Patrollers.

They descended in spasms as the rope ran over the cable. Somehow they began to spin clockwise, faster and faster, as they were lowered to the snow.

"Oh!" cried Leilani as they swung in wild circles.

He held her in a fierce embrace until they were down. The Patroller waiting to catch them stopped the spinning chair and lowered them the last few inches.

The woman was too exhausted, dizzy, and frightened to stand upright on her skis. Howie had to hold her steady so she wouldn't fall.

"See, that wasn't so bad," he said, as she collapsed into his arms.

***

Leilani gradually found her balance.

"I can stand, I think," she told him, clutching onto his arm.

She was breathing hard. Howie kept a grip on her right arm so she wouldn't tumble into the mogul that was only a few inches below where she was standing.

"How's your skiing?" he asked. "What level would you say you are?"

"This is only my third time on skis. But I'm quite athletic. I'm a pretty good surfer."

"Surfing, that's great. Skiing's a little different, of course."

Howie was babbling. He was exhausted, too.

He turned to the Patrollers. "What do you say we get a snowmobile to take Leilani down the mountain?"

"Howie, all the mo's are in use, every last one of them," said the Patroller in the harness. "I could get a sled to take her to the base but I don't think there's anybody free who can ski one down to me. Look, all you have to do is traverse through the trees for a few hundred feet and you'll be in Bluebird. I can have a mo meet you there. I'll call it in as Code Red."

Bluebird was the next trail over, the gentle intermediate run. It beckoned from only a few hundred feet of trees.

"I guess we'll have to do that," Howie agreed.

"Stay high," the Patroller advised. "If you go low, there's a cliff you'll have to watch out for."

"A cliff!" said Howie.

He turned to Leilani and did his best to be cheerful. "This shouldn't be too hard," he lied.

Howie stepped into his skis, gave Leilani her poles, and told her simply to traverse across the trail toward the trees. He would follow, ready to catch her if it was necessary.

"It will be good," he said, "if you can use your edges to get a grip on the hill. Do you know where your edges are on your skis? Remember, we're going to try to go across, not down."

The traverse was uneven, which made it difficult for someone who had only skied three times. There were a few ups and downs in it. Leilani only managed a short distance before she lost her balance and flailed backward. Howie came up from behind and caught her. She was light, fortunately. He was able to hold on to her waist, put his own skis around her shorter ones, and ski for both of them.

Hoping for the best, Howie traversed with Leilani into the trees at a shallow downward angle. Skiers had been through here since the last snow so he didn't have to break a fresh track. This made it easier, but it was a challenge for Howie to keep them from crashing into a tree.

"You're doing great," he told her, out of breath, just as the tracks they were following took a roller coaster dive to avoid a large fir.

Howie couldn't avoid the crash. At least they didn't hit a tree. They fell together, heads upward into the hill, rather than heads downhill. This was good. It was awkward getting up, but though she could barely ski, Leilani proved to be agile. He was able to pull her to her feet.

"Okay, just a little more!" he urged. And managed, more or less, to continue skiing for both of them. But it was touch and go. Howie had raised his goggles earlier in order to see better, but the light was fading fast and with the weight of Leilani between his skis, he nearly lost his balance several times.

It was completely dark by the time they got to Bluebird, but a snowmobile was there to meet them with its headlight guiding the way, shining into the trees. From here, it was only a short ride to the base. They rode three together on the seat, the Patroller in front, Leilani in the middle, Howie in the rear keeping her from falling off.

As soon as they arrived at the base, Howie took both their skis, put them in a rack, and led Leilani to the closest indoor space he could think of that had a roaring fire—Edges, the expensive bar on the ground floor of the new hotel, the Hamm Haus.

"I'm freezing!" she cried.

"We're almost there. Come on, we'll be warm in a second."

The bar was crowded. The heat of the closely packed room greeted them with a warm wash. Every table was occupied but Howie was ruthless. He went to the nearest table and told a young kid that they had just been through a harrowing evacuation on the Wolf Lift, life and death, and Leilani needed to sit.

She was clearly exhausted. She sat and breathed for a minute before at last she took off her helmet and shook loose her long black hair.

Howie expected her to be pretty, because he had sensed that from the start. But she was more than that. She was maybe the most beautiful Polynesian girl he had ever seen outside of his South Seas daydreams. She left him speechless.

She looked at him and smiled. She appeared to know the effect she had on men.

"Thank you," she said, standing up. "I'm all right now. But I must go."

"Can't I buy you a hot drink?"

"No, I'm sorry. I'm very late and my godfather will be worrying about me."

"Your godfather?" There was something vaguely mafioso about the word.

"Howie, thank you so much," she said, offering her hand to shake. After what they had gone through, it seemed an oddly formal gesture. They pumped hands up and down exactly three times and then she turned to leave.

She went only a few steps before she turned back to him. Impulsively, she rushed forward to give him a kiss on the cheek, a more substantial thank-you than a handshake. But she missed his cheek. Probably her aim was off. Instead of his cheek, her lips landed on his lips and lingered there fully—briefly—before she turned and hurried off.

Howie was stunned. It was all he could do to watch her vanish down the hall into the hotel part of the building.

She turned back to him as she waited for the elevator, knowing she would find his eyes. She smiled slightly.

Then the elevator opened, gobbled her up, and spirited her away.

Chapter Three

On the afternoon of January 7th, while Howie was on San Geronimo Peak helping with the lift evacuation, Jack Wilder—once Howie's boss—was having an adventure of his own.

At a few minutes past 2 o'clock, after months of preparations, Jack and his new guide dog, Gypsy, set off on their maiden voyage together into town—Jack in his battery-powered wheelchair, and Gypsy leading the way in a specially rigged harness.

They left home and rode on the sidewalk through a quiet residential neighborhood that became increasingly busy as they approached the historic district. It was a bright, gusty afternoon and Jack was bundled up. The air was cold but the sun was warm on his face. The harness had two rigid bamboo poles that kept the distance between dog and man a constant three feet. With his wheelchair and dog, he felt like a Roman emperor racing into battle in his chariot, an imperious figure with his white hair, large belly, and white cane held high in his right hand, ready to fend off anyone who got in his way.

Jack was feeling pretty good, all in all. Though he was blind, he was still in the game.

The trip into town was less than two miles but it was a major step in his rehabilitation. Two years ago he'd had a stroke. Six months before that, Katya, his beloved guide dog of many years, had died. Jack had fallen into a deep depression and had vowed never to have a dog again. He was old and frankly he'd had his fill of Planet Earth. He believed it was time to fade away into the great beyond.

But the days passed, the boredom of being an invalid led to a new resolve, and a time came when he found an excuse to reenter life. Getting himself a new guide dog wasn't something he was doing for himself, he decided, it was for Emma. His wife was a librarian, which had become a dangerous profession in America. He thought it wouldn't be a bad idea to have a dog in the house for protection.

Gypsy, in fact, wasn't much of a guard dog. She was a sweet yellow lab and Jack had come to like her. He wasn't sure he adored her yet, but maybe that was coming. He still felt some resistance that she wasn't Katya. But recently it occurred to him that Katya would have wanted Jack to have a new dog—a replacement, if she couldn't be there herself.

Guide dogs were expensive animals who went through at least two years of training. Because Jack was in a wheelchair, Gypsy had to undergo an additional three months. As for Jack, he had been required to spend a month in Albuquerque learning how to pair with her.

That had been an ordeal, but by the time he was back home in San Geronimo with Gypsy, he felt stronger and more focused than he had in years. He was also doing extensive physical therapy to recover from his stroke, and by the new year, he often stood from his wheelchair and walked carefully about the house.

Gypsy navigated the increasingly busy streets of San Geronimo with shrewd intelligence. She stopped at corners and kept a lookout for danger as they came into the historic district. Tourists scattered to get out of their way. Using his phone and Google maps, Jack directed Gypsy to the Wilder & Associate Private Investigations Agency office on Calle Dos Flores.

"Turn left at the next street! . . . now right!"

Together they made their way across the town Plaza and down a narrow street, hardly wider than a donkey cart, to the two-hundred year old adobe building that the agency called home.

He paused by the front door to catch his breath. He was exhausted from the effort of getting here, but he had done it! He was mobile again! He felt alive.

He checked his phone for the time. He had made it from his house to the office in 1 hour and 12 minutes. That could stand improvement, but it was a good start.

"I'm back!" he said to Georgie, maneuvering his way through the front door.

***

Georgie rose from behind her desk to help Jack, his wheelchair, and Gypsy through the front door. The building was from a time before junk food when people were smaller, and doorways were narrow. Georgie greeted Gypsy with a big hug, and she wagged her tail ecstatically in return.

"Oh, you lovely dog!" Georgie cried.

She guided Jack's chair close to the electric heater in the reception area and then sat down facing him.

"Jack, congratulations! Wow, you did it! The two of you! You and Gypsy! What a team!"

"Took just over an hour," Jack boasted.

"Can I get you some coffee?"

"Does Howie keep any brandy in this joint?"

"Aye, there's a bottle of Hennessy's. Care for a wee drop?"

"Please. In my coffee. I'm surprised Howie hasn't turned the agency into some teetotaler joint. Between you and Claire, he's become disgustingly healthy—a vegetarian, I've heard."

"Well, a quasi-vegetarian," said Georgie. "He eats meat when it's around. Which is often. Basically, Howie eats anything. He's an omnivore."

"That's putting it delicately," said Jack.

Georgie was Howie's Scottish daughter, 23 years-old. Jack found her a joy, so young and smart and full of energy. But he wasn't sure what kept her in San Geronimo. Growing up in working class Glasgow, she had won herself a scholarship to Cambridge University and had graduated with a First in Greats—which Jack understood to be history, literature, philosophy, and such. To Jack's thinking, she should be running some grand venture in Silicon Valley, or at least, a fancy non-profit in Cambodia. Instead, she had gotten herself a New Mexico Private Investigator license in order to help her father run the agency, which now had more work than it could handle.

"So how's life, my dear?" Jack asked.

"Busy," she told him. "I'm volunteering at the Pueblo—I'm the secretary of a group that's trying to stop the ski resort from expanding. You'll never guess what they're up to now! They're hoping to build a revolving restaurant at the very top of the mountain that will overlook Indian land. We're determined to stop them. I'm glad to be involved, but it's taking up a lot of my time."

"Well, I hope you're taking time to have yourself a bit of fun. You're only young once, Georgie."

"I don't know, Jack—I think youth is overrated. Most of us are depressed and rather frantically lost."

"Not you, my dear," said Jack.

Georgie and Jack continued talking, room to room, as she made up a mildly alcoholic coffee. The middle room of the old adobe building had a bathroom, a small kitchen, and a storage area. Howie had put in a shower when Georgie began sleeping more often in town.

"Anyway, Jack, I have news," she continued. "Great news!"

"Oh, yeah?"

"I'm not sure what to make of it, really. I got a call this morning from somebody at—get this!—the Galactic Explorers Club!"

Georgie accented each word of Galactic Explorers Club, as though she couldn't believe there was such a ridiculous thing.

"Do you know about these people?" she demanded. She didn't wait for an answer. "They're a bunch of egomaniac billionaires who got together to build rockets and send tourists into space. They're down in southern New Mexico at Spaceport America. I mean, honestly! They plan to take tourists to the Moon like they're on some kind of Viking cruise up the Rhine! The main investor is the idiot who calls himself Captain Cosmo, the billionaire formerly known as Daniel Gluck. He's the video game king from the 90's. It's like he's turned himself into a cartoon character."

Georgie was young, idealistic, and outraged.

"He's spending billions of dollars on this nonsense when there are people starving here on Earth!" she added.

Jack sat deep in his own thoughts. There was a half-smile on his lips.

"Anyway, believe it or not," said Georgie, "You have been invited to witness their first commercial rocket launch tomorrow morning. It's a bit late in the day for an invitation like this, if you ask me. But they're offering to send Captain Cosmo's personal jet to pick you up tonight and take you down to the Spaceport. They'll put you up at their fancy hotel. Are you listening, Jack?"

"Mmm," said Jack.

"Captain Cosmo is going to be one of the passengers along with three super-wealthy tourists. Each of the tourists are paying $7 million to experience weightlessness, make four and a half orbits of the Earth, then set down safely—they hope—back where they started, at Spaceport America. The whole thing is obscene as far as I'm concerned. You're not listening to a word I'm saying, are you, Jack?"

"Captain Cosmo!" Jack said with an abrupt laugh. "My God!"

He rolled his head upward and laughed uproariously. In Georgie's experience, Jack didn't laugh often, but when he did, it was an explosion.

"I can't believe I've lived to see this!" he said to the ceiling. "Little Danny Gluck! Georgie, you should always be nice to children, especially the obnoxious kind, because you never know what they'll grow up to be!"

"You know this egotistical asshole?"

"I do," said Jack.

***

Danny Gluck!

Jack knew Danny from when he was just a pimply, annoying kid, the son of a cop under Jack's command, Sgt. Pete Gluck. Jack and Danny's father had been in the police academy together and they remained friends despite the fact that Jack rose in the hierarchy to the rank of commander while Pete remained a sergeant.

He and Pete shared plenty of laughs, some hard cases, and endless guy talks about life, marriage, work, and the meaning of it all. But then, on a very bad afternoon, Pete was killed while storming a building where two bank robbers were holed up, leaving behind a fatherless eight-year-old son. Danny.

Danny's mother was an alcoholic. A nice woman, but vague. So Jack took it upon himself to show an interest in the fatherless boy. Sometimes he'd pick Danny up on weekends and take him to 49er's games at Candlestick Park. In those days, free tickets to football games were part of being a cop in San Francisco. Nobody thought of it as graft. One time he took Danny to the Santa Rosa State Fair, and they watched horse racing together and rode scary rides. It was the sort of fun afternoon that could bond a man and a boy, but it didn't. Danny was a strange inward boy. Before Pete was killed, he had worried that Danny might be "maybe a little autistic."

A little?

Jack did everything he could think of to reach the boy, but he felt they never really connected. The kid was polite but distant. Off in his own world.

Once while watching a football game, Danny had said, "You know, this would be a cool sport if only they had monsters from outer space on one team and killer robots with ray guns on the other! Boy, would that be worth watching!"

They had seats on the 50 yard line courtesy of the 49er's general manager. It took a moment for Jack to take in what Danny had just said. He answered calmly. "This is football, son, not some battle between monsters and robots. The point of the game is to see really good human athletes playing against each other. These are just people and they practice very hard to learn to pass and run the ball and do what they do."

Danny had a glazed look in his eyes. "Bam, crash, boom!" he said vaguely.

Jack wasn't sure what to do with the kid, but he kept at it for Pete's sake. Little did he know that monsters and killer robots were going to be Danny's road to riches.

The last time Jack had seen Danny was when he was thirteen. At that age, he was in a nerdy phase, still pre-adolescent, obsessed with comic books and superheroes. Jack had tried to guide him away from the cartoon world to his neglected school work, which was earning him Ds and Fs. Jack tried to impress upon the kid that if he was going to do well in the world, he needed to study. But Jack's lectures never had any effect. Danny's grades didn't improve.

Which was funny of course, in retrospect. College would have done nothing for Danny Gluck. It was his comic book brain—people flying around wearing capes and saving the planet—that made his fortune. As a young computer geek in San Francisco in the 90's, he came up with two of the most popular video games ever made, warriors and monsters who crashed cars and died in huge amounts of blood. The Galactic Explorers Club was the hobby of a very rich man.

When he was thirteen, Danny moved with his mother back to New York City, the Bronx from where she had originally come, and Jack never imagined he would hear from the kid again. Why Danny thought of him now after all these years, Jack couldn't imagine.

He had to admit though, he was curious.

He wheeled himself into his old office at the rear of the building—Howie's office now—in order to call the number the man from the Galactic Explorers Club had left with Georgie.

***

"Thank you for returning my call, Mr. Wilder," said the man at Galactic.

He called himself Bill Williamson, though Jack imagined his birth name had a more foreign ring to it. Venusian, perhaps. His voice sounded like it was being processed by a computer, coming to him from another galaxy. "I am the captain's deputy executive assistant. He has asked me to invite you to the historic launch tomorrow at Spaceport America planned for 7 AM."

"That's very nice," Jack said. "I always enjoy an historic occasion. But I haven't seen Danny in decades, so why does he want me there tomorrow?"

"As I mentioned, it's going to be an occasion for the history books, Mr. Wilder—one that Captain Cosmo wishes you to see. This will be the first time regular people—everyday people such as you and I—will be able to orbit the Earth and witness the splendors of space."

Jack grunted. "First off, I'm blind, Mr. Williamson, so I will not be able to *see* any of this spectacle. And second, everyday people like me will never be able to afford $7 million for a trip in space."

"Please, Mr. Wilder—Captain Cosmo understands that you are blind and in a wheelchair. Along with his personal jet, he will also be sending an ER medic and several people to attend to you. He very much wishes for you to be present tomorrow morning."

"Then why didn't he ask me earlier? Why leave this 'til the last minute?"

"That is something only Captain Cosmo can tell you, sir. I believe there are matters he wishes to discuss with you. He hopes to see you tonight as soon as you arrive."

"We can talk on the phone," suggested Jack.

"He wishes to speak with you in person," said Bill Williamson. "As for your second concern, yes—space travel is expensive now, but that will change in time. Think of flat screen TVs. Captain Cosmo is on a mission to save mankind from itself. He believes space tourism will change the way people think. It will open up whole new vistas. When mankind sees our planet from space, they will understand the Great Cosmic Secret!"

Jack avoided asking about the Great Cosmic Secret.

"The Galactic XR113 rocket is the most powerful rocket ever built," said Bill. "Tomorrow it will take four passengers and a crew of two into a low orbit of Earth, but in the near future it will carry people to the Moon, to Mars, and to the great urban center he plans to build there.

Mars will be the New Jerusalem where humanity will thrive when Earth is no longer habitable."

"Mars?"

"Yes, Mars," said Bill firmly.

"Well, I won't argue the point," Jack demurred. "But I still don't get it. I haven't seen Danny since he was 13 years-old. I can't imagine why he thought of me."

"If I can offer an opinion, sir—Captain Cosmo mentions you often. In public and in private, he often says that you were the crucial mentor in his life, the person who got him started on his path to the stars."

"Oh, come on! That's nonsense!" said Jack. "I'm not taking responsibility for a kid I took to a few football games! He turned into Captain Cosmo by himself, believe me. I had no part in it!"

"His jet will arrive this evening in San Geronimo. We will send a van to your home at 7 PM, which will take you to the airport. It's a 43-minute flight to Spaceport America and there will be a medical staff and several attendants to help with your wheelchair and guide dog. We will return you home tomorrow afternoon. Of course, Captain Cosmo will pay you generously for your service. He knows you are a busy private investigator."

Jack sighed. He was not a busy private investigator. That was the problem. He hadn't worked a case for over two years. And he was bored. Stupendously bored. Bored with his life, bored with his condition, bored half to death. When he thought about it afterward, he understood that this was his first mistake. He acted out of boredom and curiosity. That was rash.

As for Spaceport America? Well, what else did he have to do?

"Dammit!" he said irritably. "Okay, but I need to warn you—I charge a thousand dollars an hour," he lied.

"I'm certain the Captain will wish to pay you considerably more," said Bill.

***

At least Emma hadn't been too difficult about it. He had expected a few sharp remarks, at the least. Emma was good at sharp remarks. But over the years, she had become resigned to Jack being Jack. Fatalistic. She merely made a few jabs.

"Tell me you're joking. You're going to Spaceport America in a private jet to see Danny Gluck blast off in his new toy? For chrissakes, Jack! *Danny*!"

Jack answered patiently. "He's no longer the nerdy kid we knew, Emma. He's not only one of the richest people on the planet, he's a prophet. He's going to build the New Jerusalem on Mars to save humanity from annihilation. This is big stuff, Emma."

"You've been following him?"

"Frankly, I couldn't restrain my curiosity. I ran an Internet check on Danny."

"He's an egomaniacal lunatic," said Emma. "Space tourism is a monstrous waste of money."

"Emma, I'll fly down there and come right back. It's going to be first class all the way, that's the nice part of being rich. You're pampered. All I have to do is sit in my chair and let people wheel me around."

"Well, go ahead if you think you can do it," she told him with a sigh. They were sitting in the kitchen waiting for the van to take Jack to the airport. "I can't stop you. But honestly, Danny Gluck! His rocket ship is beyond satire. It's beyond my comprehension how someone like that became so rich."

"He was in the right place at the right time, San Francisco in the 90's," said Jack. "The fickle finger of fate pointed his way."

"Oh, sure! You know I worry about you when you jaunt off into your ridiculous adventures."

"Cases, Emma. Not adventures. I'm a private detective. That's how I live."

"You *were* a private detective, Jack. When you were younger. Before you had a heart bypass and a stroke. I'm not going to stop you. But one of these days I'm expecting to get a call. Or a cop is going to show up at the door—"

"Emma, don't go there. Please. Don't even imagine it."

"You need to take care of yourself, Jack. Because I can't."

"Emma—"

"No, it's okay. If you want to pretend you're some octogenarian superman, that's your business. Georgie likes to say you're her hero. She thinks you're a cross between Zorba the Greek and The Old Man and the Sea. For me, I see you more as Sisyphus, trying roll a boulder up a mountain. But who am I to stop you?"

"Gypsy and I will be back by this time tomorrow," he assured her.

"I hope so," said Emma. "But I'm not counting on it."

Chapter Four

The flight south across the length of New Mexico was pleasant. Jack decided it was a definite perk of wealth, one worth having, to be able to hop from place to place in your winged limousine.

Jack smiled thinking of how Georgie would disapprove of such carbon-producing luxury, the waste of fuel and resources to support such a small percent of the global population, the ultra rich who could afford a private jet.

She had studied climate change at Cambridge and had once spent an hour explaining to Jack with mathematical equations and something she described as "modeling" how his generation had destroyed the planet.

"This is why my generation despises your generation," Georgie informed him. "We're inheriting the mess you've made of everything."

Frankly, he suspected Georgie was right. The girl knew her stuff. Maybe at his age he was more blasé about the sins of the world. And also more forgiving. Luckily, Jack wasn't here to moralize. At the moment, he would have to say that being treated like a pasha wasn't so bad.

A young woman who introduced herself as Heather helped Jack into his seat, which was a particularly comfortable armchair with a safety harness. Years ago he would have called Heather a stewardess, stew for short. Fortunately, he knew enough not to call her that now. The world kept turning and for an old man it was hard to catch up. When he was buckled in, Heather settled Gypsy in the seat beside him.

"May I get you something to drink, sir?"

Jack was about to say no, he was fine. But then he thought, why not?

"You got champagne?"

"Certainly."

"Well, okay. I'll have a glass of that. And you might get Gypsy a bowl of water. If it won't slop around too much."

"I'll put it in a special container that won't spill. Captain Cosmo often flies with his two Afghans."

"I bet he does," said Jack.

Once they were cleared to go, Jack sat back and felt the compression of gravity as the small jet revved its engines and climbed steeply into the sky. As soon as they leveled off, Heather brought him a glass of cold dry Champagne that went down very easily. The bubbles were effervescent, just right.

I could get used to this, he said to himself dreamily. Jack was tired. With the trip into town with Gypsy, it had been a long day. She put her doggy nose into the crook of his arm, from her seat to his.

"Not bad, eh?" he said to Gypsy. "If Emma could see us now!"

Jack closed his eyes and felt himself riding on the air currents. A memory from long ago drifted into his mind: an afternoon in Golden Gate Park when he was ten years old, flying a kite shaped like a bird, a large black raven, that his father had bought him in Chinatown.

Memories from childhood had been coming to Jack in great vividness since he'd had his stroke. Blind though he was, he could see that long ago afternoon in startling Technicolor, the kite in the blue sky above the green meadow darting around in the sudden gusts of ocean breeze.

The kite rose and fell, rose and fell . . . Jack fell asleep as he was hurtled south with his champagne glass, half full, still in his hand.

***

Jack woke with a start. At first he didn't know where he was.

It took him a moment to understand that they had arrived down south. He was on the ground in his wheelchair, outside on the tarmac. It was night and the air was dry and cold.

He panicked briefly wondering where Gypsy was. But then, out of nowhere, he felt her whiskers against his hand. He stroked her head and ears.

Jack sensed the enormous space of the night overhead. The breeze had the scent of sand and sage. The half-full glass of champagne was gone.

Gypsy kept nuzzling to make certain he was awake.

"You were asleep when we landed, sir," said a young female voice from behind his left ear. "I didn't want to wake you."

Jack tried to remember her name. Heather. She was pushing his wheelchair.

"Where are we exactly?" he asked.

"We're at Spaceport America, sir. I'm wheeling you toward a van that's going to take us to the hotel. We have a suite waiting."

Heather had an attractively efficient voice and Jack imagined she was an attractive woman. The kind of efficient attractive woman rich men often like to have on display.

"I was told Danny wanted to see me as soon as I arrived," he said. "I'd like to do that now. I need to find out what this is all about."

"Captain Cosmo is busy at the moment," she explained. "He's preparing for his journey into the future."

"No kidding? The future?"

"Yes, Mr. Wilder, the inter-galactic future. Captain Cosmo is leading the way to New Times."

"So this is some kind of religion, is it?"

"I can send you information, sir. There's a very good audio lecture that Captain Cosmo gave from the top of the Eiffel Tower that I think will impress you. It's brought many of us into Galactic Wakefulness. Only Captain Cosmo can take us to our new home in the stars!"

Jack laughed. "Right."

"The Captain has a number of last minute procedures he must do before the flight tomorrow morning. He has asked you to go to the suite, make yourself comfortable, and he will be there as soon as possible."

"Okay," Jack agreed. "Heather, is that right?"

"Yes, Mr. Wilder. I will be attached to you during your stay. I'm here to answer questions and offer any help I can."

"How are you at describing, Heather?"

"I don't understand."

"I'm blind, my dear," he explained. "I've never been here before and I like to be able visualize where I am. If you could provide me with a description, I'd be much obliged."

"Yes, of course!" She seemed pleased to be of use. She continued brightly. "Spaceport America is the first commercial spaceport in the world. Situated on 18,000 acres adjacent to the U.S. Army White Sands Missile Range, the Spaceport has a rocket friendly environment of 6000 square miles of restricted airspace, as well as a 12,000 foot runway, vertical launch complexes, and 340 days of sunshine! Only 59 miles from Las Cruces—"

"Heather—"

"Plus the armed security forces at the Spaceport are of military quality. Once you are inside the perimeter of Spaceport America, you can rest assured that you and all your enterprises are secure. The remote location of the Spaceport minimizes the client's public exposure and protects their proprietary interests."

"I see," said Jack. It was a memorized spiel, but it was interesting. Meanwhile, it was going to take encouragement for Heather to find her inner-poet and be his eyes.

"In other words, you can blast rockets to kingdom come and do whatever you want here and nobody will ever find out your secrets?"

"Yes!" she agreed. "And there are EMT trained firefighters in case your rocket crashes and burns!"

"Well, that's amazing," Jack admitted. "Just amazing. All this and there's a hotel too?"

"A first class hotel, sir, as you will see."

"As I won't see, unfortunately."

"Oh, I'm so . . . I'm sorry . . ."

"No matter. I was a cop for twenty years. There's nothing you can say that will bother me."

With Gypsy trotting at his side, Jack sat back as Heather pushed him across what felt like a wide concrete plaza. He felt the difference in air, a feeling of density when they came to a large building. An automatic door whooshed open and he was pushed into a lobby that smelled of something subtly jet-like and synthetic. The air seemed processed, far from nature. Another door whooshed and he rode upward in an elevator.

The hallway was softly carpeted. The wheels of his chair made only the softest sound as he was rolled to his suite.

"Here we are, sir! It's a beautiful suite. Tom Cruise stayed here once. That's what we call it now, the Tom Cruise suite!"

"Great," said Jack.

"Would you care to order dinner, Mr. Wilder? Perhaps another glass of champagne?"

Jack had to admit he was hungry. He had missed dinner.

"Do you have a menu?"

"We have anything you want."

"Really? How about lobster?" he asked experimentally.

"Yes, certainly. We have lobster flown in daily from Maine. I would recommend the Lobster Morocco. The cream sauce has just a touch of cinnamon. It's truly superb."

"Well, okay. Lobster Morocco it is. With some rice pilaf. You might give me a small hearts of palm salad and I'll let you decide on dessert. I'm partial to chocolate."

Jack listened to Heather disappear into another room in order to phone down to room service. It was fun to order lobster and champagne. The problem was, he didn't really want it.

"Excuse me, Heather!" he called into the next room. "Forget the lobster. Give me something simple. A turkey sandwich on rye. Mayo, tomato, thin onion, Swiss cheese, pickle, hold the lettuce."

After a moment's thought, he added, "But let's keep the champagne coming."

Chapter Five

In his dream, someone was calling his name.

"Jack!"

Gypsy was growling. It wasn't a serious growl, but serious wasn't far away.

"Jack, wake up! Tell your furry friend I'm okay."

Jack struggled to rise from the fog of sleep. He was on a huge bed in what felt like an absurdly large bedroom. The bed was so large he couldn't reach the end of it with his hands or feet. He managed to sit up.

"Jack, tell doggie I'm cool."

The voice was almost a whisper, but it demanded attention. It had changed a great deal since Jack had heard it last. Danny was no longer a child. Yet there was something in it he recognized.

"Gypsy, it's okay," he told her. "Good girl!"

Jack had a memory of Heather wheeling him into the bedroom after a sandwich and a half bottle of champagne, but he didn't remember falling asleep. He managed to sit up.

"What the hell time is it, Danny?"

"Four-twenty-three. The launch is less than three hours from now and I can only stay a minute. This is my date with destiny, Jack. This is the beginning of New Times! I'm going to take the human race to the stars, Jack! The stars!"

"As I understand it, Danny, you're going to orbit the Earth four times. That's great, I'm not putting it down. But the stars are still quite a few light years away. Now, why did you send for me?"

"Jack, I wanted you to know how important you were to me when I was a kid. You stirred my imagination. You dared me to dare. You were the first grown up to look at me and say, Danny, you're not a fucked-up little creep, you're a genius!"

"I never told you that, Danny."

"Not in so many words, but you were the one, Jack. You gave me faith in myself."

Jack sighed softly.

"Plus you're the only person in this entire galaxy I trust completely," Danny added. A more down to earth tone had come into his voice. "When you live at the heights that I do, Jack, it gets harder to find someone you really truly trust. And I trust you."

"Danny, no—"

"Don't interrupt, Jack. I want to give you something, just in case I don't survive this rocket ship ride. If I die, I want you to do something for me. If I'm still alive afterwards, you can forget it. However it goes, I'll pay you very well for your service."

"Danny, hold it. First of all, if you have any doubts about your flight, you should call it off. Second, I'm an old man. Look at me, I'm a wreck. So if you want someone to do something, you need to find someone younger."

"Jack, it's not my rocket. XR113 is the most beautifully designed flying machine ever made—it's perfect! I made it and it's mine!"

"Danny—"

"No, it's not my gorgeous rocket that's the problem. It's that asshole Hamm. He wants to kill me and he won't stop at anything. You have to help me, Jack. Do you know who Leonard Hamm is?"

Jack had to think for a minute. "Hamm . . . Hamm . . . that's the guy who bought San Geronimo Peak. He owns our local ski resort."

"Exactly. He's in your backyard. Which is why you can help me. I'm going to give you a flash drive and it has all the instructions on it in case I'm killed. You'll be my revenge."

"I am not going to be your revenge, Danny. This whole thing is ridiculous."

"It's survival of the fittest, Jack. It's Darwin in action. Now, everything you need to know is on the drive. You can destroy the drive as soon as I'm down safely, but make sure nobody ever finds it. I leave that to you. I know how smart you are. Captain Cosmo wants to keep his secrets."

"For God's sake!" cried Jack, more and more irritated. "And what's this Captain Cosmo business? I mean, come on, Danny! Have you become a comic book character?"

Danny laughed. "You haven't changed a bit, Jack! In New Times, either you're a hero or you're a villain. Truth doesn't matter. It's mythmaking that's important. And I'm aiming for mythical, my friend. This morning is only the beginning."

"Danny, you're not an astronaut. You invented a few video games, that's it. If I were you, I'd come down to Earth and cancel this tourist trip to space. I'm sure it's not too late."

"Bye, Jack. I gotta go now, I have to get ready. But thank you for coming. It means a lot to me for you to be here in my moment of destiny—"

"Danny! Captain Cosmo is a made-up character. He comes from your imagination. So for chrissakes, don't believe your own make-believe!"

"Here's an envelope, Jack. The drive is inside. Take good care of it. Keep it with you at all times until I'm safely back at the Spaceport."

"Danny, no—I mean it, don't give this to me. I'm not the right person to do any kind of job, especially this."

Regardless of his objections, Jack was helpless to refuse the envelope Danny put in his lap.

"Goodbye," he said a final time. "Wish me luck."

"Danny, come back . . . Danny, no, I'm not doing this!"

But you don't become a billionaire by listening to people who tell you no. Captain Cosmo—the fantasy version of Danny Gluck—left the bedroom, closing the door behind him, with the envelope on Jack's lap.

***

Jack couldn't fall asleep after Danny left. Sleep was always a delicate matter for an insomniac, and to be woken at four in the morning put an end to any possibility of a restful night.

"Damn!" he said to Gypsy who was sprawled at the foot of the bed.

Heather came for him at 5:30. She was irritatingly cheerful.

"Good morning! Good morning!" she cried. "Are you ready for the big day?"

"Give me a moment to get dressed," he growled.

Ten minutes later, she wheeled Jack from the suite down the hall and out of the building into a cold winter morning. Jack had Danny's envelope in a side pocket of his overnight bag, determined to give it back to him at the first possible moment.

"So this damn rocket," he said, "tell me about it."

"It's 489 feet tall and weighs 8 million 5 thousand and 37 pounds," she answered promptly. Heather had memorized her facts. "To give you a comparison, Apollo 11—the first rocket that took people to the moon—was 363 feet tall and weighed 6 point 2 million pounds fully fueled. One of the remarkable features of the XR113 is that both the cabin and the main body of the rocket can be reused. On re-entry, the rocket and the passenger capsule will separate. The rocket will parachute harmlessly to a landing site in the Mojave Desert, and the cabin will extend wings, transform itself into an atmosphere-friendly flying machine, and land gently right back here at the Spaceport."

"If everything goes right," he said.

"Yes, of course. But we wouldn't be sending passengers if there was any doubt."

Jack scratched his beard. "I don't know, Heather. Sometimes doubt is appropriate."

The air was crisp and dry. Gypsy trotted at Jack's side, sniffing happily. Deep in her doggie soul she wanted to run and play. Jack reached to the left of his wheelchair and let her off her leash. Gypsy bounded away across the open tarmac delirious with joy.

"Sir!" cried Heather. It was the first negative intonation he'd ever gotten from her. "All dogs must be on a leash at Spaceport America! It's a strict rule. All animals. Especially the monkeys!"

"Monkeys?" Jack queried.

"Oh, I shouldn't have said monkeys, sir. Spaceport America strictly prohibits launching test animals on rockets!"

"Do they? Well, why don't we give Gypsy a few minutes to run around, sniff and stuff? She'll come back when I call her."

"It's highly—"

"Yes, I know, Heather. And you need to stop calling me sir. Call me Jack."

They crossed a concrete plaza toward a tram. Jack once again felt the enormity of the desert plain. The early morning sky was already hot. He felt the sun on his face. The land here was harsh and primal.

Gypsy came running when Jack whistled and they rode on padded benches beneath an awning with open sides for nearly ten minutes.

"So, Heather, can you describe where we are?"

"Oh, it's lovely! Just stupendous. There's nothing like the desert!"

"Truly? I imagined this land as quite barren. More suitable for rattlesnakes than people."

"Well, you need to like the desert, I guess, to see the beauty of it."

"And do you like the desert?"

She lowered her voice.

"Honestly, this is my idea of hell, Jack." Heather laughed self-consciously and she seemed to change into quite a different person. "The desert, the mountains . . . it scares me somehow. It's such dead land. Only cactus and snakes and coyotes. . . how they howl at night. It's unearthly!"

Once she opened up, Heather was good at describing. Which was exactly what Jack needed from her.

They disembarked at a large square building, Launch Center A. The building was metal, top to bottom, three stories, more of a bunker than any place you'd want to call home. There were three tiers of windows in the front that looked out onto the XR113 rocket, which was still attached to the launch superstructure on the tarmac a few hundred yards away. A small stream of white smoke was already coming out of the bottom. Jack pictured the rocket from his 1950s childhood as a kind of blimpy thing with fins and a bullet-like nose. Heather assured him that this was basically the right idea. Only not so blimpish. More stylishly thin.

"Is Danny on board by now?"

"Yes, the astronauts and the passengers have been on board for nearly an hour. They're all strapped in and the medical team is monitoring their vitals."

Heather guided them from the tram to a security checkpoint at the base of the building. There were four security officers and two different metal detectors. The security was thorough. Gypsy was briefly a matter of some concern. Ordinarily—for a number of reasons—dogs weren't allowed at rocket launches. Jack needed to remind them of the Americans with Disability Act.

An elevator took them up a floor from where he was pushed down a hallway to a narrow room that had two rows of comfortable theater seats that looked through a wall of glass to the rocket on the launch pad.

Jack was seated at the end of the row in his wheelchair with Gypsy beside him. Heather was on his right.

A buzzer sounded and the launch scaffolding began to slowly move backward on rows of large wheels leaving the rocket in place pointed toward the sky.

"Counting fifteen minutes!" came a voice on a loudspeaker. The voice continued counting backward: "Fourteen fifty-nine, fifty-eight, fifty-seven, fifty-six . . ."

Despite himself, Jack felt his heart beating faster as the clock wound down.

". . . seven minutes, six fifty-nine, fifty-eight . . ."

At five minutes, different voices began announcing a series of computer readings, how the various systems were working and at what level. Jack understood none of it but there was something in a countdown that heightened the suspense as the numbers dwindled.

At two seconds to take off, Gypsy began to howl.

There was a roar as the rocket ignited and lifted slowly off the launch pad. The ground shook, the engines thundered. But something was wrong. The rocket rose only a few feet before it exploded in a blinding flash of light so intense that Jack felt the heat of it on his face.

All around him, people were screaming.

There came a percussive boom, a sonic wave of destruction that nearly sent Jack and his wheelchair tumbling backward.

He wasn't sure what had happened, but he knew the six people on board were dead.

There were cries of dismay, voices shouting. A siren was wailing. A woman nearby was weeping and saying no, no, no again and again.

Jack's ears were ringing. "Gypsy, where are you?"

She was excited, whimpering, but she seemed okay. She put her head in his lap as though in need of protection. Jack held her tightly.

"God dammit!" he swore, knowing the hard drive Danny had forced on him was now his problem, like it or not.

Chapter Six

It snowed heavily throughout the night, and it was still snowing when Howie opened his eyes Friday morning at close to 10 o'clock.

He had been dreaming about Claire—a disturbing dream, though he couldn't remember it entirely. He decided to phone her, they needed to talk. It was eight hours later in Berlin and if he phoned now, while he was still in bed, he would be able to get her before her performance tonight at the Berlin Philharmonic where she was set to play the Prokofiev Cello Concerto in E minor.

They used a free internet app for their international calls. Howie dialed the country code, then her number, and he listened to her phone ringing halfway around the world. After six rings, her voicemail came on.

"Hello, I'm not available right now," said Claire's voice. "Please leave a message and I'll get back to you as soon as I can."

Right, Howie grumbled to himself. The way he was feeling, he could have used a hit of Claire. BEEP, said her phone.

"Hi, it's me. I was just thinking about you so I thought I'd call. I had a crazy experience on the Peak yesterday. The Wolf Lift broke down with 67 riders on it and we had to do a lift evacuation with night coming on and the temperature in the teens. We got everyone down but it was a lot of work and dicey at times. Anyway, I hope you're doing well. Call me when you can. I love you," he said across the many miles. It was an empty feeling to say I love you into an electronic void.

He groaned as he climbed down the steep ladder from his sleeping loft. He was sore in every joint, every muscle. Standing barefoot in his tiny sitting room/kitchen, he peered out his south facing hatch to take stock of the weather. He couldn't see a thing. The glass was covered with snow so he had to open the front door to look outside. The forest had turned into a winter wonderland overnight. There was at least a foot and a half of fresh powder and it was still snowing heavily, large flakes falling from a white windless sky. Every branch was covered with snow, every tree.

Howie sighed thinking of the shoveling that lay in front of him. Generally he liked new snow. There was an enchantment to the forest, everything hushed and white and beautiful. But this morning he was tired and cranky. The first thing he needed to do was find his snow shovel. He hadn't used it since last winter. Where had he put it? He wasn't very organized about such things. Hopefully it was in the utility shed by his snow-covered vegetable garden.

As he stood in the open door, he heard a meow behind him. It was Orange, his large, overfed cat, letting him know that she was cold.

"Sorry," he said, closing up. When all you had was a cat for companionship, you needed to be nice to her.

"Well, come on, Orange, let's make ourselves breakfast," he told her.

***

Howie lived in a small space, egg-shaped, less than 200 square feet—an eco-pod, as it was called by the two anarchist German architects who designed it. The pod had been built with the end of civilization in mind, shelter in which to survive the coming collapse. When the power grid was gone, the supermarkets empty, eco-pods would be just what were needed in the post-apocalyptic world.

Howie wasn't quite so pessimistic. He presumed that humanity would somehow muddle on. But the eco-pod kit was perfect for his situation. He didn't have much money after buying his ten acres of forest in the foothills north of town and the kit was way cheaper than the average price of a house in San Geronimo County. Fitted with solar panels, it seemed just the thing to put down in his forest of fir and aspen. The only source of water was a year-round creek.

The pod bristled with electronics, retractable antennae and odd satellite dishes that poked and prodded the heavens. Howie was going to need to replace the lithium battery at some point, and that would be expensive. But besides the battery, the pod was self-sufficient. It was the perfect home from which to watch the snow fall as you were having breakfast, just you and your cat.

Claire called the pod the Egg, because of its shape. Howie thought of it more like a Mars landing craft. There were four skinny mechanical legs that held the pod in place on the ground. The legs shortened and expanded with a jack-like device on the outside. Inside, there was a sleeping loft above a compact living area and a miniature bathroom that wasn't much larger than a telephone booth. Howie was okay with that, in fact he was quite comfortable. He liked being off-grid. When his life as a P.I. felt sleazy and dark, the natural world restored him. But living in the woods was better when Claire was here. Over the years, he had built several outbuildings, including a small cabin for his daughter. But she was gone too, most of the time, staying in the office in town. He understood, of course. He supported her entirely. Georgie was twenty-three and she needed a life of her own.

He got some coffee going and while he was waiting for it to brew, he opened the front hatch to take another look at the snow. It was beginning to taper off, thankfully. Nevertheless, he saw he had a long day's work ahead to get himself unburied.

"All this exercise, I should be losing weight," he said to himself. But he wasn't. Howie had a way of replacing calories lost with calories gained.

I should go on a diet, he was thinking—no more bear claws—when his phone rang. For a second, he thought it might be Claire returning his call. But it wasn't.

It was Sean Basset, the head of Ski Patrol, and it changed everything.

Sadly, he would need to put off shoveling snow until another day.

***

"I need you, Moon Deer," Sean told him. "Leonard Hamm phoned me a while ago from his jet. He does that sometimes, calling from 30,000 feet like he's some god in the sky ordering people around."

"Really?" said Howie. He imagined the Sistine Chapel, God pointing down with his finger, Sean giving God the finger in return.

"Hamm was over Iowa. He's flying here from New York to deal with the lift disaster—that's how serious this is—and he asked for you by name. Could I get in touch with Howard Moon Deer, he demanded. I told him yes, I could. He would like you to meet his plane at the airport when he arrives in approximately forty-five minutes. He wants to talk with you as soon as possible."

"Forty-five minutes? Are you serious? I've never met the guy. What does he want with me?"

"I don't know, Howie. I only know what the big man told me. The voice of Leonard Hamm from the sky. Obey, obey, or else. He wants you at the airport when he lands and I'm supposed to make sure you're there, hell or high water, no excuses. So please do it for me, if not for yourself."

"What do you mean, for myself?"

"Well, the guy's a billionaire! Do you know how much money that is? Try to get your head around one thousand million dollars. If he wants to hire you for something, you can soak him, buddy."

"I'm not so sure," said Howie. "My experience with rich people is that they're tighter than clams."

"Well, just go see what he wants, okay? Then report back to me. I'd like to be kept in the loop."

"Sean, I'm not sure I want to get mixed up in mountain politics."

"Look, Howie, I have to tell you, they found a small explosive device by the cable at Tower 7. This wasn't a mechanical failure. Someone did it. Meanwhile, Patrol is being left in the cold. We don't know what's going on. So, please, after you see Hamm, stop by the Patrol shack and tell me what he's planning. You have to come by anyway. I have some forms I need you to fill out, a witness statement."

"A bomb? You're kidding! Now I'm sure I don't want to get involved in this!"

"You are involved, Howie, whether you like it or not. You volunteered, remember? And no good deed goes unpunished. You were helping to lower people to the snow and there are three different insurance companies and a host of New York attorneys who want to know all about you."

"*Me*?" said Howie incredulously.

"In any case, these witness statements are nothing to worry about. You only have to say what you saw and did yesterday. Tell the truth, that's all. We have to document everything."

Howie remained dubious. A little voice said, don't do it, Howie! Don't get mixed up in this. He remembered that afterwards.

"I tell you what, Howie," said Sean. "If you do this for me—meet Hamm at the airport, give me your statement—I'll make sure that you never have to pay for a ski pass again. You'll go on the Legacy list. Free skiing for the rest of your life."

"Really?" said Howie. This was temptation. His eyes went somewhat dreamy. He pictured himself floating down the mountain in long easy turns, lungs full of mountain air, a wake of snow flying up behind him. "For the rest of my life?"

***

By late morning, the snow had stopped and the clouds were lifting. There was a sliver of blue in the west, a promise of sun. But the air was cold. The outside thermometer said it was 19 degrees.

Howie found his snowshoes in the storage area under Georgie's cabin and plodded his way along the forest path to the snow-covered road where he had a primitive parking area. The trail crossed all ten acres of his land and it was twisty and sometimes steep. Under the trees, there were deep patches where his snowshoes sank into bottomless fluff, other places where the snow barely covered the ground.

It took some time to dig out his car, but he was soon mobile, thanks to good snow tires and all-wheel drive.

The three-mile stretch on the dirt road between his land and the highway hadn't been plowed, but several vehicles had gone through and he was able to ride on their tracks. His Outback skidded here and there, but with only a few nervous moments he made it to the highway. He was curious to meet the legendary billionaire, Leonard Hamm. Very few people in San Geronimo had met the man. Hamm was only here infrequently and he kept to himself. Why he suddenly wanted to meet Howie was a mystery.

The airport was in the desert west of town. The snow here lay in patches with bare ground and sagebrush showing. Howie had the car radio set to the public Albuquerque station. The big story on the radio was the dramatic explosion at Spaceport America in southern New Mexico. At 7:01 this morning, the XR113 rocket had exploded, killing its two-person crew and the four paying passengers. The flight was to be the launch of space tourism, the first passenger flight into space. Notably, Daniel Gluck, the video-game billionaire and majority stockholder of the Galactic Explorers Club, was among the passengers who died in the explosion.

It was an important story, he supposed. The explosion would set back space tourism for at least a few years. But at the moment, Howie couldn't care less about space tourism, and he listened with only half his attention. His mind was on Claire. Usually, they talked at least every other day, but she hadn't answered the last two times he'd tried.

The problem was their long separations—Claire in the great cities of the world with her cello, and Howie in New Mexico. Biology didn't automatically stop when you were separated from your lover. He had felt the odd attraction himself once or twice. For example, that Hawaiian girl yesterday. When she kissed him, her lips had set off a kind of shiver that vibrated up and down his spine. Pure lust, he admitted to himself.

No, no, no! Howie told his body.

Yes, yes, said his body back.

What he really needed was for Claire to answer her phone . . .

Howie made it to the airport just in time. He came into the parking area as the sleek little jet was making its final descent onto the runway. The San Geronimo airport, once a sleepy single runway in the desert, had expanded as the town had grown. Many locals didn't like that. Whether to build or not to build was a hot political issue up and down the Rockies. Pro-development, anti-development. Howie saw it as a yin/yang opposition of viewpoints that would never be resolved. Not in America. Maybe not anywhere.

Howie had to run from the parking area, through the deserted terminal, and across the ramp that led down to the tarmac.

He slowed to a walk just as he came to the gate in the chain link fence. Beyond this point, you needed to enter a code to get through to where Hamm's jet was coasting toward the terminal.

He waited at the gate as the jet came to a stop. It was a beautiful flying machine, a winged miracle that could take someone anywhere they wanted.

As he watched, a hatch door opened near the cockpit and a flight of steps tumbled out. Four blank looking men came out first. They walked quickly down the steps and stood flanking the bottom of the stairs. They had earphones in their ears. To Howie, this seemed an excess of security.

A small pale man appeared in the door of the jet. He was dressed in a black overcoat and a black hat. With his black clothes and bad posture—his neck, head, and shoulders slumping forward—he looked like a hungry raven. A woman in an ankle-length fur coat walked out of the plane behind him. Howie assumed this was Mr. and Mrs. Hamm.

Leonard Hamm descended the steps carefully, one step at a time. Mrs. Hamm was a good deal more spry. She followed her husband impatiently, and to Howie it looked like she wanted to give him a shove. Two men—more security—followed at a respectful distance.

Hamm and his retinue walked toward the gate where Howie was waiting for them.

"Are you Howard Moon Deer?" asked the first security man as he approached.

"That's me," said Howie.

Howie's identity was repeated into a small lapel mike. "Howard Moon Deer is here," said the security man.

"Howard Moon Deer!" said the next in line, passing along the name.

"Moon Deer," said a third.

The group came closer until Howie was even with the big boss himself.

Leonard Hamm was a short man. He had a prominent Adam's apple and a beak-like nose. Howie felt dark eyes scanning him from beneath his black hat. They were eyes that had seen the world but liked nothing they saw.

"Come with me, Moon Deer," said Hamm shortly, without pausing in his stride. "We'll talk in the car."

Chapter Seven

Howie was shown into a jump seat in Leonard Hamm's black 4X4 SUV limousine by one of the security guards.

It was the fanciest limo Howie had ever seen. It had huge snow tires and most likely bullet proof armor. Along with luxury, it had enough power to climb every mountain and keep on going. It was a tank.

The jump seat faced Mr. and Mrs. Hamm who were ensconced in great comfort in the cavernous back with a blanket across their laps. Dressed in black, Leonard Hamm was funereal. The little hair he had was combed carefully to the left, covering a bald spot. His wife, for her part, looked like she had just stepped off a stage in Las Vegas.

"Excuse me if I barf," said Mrs. Hamm unexpectedly to her husband. She had a low husky voice. "I hate snaky mountain roads 'cause I get car sick," she added, turning her attention to Howie. "But oh, no—he doesn't care what I go through! We have to fly halfway around the world to see what's going on with his new toy!"

"It's not a toy, Gloria," Hamm said patiently to his wife. "It's a ski resort. And I'm going to make it the greatest ski resort in North America."

Mrs. Hamm gave Howie a closer look, bending forward from where she sat in a nest of cushions. Howie felt at a social disadvantage, riding backward in a jump seat.

"I told him to buy Vail, for chrissake," she confided. "If he'd bought Vail, we wouldn't have had this goddamn drive fifteen miles up a shitty mountain highway in a snowstorm!"

"The snow has stopped, Gloria," said Hamm again patiently.

"Plus, I *know* people in Vail!" Mrs. Hamm continued to Howie, as though her husband didn't exist. "I don't know anyone in this goddamn place!"

Up close, Mrs. Hamm was a hard-faced woman in her late fifties with short, perfectly cut, perfectly blonde hair. She was maybe a year or two older than her husband. Her hair was young, but her face was not.

"Tell me something," she demanded. "What's your name again?"

"Howard Moon Deer."

"Well, Howard, give it to me straight. Is there any life in this pathetic town?"

In fact, there *was* a good deal of life in San Geronimo. But Howie knew that the old people chatting on benches outside Walmart and arty New Agers contemplating their horoscope weren't quite Mrs. Hamm's idea of life.

"There are plenty of interesting people in San Geronimo," he answered patiently. "And of course there's always a party going on up at the ski mountain. People passing through on expensive vacations like an excuse to get a bit wild at night. You won't be bored."

She looked at him more closely. "What is it you do again?"

Before he could answer, Hamm broke in. "He's a goddamn private detective, Gloria! I told you that. I sent for him. We're having problems on the mountain and I need to find something out. So I hired him."

"Mr. Hamm, you haven't hired me yet," Howie interrupted as politely as possible. "Right now, I don't know exactly what you want, so I'm not sure if I'm the right person."

"Okay, okay," said Hamm. "We'll talk about that when we reach the office, not now. Now I'm going to shut my eyes and take a power nap. I need to restore myself."

"Leo takes a lot of power naps," confided Mrs. Hamm. "He says it's the secret of all success. Leo says everybody can be a billionaire—it's all in your attitude."

"I'll keep that in mind," said Howie.

The highway had been plowed and sprayed with red ice-melt, but the road remained snow-packed and the long slow line of cars climbing the mountain drove carefully. Halfway up, a car with Texas plates had spun out. Further along, a UPS truck was having trouble. The cops were out, lights flashing. The limousine proceeded past the trouble spots at 10 miles per hour.

"So, tell me about yourself, Howard," said Mrs. Hamm. But before he could open his mouth, she spoke first: "Myself, I was born poor. Brooklyn. Can you believe it?"

He did believe it. But didn't say so.

Mrs. Hamm—call me Gloria—recounted her early years in Brooklyn, and how she had skipped school to go to the Metropolitan Museum in Manhattan in order to see the great art there. Her other friends were interested in jewelry, mink coats, sex, whatever, but what Gloria Hamm adored was Culture. She had been a sensitive child with the soul of an artist.

Howie listened politely, absorbing enough to ask occasional questions. He didn't want to cut off anyone's autobiography. But his thoughts were elsewhere. With Mr. Hamm taking a power nap and Gloria Hamm recounting her childhood, he was starting to wish he was somewhere else too. Among other things, he was going to be stuck on the Peak without his car, which he had left at the airport. He would need to phone Georgie to rescue him.

They pulled into the resort through an entrance that was closed to the public. The utility road went all the way up to the central plaza at the base area where the new hotel, the Hamm Haus, was located.

The snow had transformed the resort since Howie was here yesterday. Every rooftop, every tree, every vehicle was buried. Monstrous earth-moving vehicles with flashing orange lights were attempting to plow the main arteries while snowblowers worked on clearing the paths. The sheer weight of the snow seemed to smother the valley, bringing all usual activity to a halt.

Howie zipped his parka to his chin as he climbed out of the limo behind the Hamms. The chairlifts weren't running yet—Patrol was still doing avalanche control—but there was a line of at least a hundred skiers and boarders at the bottom of the Coyote Lift, powder hounds waiting to be first in line for freshies on the mountain.

"Leo, slow down!" Gloria called after her husband who was marching ahead toward a side door to the hotel. "I'm going to slip and fall on my tush if I go any faster!"

Leo slowed down. He was an attentive husband. Howie followed the couple into a side entrance to the hotel. From what Howie could see, the Hamm Haus sported a lot of dark wood and frontier chic. It was the Rocky Mountain West as imagined by an expensive designer in New York.

Mr. Hamm shielded the keypad with his body as he punched in a code to the elevator. They rose to the 6th floor where the door opened onto a spacious reception area. There were huge windows on two sides looking out onto the mountains and the base area. It was a Vista-Vision view, Technicolor blue sky, brilliantly snow-covered mountain—all seen from great comfort with a fire burning in a huge stone fireplace.

A young woman sat at a large desk half-hidden behind an array of computer screens.

"This is my goddaughter," Hamm said brusquely as he led the way into his private office. "She'll have the contract for you to sign on your way out."

Howie was about to say hold on a second. They had matters to discuss before any contract was signed. But just then the woman looked up and he experienced a kind of electric shock.

It was the Polynesian damsel in distress he had rescued yesterday from the chairlift. Leilani.

He didn't know what to say. She was dressed in what seemed to be a kind of sari, white silk with a pattern of pink flowers on it. The sari hugged her body. One shoulder was bare. She looked at him gravely but gave no sign of their earlier encounter.

He stared at her foolishly as she went back to work.

"Come on, Moon Deer," said Hamm, storming forward. "Into my office!"

***

"God, that woman!" Hamm exploded, once the door to his private office was closed behind them. "There's times I'd like to kill her! Wring her goddamn neck!"

Howie couldn't think of an appropriate comment. "Your, uh, wife?"

Hamm became cautious. "I was joking, Moon Deer. I was speaking with poetic emphasis. Obviously, I love my wife. She's the apple of my Eden . . . what more could I ask from a woman? I've known her since I was six!"

"Sounds romantic," said Howie.

With a sigh, Leonard Hamm collapsed into a huge chair behind a vast desk. He pointed Howie to a leather armchair.

"Sit," he said.

Howie sat.

In the tinted window behind Hamm's head, Howie could see that the Coyote Lift was loading. Happy skiers and boarders were heading up the mountain. He wished he was one of them.

Hamm was studying him intently. Again, Howie had the impression of a large black bird, a raven who was considering whether to swoop down from a branch to snatch something to eat. Ravenous, thought Howie, understanding the word in a new light. Always hungry, never satisfied. Insatiable. Perhaps that was the definition of a billionaire, someone who forever wanted more.

"We're confidential here, aren't we?" Hamm asked softly.

"Yes, of course, Mr. Hamm. Even if I don't take the case, you're meeting with me this morning. Whatever you say is completely confidential . . . as long as you don't tell me something that's against the law," Howie added.

Hamm smiled grimly. When it came to sailing close to legal limits, he clearly knew the law better than Howie.

"I'm going to tell you a secret," he said. "I have an enemy. A very serious enemy who has caused me great harm." His smile was malicious. "I bet that surprises you, doesn't it? You probably imagine that I'm loved by all."

"Well—"

"Don't talk, listen. Daniel Gluck. Gluck the Fuck, that's what I call him—don't tell my wife, she doesn't like me to use the F word. You've heard of this pile of shit, I assume. The explosion this morning. Daniel Gluck? Dead, dead, dead!" he said merrily. "The asshole blew up in a million pieces!"

"Right," said Howie, remembering what he had half-heard on the radio. "The rocket that exploded this morning with tourists on it."

"Captain Cosmo!" Hamm cried gleefully. "The billionaire formerly known as Daniel Gluck!"

Howie thought Leonard Hamm was about to burst into song.

"So, Gluck is the person you say was your enemy?"

"It's our game, you see. It's complicated, but it's something you need to know about if you're going to work for me."

"Mr. Hamm, I haven't agreed to work for you," Howie insisted, not for the first time. "I need to know first what you want me to do."

"Here's what's happening. I plan to get revenge and you, my friend, are going to help me."

"Hold on. I'm not a big fan of revenge, Mr. Hamm. Besides, your enemy is dead," said Howie. "The game, as you call it, is over."

"No, this game isn't over until I can piss on his grave! He's left me wounded, you see. He's hurt my brand. He's like a dead rattlesnake that can still bite. What happened on that lift yesterday is going to cost me a lot of money, but I don't care about money. What I care about is winning. I care that people will think I'm weak if I let this go unanswered. This is *my* resort, *my* paradise in the mountains, and people aren't going to ski here if they think the chairlifts are vulnerable. So I want you to prove that Gluck was behind that attack. Get the evidence and then I'm going to sue his estate for everything he's got. I'm going to ruin that asshole!"

"You can't ruin an asshole who's dead," Howie repeated. "I'd say he's ruined enough already."

"Not dead enough. Now, Leilani is printing out our agreement. You'll be required to sign a confidentiality clause, of course. But you'll say yes when you see what I'm going to pay—"

"Mr. Hamm—"

"Listen to me. Listen to this story first, and then I'll let you decide. I know you'll see my side of the story."

"Mr. Hamm—"

"No, listen!"

***

"This whole thing with Gluck began in New York City in the late 1990s. He had the penthouse next to mine on a rooftop on Central Park West.

"We shared the entire 18th floor, the top. I had the north side of the building, he had the south. Our terraces met at a high metal fence with spikes on top. There was a good deal of vegetation as well, potted trees and shrubs, that gave us each privacy. But it didn't shut out the noise and the idiot had a party going every night. Loud music, drugs, girls. People shrieking and shouting. I'd get home from downtown and all I wanted was to stretch out on my part of the terrace and listen to Chopin. Do you know what I mean?"

"I like Chopin," said Howie.

"But you can't listen to Chopin, you can't even relax when your goddamn neighbor is shrieking and carrying on like it's the last days of Sodom and Gomorrah!"

"I can see that could be a problem," Howie conceded. He tried to picture the last days of Sodom and Gomorrah. He thought Hieronymus Bosch might have painted something along those lines. "But it's not the end of the world, after all. It's only a noisy neighbor."

"Not the end of the world? You don't understand! My God, it was torture, Moon Deer. It consumed me. It nearly drove me mad!"

"Did you complain?"

"Of course, I complained! I gave the jerk a courtesy phone call—just one phone call, mind you—to let him know that he was sharing the roof with another tenant and there were legal constraints in the co-op agreement from disturbing the other owners. He just laughed! You know what he called those parties? Bunga-bunga parties—after that idiot politician in Italy! It was a nightmare to have this Gluck, this loud monstrous infant next door. It may seem like a small thing, a noisy neighbor, but Gluck was destroying my perfect paradise!"

"I see," said Howie.

"He consumed me!" Hamm admitted. "So do you know what I did next?"

"What did you do next?" Howie asked cautiously.

His smile was dark. "I got Gluck kicked out of the building. Know how I did it?"

"Maybe you'd better not tell me."

"I hired an underage girl to go to one of his parties. She was fifteen. Then I arranged for the cops to break down the door. Cannabis, cocaine, underage girls, everyone ended up in jail. Which was the end of Mr. Gluck's brief sojourn in New York City. For a few months, I believed I had won."

"Won?" said Howie. "This was a contest?"

Hamm leaned forward. His eyes blazed with intensity. "Of course it was a contest! What do you think life is about? Power to the victor and losers lose. That's it!"

Howie shook his head.

"But the feud didn't stop there. Some months after the penthouse dust up, he managed to pull off a hostile takeover of one of my companies. I owned 49 percent of the stock, but he blindsided me—before I knew what had happened, the company was his. Well, you can imagine my fury. So I got even. Three months later I took over one of *his* franchises, video game outlets in shopping malls. But then my pet elephant died in mysterious circumstances."

"You had a pet elephant?"

"I loved my elephant. He made me feel like a rajah. I kept him at my Florida estate. But here's where it gets fun. Gluck's house in Big Sur burned down with his entire comic book collection in it! Can you imagine that? A grown-up collecting comic books! He blamed me, of course."

"Mr. Hamm, perhaps you'd better not tell me about this."

"Oh, nobody can prove anything! But from here it became a fight to the death. Let me tell you about Hawaii."

Howie sighed. As F. Scott Fitzgerald had put it, he was starting to suspect that the rich were indeed different from you and me.

***

"Hawaii!" said Hamm with a dreamy look in his eyes. "I sailed there in my yacht. That's the only way to see Hawaii, you know. Under sail after a long ocean voyage. Salt and sea, the stark awesome beauty of it! There you are on the blue water and all at once there's a speck of volcanic land, mountains rising from the sea."

"Sounds thrilling," said Howie. And he supposed it was. All you needed was a yacht.

"This was ten years ago. I was going through my sea-faring phase. *The Valhalla,* that was my ship. Three masts, a hundred and ten feet. Crew of seven. Our life on the water was entirely democratic. The crew and I had dinner together every night and usually a bit to drink. I even stood watch one night. And my God, did I love it! Here I am, I thought, enjoying life for the first time! I found a whole new version of *me* on that trip. *Me* the bold! *Me* the pirate adventurer! We sailed from Palm Beach through the Panama Canal to the Big Island, nearly a month on two different oceans.

"By the time we anchored off Kona, I was a true believer in the healing power of islands. I said to myself, I'm rich, I've won the race, why settle for less than this heavenly land? So I bought fifty acres north of Cook Bay. It was a very exclusive development, only four parcels. I had nearly five hundred yards of private beach and my own small lagoon. Palm trees, white sand, turquoise water! I guess I went a little native. I let my hair grow. I started wearing shorts and flip flops. I learned to play a ukulele. People started calling me the Hippie Billionaire!"

Howie managed a strained smile.

Hamm didn't smile back. His pale complexion glistened as sweat broke out on his forehead. "Unfortunately, as is sometimes the case with paradise, there was a snake in the garden," he said darkly. "Only in this case, the snake was a crocodile."

Howie tried to picture a snake that was a crocodile, but his imagination balked.

"Go on," he told the billionaire, with some misgivings.

***

The crocodile appeared mysteriously in Hamm's private lagoon late one afternoon. The reptile was a prehistoric monster at least 20 feet long with a mouth full of enormous teeth. His appearance was baffling because crocodiles weren't native to Hawaii, they didn't exist on the islands. Whoever this crocodile was, he'd been imported.

Hamm's tropical mansion sat on a small river that came down from the uplands and flowed into the lagoon. The house was designed with the South Pacific stories of Somerset Maugham in mind—a white two-story colonial plantation building with wide verandahs and coconut palms. The water of the lagoon was a luscious transparent blue, almost as warm as a swimming pool, you could see the sandy bottom. But the river water was brackish and for a short distance that ran alongside Hamm's beach, you couldn't see below the brown surface.

"*My* lagoon," Hamm liked to say on the phone to his employees back East. He loved having his own lagoon. For him a lagoon of your own meant that you had arrived.

On the day the crocodile appeared, Hamm received an odd gift anonymously in the mail: an old-fashioned time piece that ticked loudly. A clock. It was only later that Leonard Hamm understood the meaning of this gift.

The crocodile appeared from the brackish water of the river while two young women who worked in the kitchen were sitting on the sandy bank smoking pakalolo, hidden from the house.

The attack came out of nowhere.

A giant reptile emerged thrashing from the water, took a bite of the nearest leg, severed the leg completely, and disappeared with it into the river.

The girl who lost her leg was Pua Kalawai'a, twenty-five years old, pretty, the single mother of an 8-year-old daughter. Her friend screamed for help, and they put a belt around Pua's right thigh to try to stop the bleeding, but the wound was too large. Pua bled to death on the way to the hospital, thirty-two miles away.

"That crocodile was meant for me!" said Hamm with a frown that burned. "It wasn't meant for that girl. I swam in that lagoon every day," he said moodily. "Until that crocodile! Hawaii was ruined for me after that."

"I presume it was also ruined for the kitchen maid," Howie muttered.

"Oh, you can always find another kitchen maid! But once paradise is lost, it's lost forever. Did you know that? Gone forever! I couldn't even sleep in my house anymore. Every time I closed my eyes, I imagined huge teeth coming up from the depths of the water. So, I went back to New York after that, then Singapore. I was in exile. I roamed the Earth. And now here I am in New Mexico. And yet . . . wherever I go, that crocodile is always there in my mind, coming for me. Do you know what that's like?"

"I've had ghosts," said Howie. "But never crocodiles."

"They're bad," said Hamm.

"Did you keep the clock that you got in the mail?"

"I did."

"And you think someone was playing Captain Hook on you?"

"You bet I do! And there's only one person I know who's into games like that. Only one. Daniel Gluck. It took me two years, but I discovered Gluck owned the investment group that owned the corporation that had developed that beachfront for luxury lots. There were a bunch of shell corporations and I've never been able to prove it, but I know Gluck put that monster in my lagoon. I hired a team of detectives to discover where the creature came from. They learned that someone purchased a live crocodile in Costa Rica and had it sent to the Big Island. It took a special permit, of course. On the bill of lading it was supposed to be going to a Chinese restaurant in Hilo."

"A restaurant? Are you serious?"

"Crocodile isn't too bad, actually. Tastes a bit like chicken."

"Sure," said Howie.

"No, truly. But this croc never made it to Hilo. It disappeared en route. That's enough evidence for me."

"Mr. Hamm, this isn't something that would stand up in court."

"I don't care about courts. I only care about *me*, get it? And this changed *my* life. I've never been back to Hawaii, I never want to see it again. I have only one consolation. I brought Pua's little girl with me, I've brought her up. She's my island sunshine."

It took Howie a moment to connect the dots. "Leilani? She's the daughter of the woman who bled to death?"

"Leilani! I took care of her after her mother died. I raised her like she's my own. She's my legacy."

"I see," said Howie, absorbing this news. "You're her godfather."

"And you saved her yesterday on that damn chairlift! Now, here's what I want you to do. You're a private detective, you know this mountain, I want to nail the bastard who put Leilani's life in danger. The moron who sabotaged my chairlift. And you know who I'm talking about. Gluck the Fuck! My God, a poison dart! It's exactly the sort of thing that comic book bozo would dream up!"

Howie hadn't heard about the dart. "I'm sorry? What's this about a poison dart?"

"The cop told me. What's his name? Something to do with a sandwich."

"Ruben? Lieutenant Santo Ruben?"

"That's it. The lift supervisor, the one who climbed Tower 7, was killed with a poison dart. Who else but Gluck would dream up something like that?"

Howie was sorry to hear that Tomás was dead. Murdered. Howie had met him several times and always found him the embodiment of a wise elder from a bygone era—patient, humble, living in harmony with the land—qualities that had been lost with the younger generation. But death by a poison dart? If true, it was certainly an exotic way to die. He would need to ask Santo about this.

"Well, perhaps you're right about Gluck, I don't know. But Gluck is dead, Mr. Hamm," said Howie once again. "And clearly law enforcement is over this already. The State Police, FBI—those outfits have resources I don't."

"Then *get* the resources. I don't trust government agencies, I want my man in the mix. I'll give you the money to hire a staff, whatever you need . . . within reason, of course," he added more cautiously. "Look,

Moon Deer, you know people on this mountain. Patrol likes you. They'll tell you things they won't tell me. From what I hear, you're an insider."

"Really, I'm not," Howie assured him. "And if you want me to spy on Patrol the answer is no."

"I'm not saying spy on Patrol. I'm saying use your eyes and ears, your special access to find out who committed this crime. Is that wrong? I don't think so. All I want is the truth."

"Mr. Hamm, truth can be tricky. And in this case, the truth might be that Gluck had nothing to do with what happened at Tower 7. Would you be prepared for that?"

"If it *is* the truth and you can prove it. Yes, I will accept it. I'll think of a different way to come out on top."

Howie sighed. *Come out on top!* Was that all this man cared about?

"Now, here's another thought," said Howie. "If it turns out that Gluck hired someone to sabotage your chairlift, it will give you a good motive for blowing up his rocket with six people on board. This could come back to bite you. You could be accused of murder. Are you prepared for that?"

Hamm smiled grimly. "Why don't you let me take care of that angle. I can hire my own experts to prove the design of that rocket was badly flawed. Nobody is going to pin that on me. So let's not waste time haggling, Moon Deer. How much do you want? Give me a figure and I'll make it come true."

"I need some time to think about this, Mr. Hamm."

"What would you say to a twenty-thousand-dollar bonus for you to say yes, right now, this very moment!"

Hamm was like a car dealer delivering the final punch of salesmanship.

Howie had to admit twenty thousand dollars would be very useful right now. He'd be able to pay off his building loan . . .

"Plus, you charge me your usual fee and we'll double it," Hamm added. "Your expenses as well. I'll trust you. I know you'll do your best."

Howie didn't like Leonard Hamm. But he had to admit, he too was curious to know who planted that explosive device and shot Tomás Romero with a poison dart. Leonard Hamm had called San Geronimo Peak his mountain because he had bought it for cash. But Howie took a different view. Mountains belonged to themselves and those whose imaginations had been fired by the majestic beauty of their granite cliffs and snow. As a skier, he was personally offended by whoever had come here to put lives in danger.

If Howie had a client, he would have standing to investigate the crime. Without a client, he would be on the outside.

"All right," he said at last. "But I will decide how I'm going to run the investigation. I'll need to do this my way. As long as that's clear, I'll take the job."

"Good! You can go now, Moon Deer," said Hamm, dismissing him with a nod. "Give me a report as soon as possible. Leilani has some papers for you to sign and a check to give you. She's very good, believe me. You can put yourself entirely in her hands."

Chapter Eight

Howie found Leilani alone in the spacious reception area. She was standing next to a blazing stone fireplace in a corner of the room where two floor-to-ceiling glass walls met.

She seemed to be trying to absorb as much heat from the fire as possible. She looked cold.

"You should wear a sweater," he told her. "Or a fleece. We're not in Hawaii. We're in the Rocky Mountains above 9000 feet."

He hadn't meant to lecture, but she made him nervous. She looked at Howie with astonishment and an expression he couldn't read.

She put a slender finger to her lips to keep him from saying more.

"Please have a seat, Mr. Moon Deer," she told him. Her voice was friendly but impersonal. She led him to a small desk at the side of the room. "Here is a contract for you to sign, and a receipt for the bonus Mr. Hamm has promised."

Her voice was soft as a tropical breeze. Soothing. She looked like she should be riding in an outrigger canoe to meet a sailing ship, a flowered lei around her neck, her breasts bare. There was something innocent about her despite her almost indecent sexuality.

He watched as she placed a number of forms on the desk alongside a fountain pen. He saw that she already had a check in hand that appeared to be made out to him for $20,000.

"When did Hamm make out that check?" he demanded. "I only just accepted this job."

"Mr. Hamm always gets what he wants," she told him flatly. "Always, without exception. And at the moment he wants you. He wrote this check earlier on his plane."

"Really? He can see that far into the future?"

"Mr. Hamm can see what he wants to see," she answered obliquely. "Thank you very much for taking this investigation, Mr. Moon Deer. I too want to know why I nearly froze to death on that chairlift. Before . . . before you rescued me," she added with some reluctance.

It was nothing, he wanted to say. But for the moment he couldn't think of any words at all.

He read the contract, which was standard except for two things. First, a number of places were left blank for him to write in his hourly fee.

"You can ask for whatever you want," Leilani told him, looking at him directly.

"$400 is the high end of my adjustable hourly rate. I'll charge you that."

"You can bill us," she told him. "Any time."

The second exception was his insistence on secrecy. There were several pages assuring Howie that if he ever blabbed about his work for Leonard Hamm he would be thrown to the wolves, torn up in pieces, ruined forever. Since, generally speaking, he kept the confidentiality of his clients anyway, this was a bit extreme.

Howie signed. He took the check.

"Thank you," she told him, their hands meeting briefly as he handed her the pen. "Let me show you out."

She left the fireplace reluctantly and led the way across the room. Before they reached the elevator, Leilani stopped and faced him.

"You know, I forgot to get a receipt from you."

"A receipt? But I signed the contract. Isn't that enough?"

"No, it isn't."

Suddenly, she had opened a nondescript door and pulled Howie in after herself, shutting the door behind them.

In the blink of an eye, she was in his arms, her body against his, kissing him almost violently on his lips. Their tongues touched and did a little dance. Howie was so surprised that he didn't break off as quickly as he should have. They were in a guest bathroom, with a sink and a toilet.

"You saved me!" she said passionately. "Please, will you save me again? Will you help me escape?"

"Leilani, stop that! What are you talking about?"

"They think of me as their pet! I'm their slave. They like having a poor waif to take care of, and they never want to let me go. I'm a prisoner! Will you help me, Howard? Please!"

Though Howie believed in saving damsels in distress, a damsel who needed to be saved a second time within two days was pushing the envelope. But before he could answer, there was a loud knock on the bathroom door.

"Mr. Moon Deer, this is security! We need you and Miss Kalawai'a to come out of that room! You must come out immediately!"

Chapter Nine

At 2 o'clock Friday afternoon, Georgina Moon Deer sat in the office working the phone, promoting an event that evening at the Pueblo Community Center.

This was a personal crusade for Georgie, not connected with her work for her father's detective agency. She was the secretary of the newly-formed non-profit, Forest Friends, who were fighting Leonard Hamm, determined to stop a revolving restaurant that was planned for the top of San Geronimo Peak overlooking sacred Indian land.

The restaurant would stand at 12,136 feet and be reached by a gondola that ran throughout the year, bringing in untold thousands of tourists. From the Native perspective, this was beyond outrageous. It would be a crass assault of commercialism that would destroy the sanctity of the mountains, not only for the Indians but for everyone. San Geronimo would never be the same. Georgie was determined to wake the community up to the tidal wave of big money that was about to transform their beautiful town into a second-rate Disneyland.

Her job as secretary was an entirely voluntary position since Forest Friends had no money. The "friends" were a handful of young Indians at the Pueblo who fashioned themselves sexy revolutionaries in the mold of Che Guevara. Georgie liked the guys. Despite their pretensions, they were very sweet. They had all hit on her at one time or another, but she'd been able to rebuff their advances without any bad feelings.

Georgie had gotten in with the young crowd at the Pueblo after doing pro-bono investigation work for MMIW, Missing and Murdered Indigenous Women, an organization she supported passionately. For the past six months she had been working with a Pueblo family whose 17-year-old daughter had disappeared, and after finding the girl in California she had become something of a hero. The guys liked having Georgie around and had been eager to rope her into being their secretary.

She gave it her best shot.

"Hi, my name is Georgie and I'm calling on behalf of Forest Friends. We're meeting tonight at 7 o'clock at the Pueblo Community Center to stop San Geronimo Peak from building a revolving restaurant on the top of the mountain. Not only will this construction destroy valuable natural habitat, but there are serious concerns about water pollution. Plus, it will bring the worst kind of tourism to northern New Mexico—more second homes, less affordable housing for locals . . ."

Georgie paused for breath long enough to notice that the listener had hung up. Her words vanished into empty space.

Undeterred, she called the next number on her list and began again.

"Hi, my name is Georgie and I'm calling on behalf of Forest Friends . . . yes, I have a Scottish accent . . . no, I am not a Marxist . . . well, fuck you, too," she told him.

Georgie had been in the United States for nearly four years now, but she still felt like a foreigner. It wasn't only her Scottish brogue that separated her. Americans, on the whole, found her accent charming. But being a Scottish Indian—Lakota on her father's side—made her a double oddity. A triple oddity, in fact, for she was half-Anglo, too. Her biological mother had been Grace Stanton, Howie's college girlfriend. "The beautiful Grace!" Howie always said with a heavy touch of irony.

The five founding members of Forest Friends, the aspiring Che Guevaras, smoked a good deal of weed, and though they could talk up a storm—expounding big ideas well into the night—they needed someone like herself, weed free, to get anything done. Basically, they needed a mother, as Georgie saw it. She was the one who convinced them that they could broaden their support if their opposition to the restaurant wasn't only an Indian cause, but a broader fight against something that was happening up and down the Rocky Mountains. All that was necessary was to bring the various groups together into an unstoppable coalition. Anglo, Spanish, Indian, environmentalists, ranchers, artists, hippies, anarchists, and those who had simply come to San Geronimo to escape the tumult of modern times, searching for peace of mind.

There would certainly be no peace of mind if the sacred mountain was turned into a cheesy tourist attraction. What next, a Santa's Village with fake reindeer? It didn't matter if Leonard Hamm had hundreds of millions of dollars to throw at them, they would have the will of the people. They would win.

Georgie's fervor was founded on anger. Like many of her generation, she was furious that her parents' generation had bequeathed them a broken world. Climate change, racism, horrible wars, pollution, fascism, rising inequality, lies, hate . . . the ills went on and on. More prosaically, rents were sky high and no one her age would ever be able to afford to buy a house (unless mommy and daddy were loaded.)

You had to fight back. Georgie lived by the adage that when a butterfly flapped its wings in Australia, it changed the weather in Montana. Or maybe the butterfly was in the Amazon jungle, she couldn't remember. The point was everything you did affected everything else, no matter how minutely. Everything you did mattered. You had to fight for the good. And if millions of butterflies began flapping their wings in unison, God help the ruling class!

Georgie Moon Deer, 23 years old, brimming with idealism, closed up the office at 5 o'clock, unburied her battered, snow-covered Subaru in the alley behind the building, and set off on the treacherous roads to the Pueblo to do battle with Leonard Hamm, the arch-enemy.

**

Georgie had not learned to drive until she came to America. With plenty of public transportation in Britain, it hadn't seemed necessary. After moving to San Geronimo, she had been happy to get around at first by bicycle until Howie kept pressing her to get a driver's license. After some initial resistance, she had discovered that she liked to drive. In fact, she loved it. It meant freedom. You could get out and about whenever you liked. Howie had even given her his old Subaru.

The temperature outside was 16 degrees. The winter sky was blood red in the western horizon as the sun slipped slowly into the distant mesas and mountains. As the twilight deepened, the new snow made everything fantastical, magical, and Georgie felt suddenly very happy. The first stars appeared, and Venus sparkled in the western sky like a diamond.

Georgie passed a snowplow with a whisker to spare, avoiding a van coming at her in the opposite lane, flashing its lights frantically.

"Relax, buddy. I have this under control," she said aloud, as she shimmied back to her own lane.

Once she was past the snowplow, Georgie felt herself relax. The Outback had all-wheel drive and good snow tires so Georgie imagined herself free to drive pretty much as usual. Over the past few months, she had been made to feel welcome at the Pueblo, which was normally closed to outsiders, and tonight she passed by the main entrance and turned right onto a smaller road that crossed a cattle guard onto Indian land. At the head of the road a sign said NO ENTRY ONTO PUEBLO LAND. As the secretary of Forest Friends, Georgie took the shortcut and ignored the sign.

The back road into the Pueblo hadn't been plowed but a number of vehicles had been through, creating two parallel tracks in the snow that pointed toward the mountains. It looked doable to Georgie. She put her faith in the power of Subaru.

But cars do not run on faith alone. A few hundred yards down the road, the bottom of her Outback pancaked in the snow and the wheels—all four of them, snow tires and all—spun uselessly.

Georgie was stuck, no houses in sight. She sat for a moment absorbing her situation.

Fortunately, she had Triple A, extended coverage. Her father had insisted. She found her phone and called the emergency road help number, was put on hold, and finally got through to an agent.

She gave her information thinking now she would be on the road again quickly. But the agent told her that due to the storm, there were a large number of drivers currently needing help and her wait time for a tow truck would be two and a half hours.

"Damn!" said Georgie. *Two and a half hours!*

She was feeling seriously stuck, wondering if she should abandon her car and hike. The lights of a house beckoned from perhaps half a mile away. But it was bitterly cold, the night was dark, the snow was deep, and she thought it best to stay where she was.

"*An donas càr!*" she cried aloud in Gaelic, a language she reverted to in times of stress—damn this car—just as the headlights of a monstrously large white pick-up truck pulled up behind her and came to a stop, engine running. With Georgie blocking the road, there was no way for it to get by.

After a moment, a large Indian man wearing a dark cowboy hat stepped from the truck and came her way. Georgie lowered her window and tried not to look as helpless as she felt.

The man was a little scary. His face was rugged and strong. Mid-forties, she decided. His eyes appraised her coldly.

"I'm stuck," she admitted. He had broad shoulders, he looked strong. In fact, this was exactly what she needed at the moment, manly brawn. "Can you help me get out?"

"It seems I'll have to," he said. "Can't get by otherwise. You're holding me up, girl."

"I'm sorry," she told him, flustered. She thought of telling him she was a woman, not a girl, but decided she'd better not. "I'm here for the Forest Friends meeting. I'm—"

"I know who you are," he said. He gave Georgie a look that was unreadable. Without another word, he shook his head and turned. He walked to a toolbox in the bed of his truck and set to work getting her unstuck from the snow.

***

"Put your car in neutral and take off the brake," said the brawny Indian. "I'm going to push you to the side."

She smiled. "Not too far to the side, please," she told him. "I don't want to be even more stuck in the snow."

"Then you shouldn't have used this road," he replied curtly.

He returned to his truck and edged forward so that his front bumper touched her rear bumper. The monster truck had no trouble pushing her to the side of the snow-covered road. When this was done, he backed up a few feet then drove forward so that he was in front. The engine of his truck growled like an angry beast. He stepped out of his cab and again came to her window.

"You can get out and help me fit this chain around your front end," he told her brusquely. Georgie didn't know why she found this faintly sexual. She quickly censored the thought as ridiculous.

"Take the end of the chain and slip the hook underneath the front of your car. Wherever you can find a good hold. You'll have to get on your back."

Get on my back?

"Now hurry up, girl—I have a busy night."

Georgie hadn't been dismissed like this since she was a child. As an attractive young woman, she was accustomed to men paying more deference to her. With a sigh, she lowered herself onto the snow and slid under the front of her car. It wasn't a very pleasant place to be on a night when the temperature was 16 degrees. A drip of oil plipped onto her jacket. With some difficulty, she found a place to connect the chain to his massive truck. She hoped it would hold.

"Got it," she told him.

"All right, get in the cab."

"I can ride in my car while you tow me."

"No, you can't. Do what I tell you. Get in the cab."

Emotionally, Georgie felt 13-years-old. She had gone through an awkward teenage time then when everything she did turned out wrong. Extreme ineptitude.

She climbed upward into the passenger seat of the cab. "My God, you just about need a step ladder to get into this thing!" she told him.

He gave her a disapproving look but didn't comment.

There was a CB radio and microphone on the dashboard as well as a rifle that was held in place with a bracket. Georgie wasn't sure what she had gotten herself into. Without a word, the man drove forward slowly until the chain was tight, then he sped up with Georgie's Subaru riding behind. Examining him in profile, she realized he was quite handsome in a battered, mid-40s way. He had a strong jawline and a face etched in stone. He was an intimidating presence.

He paid no attention to her as they drove into the residential neighborhoods. There were aging adobe houses alongside trailers and prefab homes. Everything looked like a wintry postcard under the snow in the moonlight.

The roads were plowed as they came to the community buildings, the small health clinic and the elementary school. The Community Center where her meeting was planned was a one-story BIA funded building that looked exactly its part, cheaply made but with good intent, a gift of the government.

Georgie turned to the man before she got out of the cab. "Thank you," she said. "I'll be fine from here, if you'll just unchain me."

She wished she hadn't said unchain me. It didn't sound right. Without a word, he slipped easily beneath her Subaru and pulled the chain loose. He stood and faced her. His eyes were like granite as they studied her.

"Now listen carefully," he said. "You need to stay on the main roads from now on. I don't want to see you in the back country again. Understood?"

"Yes, sir," she replied.

"Whew!" she said aloud as she watched his red taillights drive away.

Chapter Ten

The inside of the Community Center was plain, no frills. There was a raised stage at the far end of a bare room that had a few folding tables and chairs. Off behind a partition, there was a small kitchen and bathroom. No religious ceremonies were performed in this space, the building was strictly civic. The water board met here once a month, the center hosted after-school activities for children, and two mornings a week there were exercise classes for seniors. Occasionally a speaker from the BIA showed up to explain all the wonderful things the U.S. government was doing for Indians.

Georgie set up one of the folding tables near the front door with handouts explaining the goals of Forest Friends. She had a sign-up sheet she had printed back at the office for volunteers who wished to get further involved. Donations were encouraged. Attendees to the meeting could donate with cash, check, or with a small credit card device Georgie had borrowed from a yoga studio where she took T'ai Chi classes on Monday and Wednesday evenings.

At first it didn't look as though anyone would show up. The five young activists who comprised Forest Friends shuffled around the empty room restlessly discussing plans for a possible music festival that would bring in tons of money.

"I bet we could get Taylor Swift for something like this," said Jerry Trujillo, one of the guys, not the brightest of the lot.

"Come on, man, Taylor Swift don't care about no Indians!" said Larry White Owl. "She only cares about that football asshole!"

"Lots of famous bands are big on Indians," said Pete Day Rise. "It makes them look cool to their fans."

Pete was the alpha male of the group, the nominal leader. He was going to give a speech later and at close to seven he stepped outside for a few hits of weed in order to boost his "spirit energy," as he put it. He was buzzed when he returned inside and walked over to where Georgie was sitting at her welcome table.

"Look, did you make those phone calls we talked about?" he asked. "We're not exactly getting a stampede."

"Pete, I spent the entire afternoon working the phone," she told him. "I'm not sure what more I could have done."

"Well, we'll give it a few more minutes, I guess. Probably the snow is keeping some people away."

Pete was the oldest of the group, nearly thirty, a wiry man with light olive skin and expressive brown eyes that were slightly red at the moment. He looked more Spanish than Native. The Spanish had kept Indian slaves well into the 20th century and had been interbreeding with the Pueblo for five hundred years.

Georgie was starting to worry that the meeting was going to be a flop when gradually people started arriving, an assortment of Anglos and Indians. There were only a few dozen people all in all—several artists, a writer for *The San Geronimo Post*, someone from the Democratic Party looking for votes, environmentalists, one or two scruffy hippies, and a few types Georgie couldn't pin down.

A tall albino man with another Anglo wandered in, both of them in jeans, cowboy boots, and leather jackets. They looked more like bikers than environmentalists, not at all the sort who might come to a meeting like this. The albino was at least six foot three. He had white short cropped hair, no eyebrows. Both were heavily tattooed. Georgie felt an instinctive dislike of the two men that she did her best to repress. People, she knew, should not be judged by their physical appearance. Probably they had beautiful souls. Nevertheless, she was surprised when she saw Pete go over to them and greet them effusively.

"Cool, glad you guys could make it!" she heard Pete say. "Find yourself some chairs and make yourselves comfortable. I think you're going to like what we're doing here."

A few minutes later, she saw Pete walking importantly through the room and she grabbed him by the arm.

"Who are those guys?" she asked.

"What guys?"

"The ones you were talking with. The albino and his friend. They look like drug dealers."

Pete laughed. "Sure, well, maybe. But drug dealers have money and some of those dudes have some fairly revolutionary ideas about things. I met them playing pool in town the other day. Look, Georgie, we're looking for support from all sorts of people, not just the arty crowd. So, you need to keep an open mind, okay?"

"Sure, Pete. You're right," she acknowledged.

"You bet I'm right," he told her enthusiastically, giving her a peck on the cheek. Up close, he reeked of marijuana.

Why was she worried? She told herself to relax. She didn't want to come off as someone who had gone to a fancy university. Though in fact, that was the truth. She couldn't help it. She *had* gone to a fancy university.

Pueblo lands climbed the entire western side of San Geronimo Peak, where they met at the top with the ski resort, which occupied the entire northeast side of the mountain. In the mid-20th century, the Pueblo had won a legal fight that had returned to them much of their traditional land. But the ski resort had also expanded. They were joined at the hip, geographically speaking, though it would never be an easy match for two such different cultures to share a mountain. Hamm had the nearly imperial power of big money. But Forest Friends had moral authority, a mission.

At 7:30, Pete Day Rise stepped onto the stage and got the meeting off to a rousing start.

"So why are we here tonight?" Pete cried into the microphone he carried in his right hand. "We've come to protect our sacred land from desecration. We're here to defend our culture against the obscenity of money . . . not just our culture, but *your* culture, too," he said, pointing to an Anglo artist in the crowd. "We're here to say, no, you don't, we won't let you. You can take your bulldozers, your chairlifts, your gondolas, and go back to New York City where you belong. We're going to stop you! Our religion is our land! So we're going to roast you, Porky Pig! We're going to barbecue you for dinner!"

Georgie cringed when she heard Pete say Porky Pig, which was his pet name for Leonard Hamm. It was apt, she supposed, but she believed Forest Friends should take the high road, not the way of cheap insults.

Pete worked the small crowd as though he was in a huge stadium. He wasn't bad, but he wasn't particularly good either. He belabored his point, repeating himself often. Still, he covered the main idea, that the sacred land needed to be protected against greedy commercialism. And what was true for the Indians—the intrusion into their way of life— would be true for everyone else. With gondola rides to a restaurant at the top of the Peak, San Geronimo would be changed forever, overwhelmed with the sort of tourism that would affect the quality of the life in San Geronimo for everyone who lived there.

There was a good deal of hooting and cheering from the small audience. Georgie wasn't sure she liked this kind of rebel-rousing. What Georgie wanted was a sane, thoughtful debate where people actually listened to one another.

"So we're here tonight to raise money for the great work that lies before us," said Pete at last, getting to the nitty-gritty. "The first thing we need to do is hire ourselves a really good lawyer, and this is going to cost a bundle. But we've got a plan. We're going to put on a music festival to raise awareness as well as the cash we need to take our effort to the next step. Remember, Hamm is a pig from Wall Street. He's got lawyers up the wazoo. So if we're going to fight him, we need to have lawyers, too."

"Hey, we can hold the festival on the twenty acres next to the Cortez place," someone shouted. "We'll put up a big tent and have food booths. If we can get some big-name bands, the whole town will turn out!"

"That's bullshit, you just want to turn this whole thing into a rock concert!" someone else shouted.

Someone else called out that they would need to get permission from the Pueblo elders to sell beer and wine.

Another person shouted that a rock concert was absurd, the wrong approach, another example of what was wrong with the world.

The meeting was turning into a melee. Georgie was starting to feel frustrated. Out of nowhere, there were suddenly two factions.

"It could be a three-day festival!" said someone else in the room. "We could have craft booths—"

"Sure, sell T-shirts!" said one of the anti-rockers scornfully. "This is totally against Native values. What we want is to protect our sacred land, not have a party!"

"Music is sacred!"

"Not *your* kind of music!"

Someone in the back of the room whistled to get attention. "Calm down, everyone!" he said, not loudly, but with authority.

Georgie was interested to see that the quarreling did in fact stop. For a moment there was silence. She turned to see who had spoken. It was the man with the monster pickup truck who had pulled her out of the snow. He had some undefinable charisma, a physical presence.

"A hunk, isn't he?" whispered a woman who had come up beside her.

"I'm sorry?"

"That guy over there. I mean, *that's* my idea of a man!"

"But who is he?"

"Don't you know? He's John Concha, the War Chief. He was an Army colonel in Afghanistan. That's one tough cookie!"

Georgie turned to the woman with interest. She was an Anglo with short light brown hair, thirty-something, quite pretty. Cute. She smiled pleasantly.

"Julie North, CNN," she said introducing herself. She gave Georgie a firm handshake. "Can I talk to you a moment?"

Georgie was impressed. "Really? CNN?" This was exactly what the Friends needed, publicity on CNN. "You think this might be a national story?"

"Of course," said Julie. "Big money is buying up the West, up and down the Rockies. This is huge."

"Exactly!" Georgie was quick to agree. "It isn't fair that one very rich individual should have the power to change our lives so profoundly. You know, I wouldn't mind so much if these billionaires were philosopher kings come down from the heavens to set everything right. But they're not. They're vain, they're childish—they're very ordinary people who just happened to get lucky. I'd say some of them are sub-ordinary."

"So you're going to take on Leonard Hamm?"

"We are!"

"Good for you! My cameraman is waiting outside. If you come with me, I'd like to do an interview and you can tell me all about it."

"I'd be delighted," said Georgie.

She followed Julie outside. The night was bitterly cold. There was no moon, no stars, only a darkness so complete it was like stepping into a deep velvety box. She could see nothing, and certainly not a CNN cameraman.

"He's right over here," said Julie, taking Georgie's arm and leading her away from the Community Center further into the darkness and deep snow.

***

Georgie hated to think that people might lie to her. *She* didn't lie. So why should they? Truth was beauty, and beauty truth. But as the woman who called herself Julie North led her further into the darkness, she began to suspect that something wasn't right.

"Wait a second!" she said. "Where are we going?"

They walked over a rise and into a depression and now no lights at all were visible from the community center or other houses.

"Hold on! Where are you taking me?" she cried, refusing to go another inch. "You're not from CNN, are you?"

The woman stopped and turned. It was so dark, Georgie could only see the dimmest outline of her face.

"You're over your head, Georgie," she said. "You have no idea what you've gotten yourself into."

"What are you talking about?" Georgie demanded. "I'm not over my head with anything, thank you very much!"

"You and your father, you're in this together. But who are you working for, that's what we need to know."

"This is ridiculous. I work for my father, aye—he runs the Wilder detective agency. But that has nothing to do with why I'm here tonight. Now, you will have to excuse me—I'm going back to the meeting."

"Your Forest Friends sabotaged that chairlift yesterday and killed a lift supervisor. This is a very serious matter, Georgie—domestic terrorism. And if you don't want to spend the rest of your life in prison, you're going to need to start cooperating with me right now."

Georgie's mouth fell open, stunned by the accusation. She had heard about the lift evacuation, of course. Everyone was talking about it in town. She knew Howie had been skiing on the Peak and had been involved with the rescue, but she hadn't spoken to him and didn't know the details.

"Who are you?" Georgie demanded.

"I know this is an Indian cause," said Julie, ignoring the question. "I know you want to protect your sacred land. But someone was killed up there yesterday and this protest of yours has gotten out of hand. Now, if you cooperate and tell me everything you know, it will go a long way toward helping your case. It's obvious to me that you were duped into something you didn't really understand."

"Who the hell are you?" Georgie asked a second time.

"I'm from the FBI, Georgie, and we want to help you."

"Oh, please! Spare me the crap!"

"You're not from here, Georgie. You don't know how things work in America. There are radical left-wing people who worm their way into Indian groups like yours and take advantage of your innocence. If you help me, I'll make sure you aren't charged with a crime. But I need you to start talking to me right now."

"I haven't committed any crime. We're fighting Hamm's expansion of San Geronimo Peak for very good reasons, and we're going about it in a completely legal manner. Now, if you will excuse me . . ."

Georgie was peering across the snow trying to find the community center in order to get away, but the darkness was so thick she couldn't see a thing. Luckily her iPhone had a torch. A flashlight, as they called it here. She raised the phone and tapped the icon.

The light was abrupt and she was shocked to see two men walking their way from a dozen feet away. They were wearing strange night vision goggles strapped to their heads that made them look more like robots than men. Georgie was so surprised by their sudden appearance she couldn't speak at first, couldn't move. They had pistols in their hands that were fitted with silencers. Coming at her from the dark, they were figures from a nightmare, terrifying.

Georgie threw herself sideways onto the snow. It was an instinctive reaction, to get away, hide. The phone slipped from her hand as she tumbled and rolled nearly a dozen feet until she was stopped by a sagebrush.

A gun plipped two times and there was a cry, a wet gurgle. There was a third plip and the cry was cut short. She heard a body collapse onto the snow, brushing against the branch of a sagebrush as it fell.

Georgie scampered away as fast as she could, escaping blindly into the night. She was too panicked to think. She stayed low, crawling, sometimes on her hands and knees, other times half-risen on her hands and feet like a spider. She heard footsteps close behind her.

She picked herself up, ran, tripped, picked herself up again, ran into a sagebrush, and fell flat on her face.

She waited, her face in the snow, breathing hard, certain she was about to die. She clutched her arms protectively around her head, a useless gesture.

But now the footsteps were receding into the distance, crunching the snow as they went. They were walking away. Georgie was afraid to move. She lay as still as she could until she could no longer hear anything except her own raspy breathing. She prayed the men were gone, but how could she be certain?

Time had lost whatever meaning it once had. She couldn't say how long she waited lying face down on the snow, her head turned just enough so she could breathe. It was cold in the snow. She couldn't stay here forever, but she waited and listened until her breathing slowed. Finally, she struggled to her feet. Her body was numb with cold. She couldn't feel her hands and legs.

With a great effort, she climbed out of the gully onto the bank hoping to get a better idea of where she was. But there wasn't a light anywhere. She was lost in the snowy hills, she had no idea where. There was only the desert, with strange weedy growths sticking up from the snow.

She knew she couldn't be far from the Community Center, but she couldn't see it anywhere.

"All right!" she said to herself. "I'm alive. I just need to calm down and think."

She was calming just a little when she heard a sound that made her heart race back into high gear. Someone was walking nearby. Georgie turned and began running from the footsteps. But she was disoriented, exhausted, too cold to think coherently. As she ran, the darkness seemed to congeal in front of her into something darker still. She ran straight into the arms of huge man.

She screamed.

"Be quiet, I'm not going to hurt you," said the man calmly.

In the dark, he was nothing more than a shadow, but she recognized his voice. It was the War Chief, John Concha. Georgie wasn't sure if this was good or bad, but she was momentarily relieved to be in his arms. His strength was comforting.

"Oh, God!" she said. "Someone just shot the woman I was talking to! I got away, I don't know how. I ran and ran and hid in the snow. I don't know where I am. I've been trying to find my way back to the Community Center but I'm lost!"

"What woman?"

Georgie couldn't answer. "Oh, God, oh, God!" she said again and again. "It was horrible!"

"Tell me," he said.

"Just got to catch my breath."

"What woman?"

"Okay, okay, I'm okay . . . she said she was from CNN, and she wanted to interview me. She said let's go outside where her cameraman was waiting, but it was a lie. As soon as we got a little way off, she told me she wasn't with CNN, she was from the FBI. She started accusing me of being involved in sabotaging the chairlift at the ski resort. The whole thing was crazy. Then two men appeared with night goggles and guns with silencers. They shot Julie . . . Julie North, that's the name of the woman who said she was FBI. There were three shots and she fell down into the snow. I think she's dead. It was awful!"

Concha didn't speak for a moment. She held onto his arm, afraid she would lose her balance and fall if she let go.

"Can you take me to the body?"

"Aye, of course, I can. Do you have a torch? I'll just follow my footsteps backward on the trail I made in the snow."

Concha had a flashlight. They followed Georgie's trail and after a few minutes they arrived at where she had left Julie in the snow. There was still an imprint of where she had fallen. But there was no body. There wasn't any sign of Julie North, or whoever she had been.

"I don't know where she's gone."

"Maybe she rose from the dead," Concha suggested.

"Look, there's my phone that I dropped!" She reached down, picked up her iPhone, and dusted off the snow. "And there are the footprints of the two men with guns!"

"All right, let's follow them and see where they go."

The War Chief led the way with his flashlight. They came over a rise and the Community Center came into view less than a hundred yards away, the windows glowing with light. It hadn't been that far away. Georgie had been going in the wrong direction. If she hadn't been so frightened and disoriented, she would have found her way back quite easily.

The footprints merged with other footprints as they got closer to the building and soon it was impossible to make any sense of them.

"I guess this is where I was walking with that Julie North woman," Georgie said thoughtfully, studying the tracks. "The two men must have gone back inside. Or maybe they just left in their car."

"Maybe," said the War Chief.

"I'm telling you what happened!" she told him angrily. "Let's go back to where she was shot. I'm sure we'll find something!"

They returned a second time to where Georgie believed the woman had been killed but by now the snow was so churned up, the scene offered no clues of what had happened. They spent another ten minutes tramping around the sagebrush looking for her body but there was nothing to find. No blood, no bullet casings, nothing at all but meaningless footprints in the snow.

"This is where she was standing, I promise," Georgie told him. "I heard her get shot. She has to be dead!"

"Sure," said the War Chief.

"They must have taken the body away and cleaned up the blood. That wouldn't be so hard to do, would it?"

"Well, who knows?" said Concha stoically. "Let's get you inside someplace warm. I suppose we'd better call your father. He'll be worried about you."

"You know my father?"

"I do," said the War Chief without much enthusiasm.

Chapter Eleven

Howie's close encounter with Leilani in the hall bathroom left him feeling more than a little edgy. Morally, sexually, emotionally he was a mess.

He had enjoyed kissing Leilani, that was the problem. He had liked the feel of her body against his. His body said *more, more, more!*

But his brain said, no, no, no. What about Claire?

And then there was the embarrassment. Two security guards had burst into the bathroom while he was wrapped in her arms. He knew it didn't look good.

Howie was escorted from the building, a guard on each side holding onto his arms. The last he saw of Leilani, she was standing by the toilet rearranging her sari.

Howie blinked in the sunlight, humiliated and upset. Gossip moved at the speed of light on San Geronimo Peak and he feared he was going to be the butt of many jokes, all of them exaggerated for effect—banging Hamm's goddaughter in a hall bathroom!

But he hadn't.

I'm innocent! It was Leilani who had assaulted him. But who would believe that?

He didn't quite believe it himself. In fact, there was something off about the entire episode. It occurred to him that the Polynesian sexpot had been playing him, that he was a pawn in some game he didn't understand. He certainly didn't believe she found him so attractive she couldn't keep her hands off him. It was a flattering thought, but he didn't buy it.

Perhaps she really did want to be rescued from her gilded cage, believing that if she threw sex his way he would be more inclined to help.

Or maybe she was trying to make her "godfather" jealous, knowing the escapade in the bathroom would be reported to him.

Whatever it was, he didn't like it.

Howie stood on the plaza that led to the slopes and tried to get his bearings. It was a brilliant afternoon, blue sky, blazing white snow. Hundreds of people were milling about in colorful outfits with skis and snowboards looking for a good time. Many had a beer in hand. Howie checked his phone. He saw that it was a few minutes after 2 o'clock in the afternoon.

He expelled his breath as the tension deflated from his body.

What now? he wondered.

He felt so wobbly it took him a moment to remember that he had promised Sean to go see him after his meeting with Hamm. He was supposed to fill out a witness statement.

A witness statement was something he could deal with.

In order to get to Sean, he would need to go to his locker where he stored his skis. He hoped his legs were still capable of making turns.

***

Howie rode two different chairlifts to Ski Patrol's high mountain perch. There were two snowmobiles parked out front of the shack and the wind was blowing fiercely.

Howie stepped out of his skis and left them against the building with a dozen other parked skis and boards. A sign on the door said, NO PUBLIC BATHROOM. Which was putting it delicately. There was in fact a primitive toilet in the back of the building for Patrol to use, not much more than a seat over a pit. Smelly was putting it mildly.

The primitive condition of the mountain headquarters and the low pay were some of Patrol's many issues with the new management of San

Geronimo Peak, who were spending hundreds of millions of dollars on hotels, restaurants, and condos—but not much on those who kept the mountain safe.

The inside of the headquarters was rough and woodsy. There was a long plank table where three Patrollers were sitting drinking coffee. At the front of the building, there was a glass booth where the dispatcher sat at a large window fielding calls and responding to emergencies. There were two small offices in the rear. Everywhere there were coiled ropes, bulletin boards, walkie-talkies, avalanche beacons, all sorts of specialized mountain equipment. A jumble of signs on poles were stacked in a corner. The signs could be stuck in the snow warning skiers of cliffs, closed trails, rocks, and other hazards. Three Code Blue backpacks full of medical gear were hung on the walls ready to go at a moment's notice. Code Blue meant someone was in serious trouble.

Howie found Sean in the larger of the two office cubicles, a crowded little space with barely room for a desk, two wooden chairs, a computer, a radar weather screen, and Sean's pack—which was also ready to go at a moment's notice. The pack had a folding snow shovel tied to the back. When you were in Ski Patrol there often wasn't a moment to lose.

Sean was in his early forties, with long wheat colored hair and a shaggy blond-white beard. The room was warm, and he had stripped down to a turtleneck sweater and his work vest. The vest was loaded with scissors, tape, a radio harness, bandages, notebooks, even a candy bar for quick energy.

"Well, well, it's Moon Deer!" he greeted. "So how was your meeting with our glorious boss? What did that idiot want from you?"

"He's hired me to investigate the lift sabotage."

"Yeah? Well, stand in line. The state cops have an investigation going and the FBI has become involved as well. Someone from Homeland Security is showing up tomorrow. The incident is being regarded as terrorism. And that's what I've been doing all day, answering questions, dealing with cops and investigators and lawyers. They'll want to talk to you as well, Moon Deer, so be careful. You'll want to think carefully about what you say. You don't want to give those guys an opening."

"I'll tell them the truth, that's all."

"The truth!" said Sean with a snort-like laugh. "Good luck with that! In a virtual world, truth is anything you want it to be! I should warn you, Hamm's a paranoid freak. He has guns hidden all over his penthouse, a couple of guns in every room so he can always get to one quickly if he's threatened. I know because the cabinet maker who designed the hiding places is a friend of mine."

Howie laughed. "Well, I guess the rich have cause to worry that one day those who have-not will turn on those who have. Hamm told me that Tomás was murdered by a poison dart. It that true?"

"Incredible, isn't it? But yep, that's what they're saying. A poisoned dart. They've sent the dart to a professor at UNM who's supposed to know about such things. Hopefully we'll get a report from him soon. As for why the lift stopped, the bomb squad from Santa Fe removed an explosive device that had been stuck against where the cable passes through the runners. It was a small device but powerful. They're not sure if it was set off by a timer or remotely by someone on the ground. It's hard to imagine how it was put up there."

"Sounds like a real mess."

"It is, Howie. Now, look, like I told you on the phone, I need you to fill out some paperwork for me including a statement saying exactly what you saw and did on Thursday afternoon. The attorney from the insurance company wants all the documentation he can get. Write that up for me and I'll tell you anything you want to know."

"Sure, just one more question. What can you tell me about Hamm's goddaughter, Leilani?"

Sean seemed surprised by the question. "I haven't met her. I've heard about her though. She flew in alone last week from Singapore to get the 6th Floor ready for Hamm. Nobody knows anything about her. There's gossip that she's Hamm's piece on the side. But who knows? Is she as good looking as people say?"

"She's . . ." Howie tried to find the right words for Leilani, but he faltered. "She's pretty good looking, I guess," he agreed, as though he hadn't noticed. "Singapore, huh?"

"Lots of money there, Howie. Probably lots of pretty girls, too. The kind hoping to get a seat at the table. Now, please, get going on that witness statement. I've got to get the damn lawyers off my back!"

Howie took the paperwork out to the table in the main part of the building and went to work writing up his part of the lift evacuation. By the time he was finished, Sean was gone and he didn't have a chance for more questions. There was an accident on a slope in the lower mountain, a collision between a skier and a snowboarder, and Sean had to be there. As with the lift evacuation, this would almost certainly end up in court. Statements needed to be taken and witnessed. Skiing was a litigious sport.

Howie decided not to wait for Sean's return. He had work to do. He got into his own skis and decided to revisit the scene of the crime.

***

The Wolf Lift was still not running.

Howie skied down beneath the empty chairs glad not to have overhead spectators watching him. There was nearly a foot of new snow—eleven inches, according to the official count, which often erred on the side of exaggeration—but much of it had already been skied by powder hounds in their relentless search for fresh tracks. The lines in the snow zig-zagged down the trail, crossing each other in intricate patterns. The challenge for Howie was moving constantly from deep snow into packed snow then back again into the deep, speeding up and slowing down. His legs weren't as young as they used to be.

It was a beautiful afternoon. These were the days after a storm that skiers prayed for and Howie managed to have fun as he made his way to Tower 7. The world was white and soft and fluffy and he managed to fall only once.

The area around Tower 7 was roped off, still a crime scene. Several people were standing at the base of the tower. A technician in a white lab suit was up in the tower itself examining the cable.

Howie came to a stop by the rope. As he stood watching, a four-handled toboggan guided by two Ski Patrollers appeared from the trees, coming from the intermediate slope that ran parallel to the lift line. The sled carried a man dressed in a black State Police uniform who was sitting up uncomfortably, holding the sides to make sure he didn't fall out. He was wearing a brightly colored wool hat with a tassel on top.

To Howie's surprise, it was Lieutenant Santo Ruben. Howie had to laugh. Santo looked as out-of-place as a person could be. With the help of the two Patrollers he managed to rise in a wobbly manner from the sled and step onto the snow. He was wearing city shoes and a black windbreaker with POLICE on the back. The jacket didn't look nearly warm enough.

Santo looked uphill with a frown on his face to see who was laughing at him.

"Howard Moon Deer!" he called imperiously. "Come down here!"

Howie ducked under the rope and skied his stylish best down the last few feet to where Santo was standing.

"And don't you dare spray me with snow!" he called, "or I'll have you up for assaulting a police officer."

"I wouldn't think of it," Howie lied.

***

"I've been trying to reach you," Santo said grumpily as Howie stepped out of his skis.

"I've been busy," Howie said.

"Oh, have you? So, tell me—what exactly have you been busy at?"

"I've been up here, Santo. You probably know that. I helped with the lift evacuation."

"And?"

"And what?"

"I heard you had a meeting with Leonard Hamm."

Howie was not surprised that Santo had heard about his meeting. The Peak was a small world.

"Yeah, we spoke."

"Oh, you *spoke*? In other words, he hired you to poke around and get in the way?"

"I wouldn't put it like that."

"Hmm," Santo said with a thoughtful look. He was a handsome man of the Silver Fox variety in his early 60s. He looked like an aging Latin matinee idol. Women found him attractive, though his relationships never lasted long. He was three times divorced and had been single for the past few years. For the last several months he'd shown more than a little interest in Georgie. For Howie this was embarrassing, but fortunately Santo had struck out with his daughter. She had confided to Howie that she liked Santo, but he was way too old. She had no romantic interest in an alcoholic old womanizer—a dinosaur, culturally speaking.

"You know, you look like a spaceman with your helmet and goggles," Santo said.

"Helmets are good up here. Believe me. And so are goggles. You don't seem to have noticed that we're at nearly 11,000 feet in the mountains after a big snow."

"I got up here just fine without skis and goggles," said Santo. "Now, listen to me, Howie—somehow you're always involved when there's trouble. This is a major case, and I don't want you interfering. Have you got that?"

"Totally. I was skiing Thursday afternoon when the Wolf Lift stopped. Patrol asked me to help with the evacuation and I was glad to volunteer. I was the talker. I talked people down onto the snow, telling them what to do. And that's it."

"Did you see Tomás get shot?"

"I did not, Santo. That happened before I got there. When I skied down to Tower 7 I saw there was a body in a sled wrapped up in a lot of blankets, but Patrol told me to keep going. There were multiple ongoing situations on the mountain and we each had to keep our narrow focus. My job was to help Patrol get people down before they froze to death. I didn't find out about Tomás until today."

"Do you know who did this, Howie?" Santo asked bluntly.

"I do not."

"So what's your theory?"

Howie laughed. "I don't have one, Santo. You know what Jack says. Never start a case with theories. Begin by gathering information. Keep an open mind. That's the scientific approach. Theories come later."

"God, I hate it when Jack starts pontificating!" Santo said grumpily. "You start a case with whatever you can get, and it's different every time. Now, tell me, did Hamm hire you?"

"Santo, my clients are a confidential matter."

"Oh, are they? We'll see about that!"

Fortunately, Santo didn't have time to linger. He was called away by an attorney in a fancy ski suit who had just appeared and the bomb specialist who had finally climbed down from the tower.

"I'll talk to you later, Moon Deer!" Santo said before he joined the two men.

Howie skied away before anyone else could stop him. He spent the rest of the afternoon skiing and thinking. Every now and then, he stopped at the foot of a chairlift tower and gazed up wondering how an unauthorized person could climb up unnoticed to the cables overhead and plant an explosive device. It seemed to him that it would have to be done at night after the resort had emptied out, but that would be difficult to do. They would need to herringbone up the mountain on skis. This wouldn't be impossible. You could put skins on telemark skis that gripped the snow. But at night?

Maybe, thought Howie. But not likely.

As the afternoon progressed, an idea took hold, a better possibility. At close to the 4 o'clock closing time, he rode the chairlift to Ski Patrol headquarters at the top of the ridge line, took off his skis, and went inside. The old wooden building was crowded, full of Patrollers coming in from the cold to gather for the day's closing rituals. The long plank table was full, shoulder to shoulder. Howie poked his nose into the glass booth where the afternoon dispatcher, Burt Swinton, sat in front of a radio listening to a call about a snowboarder who had stopped to smoke something that probably wasn't tobacco and somehow had lost his board which had sped off downhill into the woods. Burt directed one of the Patrollers to ride a mo down to the hapless boarder and get him off the mountain. As for the lost snowboard, that was just his bad luck. The light was fading fast, the woods were dark and deep, and maybe he would find his board when the snow melted in the summer. Probably not.

"Hey, Burt, do you need sweepers?" Howie asked when there was a pause in the radio traffic.

"Sure do. We're short handed. What would you like?"

"Lift Line," said Howie.

"You got it," said Burt, writing down Howie's name in magic marker on the white bulletin board.

Sweep was the final ritual of the day and Patrol often needed volunteers. There were 132 trails at San Geronimo Peak and each one had to be closed and "swept" so that no one was left overnight on the mountain. It was especially important to ski under the chairlifts to make certain everybody had been unloaded. At designated places, sweepers needed to stop and shout loudly into the trees, "Last Call! Last Call!"

At 4:20 exactly, Dispatch turned on loud rock music which was the signal for all the Patrollers to hoist their heavy packs and head out on their separate runs down the mountain. Howie enjoyed doing sweep and volunteered whenever he had the time. The mountain was magical in the fading light when the guests were gone, and you had a trail all to yourself.

For the second time that afternoon, Howie headed down Lift Line beneath the Wolf Lift and made his way to Tower 7. Every part of sweep had to be done correctly with designated stops where you had to sight up or down a trail, raise your poles, and call out to the Patroller on the next trail over, "Wave, wave!" On San Geronimo Peak, no injured boarder had ever been left overnight on the mountain, not ever.

Howie stopped briefly at Tower 7 with two questions that were bothering him. How had someone managed to shoot a poisoned dart at Tomás Romero without being seen? He imagined a blow gun of some sort. The shooter would have had to be hiding in the trees next to the trail, but the distance from the edge of the woods to the top of the tower was at least 75 feet. It didn't seem possible that a blow gun could be accurate at that distance. But of course there must be a more updated version of guns that shot darts. Gas propelled? He didn't know. He would need to investigate this.

He turned from the woods to study the cables overhead and here at least he had an idea how the explosive device had been planted. But he couldn't linger. He needed to keep going to get down to the next wave spot where a Patroller would be waiting for him.

Once Howie was down the mountain, he left his skis in a rack and made his way to the employee locker room. Howie knew the code. The locker room was coed and it was full of body steam as instructors, lifties, and Patrol—everyone whose job took them up the mountain—stripped out of their snow gear and boots and got back into their civvies.

He found Sean in one of the locker bays. He was sitting on a bench in front of his open locker with his boots unbuckled but still on his feet. He looked tired.

"I've got just one question, then I'll leave you alone," Howie promised. "Do you know who swept the Wolf Lift Line on Wednesday night?"

Sean looked up. "Have you found something, Moon Deer?"

"I don't know. It's just a theory right now. Who swept the Lift Line Wednesday?" he repeated.

"Why do you want to know?"

"The Wednesday sweeper was alone at Tower 7 and had enough time to stop, grab the device from his pack, climb the tower, place the bomb on the cable, climb down and ski to the base. He would be a few minutes late, but not late enough so anyone would notice."

"That's kind of arbitrary, isn't it?" Sean seemed defensive.

"Well, it's just a thought. But it's the simplest way I can imagine that device being planted. So, who was the sweeper?"

Sean didn't answer at first. He shook his head.

"Sean?"

"Well, that's easy enough to find out," he said at last. "We keep records. In case anyone is left on the mountain and the family sues. But in this case, I was dispatch that afternoon so I know. It was the new guy. His name is Matt Wilson. This is his first year on Patrol, so I don't know him real well. But he's been solid so far, a good worker. Ex-military. One of those special ops guys, I think. A good skier, nothing scares him."

"Is he here today?"

Sean seemed uncomfortable. "He hasn't shown up for the last two days. I've been trying not to over-react. I mean, he's a vet and I wanted to give him the benefit of the doubt. I don't like to be so wrong about anybody."

"Matt Wilson? You haven't seen him since he swept on Wednesday afternoon?"

"He was on the schedule for Thursday and today, but he just didn't show up. I don't like someone missing work without calling."

Howie was muttering half to himself. "Missing since Wednesday . . . ex-military, special ops . . . you know, Sean, this sounds like our guy."

Before Sean could answer, Howie's phone rang with Chopin's Funeral March, which was his assigned ring for Jack. Howie was still in his ski clothes, so it took a few seconds of fumbling through several layers to locate his phone.

"Where are you?" Jack demanded with his usual boorishness, no hello, no how are you.

"Hey, I'm fine, Jack. Since you're asking, I'm up on the Peak in the locker room, still in my boots and ski gear. Where are you?"

"I'm at Spaceport America waiting with Gypsy to board a jet to get home. We'll be in San Geronimo around 6 o'clock and I need you to pick us up at the airport."

"What are you doing at the Spaceport? Is somebody about to launch you into the asteroid belt? Or is that hopeful thinking?"

"Howie, I'll tell you when I see you."

"I don't have my car, Jack. Let me see if Georgie can pick you up."

"No, we need to talk. Hitchhike if you need to, but get there. We have work to do."

"Jack, for chrissake —"

But Jack had disconnected.

Chapter Twelve

Sean gave Howie a ride down the mountain to the airport, where he arrived at a few minutes before six. After rushing to get out of his boots and ski gear, Jack's plane didn't arrive for another forty minutes.

Howie was not pleased. He loved Jack. The man was like a father to him, which was both the good and the bad of their relationship. There were times when Jack pissed him off more than anyone he had ever known. He was arrogant, conceited, totally impossible. How the old fart had gotten his wheelchair, his dog, and himself to Spaceport America in southern New Mexico was beyond imagining.

The winter night was already dark as midnight, bitterly cold, breathlessly still. Howie found his abandoned Outback in the parking lot. He tossed his daypack inside, locked it up again, then hurried to the terminal in order to get out of the cold.

The small-town airport was quiet this time of night, operated by a skeleton crew. No planes had flown in or out for hours. Howie sat alone in a brightly lit waiting room. The small café was closed as well as the San Geronimo Air ticket office. No one was at the information booth.

He tried to get Georgie but only reached her voice mail.

"What a day! I'll tell you about it when I see you! I hope everything's going well. I'll try again to get you later."

Whenever Howie left a message for Georgie, he always had to resist adding, "My God, I can't believe I have a daughter! I love you so much!" He didn't want to scare her off. To be a parent these days required icy calm. Howie had only discovered he was a parent a few years ago and he was still getting used to the idea.

With time to kill before Jack arrived, he checked the *New York Times* on his phone. He hadn't been paying much attention to the story he heard on the radio that morning about the tourist rocket with six people aboard exploding shortly after it was launched. Billionaires in space didn't interest him particularly and this morning his mind had been on Claire. He assumed the rocket explosion was what Jack was in such a tizzy about, flying home from the Spaceport, so he thought he'd better catch up on the news.

The story was the lead article on the front page. The explosion had set back space tourism for years, said the *Times*, perhaps a decade. Too bad, thought Howie. The very rich would need to find new ways to get their kicks. A number of experts were quoted speculating on the cause of the accident. The most likely theory was a leak in the fuel line but nobody would know for certain until a thorough investigation had been completed which might take months. A good portion of the article concerned the six people who had died, the two astronauts who were piloting the craft as well as the four paying customers—the head of a newspaper empire, the heir of an upscale department store chain along with his 12-year-old son who had demanded a ride on a rocket ship for his birthday. And of course, the colorful founder of the Galactic Explorers Club, Captain Cosmo, the billionaire formerly known as Daniel Gluck.

So Gluck was dead, and Hamm had won the game, as he called it. Howie reflected on this with some incredulity. The gloomy little fellow in black with the beaked nose was king of the mountain, top dog, master of the universe—whatever you called it, it seemed to matter tremendously, the competition of egos in a world gone mad.

Or was this simply an ancient aspect of life on Earth? Howie remembered reading that in colonies of sea lions, the alpha male had a harem of females that he needed to guard from all the other males who wished to supplant him. It wasn't easy to keep all those females for yourself alone, but when you were the top dog it had to be done. The alpha sea lion often lost more than half his weight during the mating season fending the others off.

Howie could only shake his head. He guessed he simply didn't possess the competitive spirit. One female was quite enough for him, and even that often more than he could handle.

The big question was whether Hamm had been responsible for the rocket blowing up. Was it possible? It seemed to Howie that it would be difficult to sabotage such a complicated piece of machinery. But of course, he knew nothing about spaceships. Perhaps if you had enough money—and hatred for your enemy—you could bribe an engineer with a hundred million dollars to put Wire A in the socket meant for Wire B. He had no idea. His entire knowledge of the subject came from watching sci-fi shows like *Star Trek*.

Beam me up, Scottie—I've had quite enough of this planet!

Howie became aware of the strained whine of a jet engine, distant at first but getting louder, as a plane came in for a landing. He hurried from the terminal and down the glassed-in corridor that led to the gate.

Howie watched as a sleek private jet floated down from the sky with two blazing headlights pointing the way, set down on the runway, and taxied toward the terminal. GALACTIC EXPLORERS CLUB was written in large letters on the fuselage. It took a few minutes for the aircraft to reach its final position by the gate. The two engines emitted a deep sigh and went silent.

A door opened from the back of the plane and Jack in his wheelchair was lowered to the ground by an electric lift. A young woman appeared on the tarmac with Gypsy on a leash and helped Jack get oriented on the ground. She was attractive, Howie noticed, and very helpful. She fussed over Jack like he was her special charge. She pushed him with Gypsy following at her side toward where Howie was waiting by the gate.

"I'm Heather," said the young woman, letting go of Jack reluctantly. "You must be Howard Moon Deer."

"I am," said Howie. "I hope the old codger has been behaving himself."

"He's been an absolute darling," she said.

"I bet," said Howie.

Jack snorted. "Let's get out of here!" he grumped.

"So did you have a fun time down south?" Howie asked as he steered Jack toward the parking lot.

"It was a riot," said Jack. "It may surprise you that some of us are working while others are off playing in the snow."

"Yep, I'm a loafer," said Howie. "That's the problem with us Indians, you see. We lack ambition."

"Cut it out, Howie. I've had a long day and I'm not in a good mood!"

"Really?" said Howie. "I couldn't tell."

***

When they reached the car, Howie helped Jack into the passenger seat. He collapsed the wheelchair and slipped it into the cargo area, then opened the back door for Gypsy to hop up onto the seat. Gypsy wagged her tail and seemed glad to be home.

"So what's this about a chairlift breaking down?" Jack asked as they drove through the desert night toward town.

"The lift didn't break down, it was sabotaged. Someone put an explosive device next to the cable. The head of Lift Ops, a guy by the name of Tomás Romero, was shot with a poisoned dart when he climbed the tower to see what was wrong. So we're talking murder."

"A poisoned dart . . . well, well," said Jack with a meditative nod of his bushy head. "Sounds like something from a comic book. Tintin, perhaps."

"Excuse me, but Tintin isn't a comic book. I grew up with Snowy and Captain Haddock and Professor Calculus. And the unforgettable detective team of Thomson and Thomson. This is literature, Jack."

"Howie, for chrissake!"

"However, I get your point. You know what this is all about, don't you?"

"I have a general idea. Though it's early to jump to conclusions."

"I'd say the conclusion is unavoidable. Two super-rich egomaniacs playing king of the mountain. These guys never grew up. I'm not sure they started out crazy, but all that money and power, a life without limits—it goes to your head."

"Not for everyone," said Jack. "You should avoid generalizations, Howie."

"Yeah? Well, let me tell you, I just spent the morning with a billionaire and cuckoo just barely begins to describe the guy. Sure, there are exceptions. But the rule remains. Power corrupts, absolute power pushes you over the edge. Before you know it, you're in a toga playing the fiddle as Rome burns."

"All right, Howie. Enough nonsense. We need to get serious. Tell me what you know."

Over the next forty minutes, as they drove into town, Jack and Howie exchanged stories of their activities over the last two days. Jack recounted how he had known Danny Gluck as a child in San Francisco and had received a last-minute invitation to attend the rocket launch at Spaceport America. Jack lingered fondly over the luxuries of flying ultra-first class, the champagne, the gourmet food—whatever you wanted, whenever you wanted it.

"Sounds decadent," said Howie.

"Oh, I don't know. It sure beats flying in those little seats with a packet of pretzels."

Howie shook his head. "No, Jack. Live simply so that others can simply live—that's how Georgie puts it."

"Well, Georgie's young. She can squeeze into those seats."

Howie for his part recounted his experience in the evacuation of the Wolf Lift and his meeting with Leonard Hamm earlier in the day, as well as how he had figured out how the explosive device had been planted by a Ski Patroller who had conveniently vanished. He left out only the steamy bits about Leilani on the grounds that it was none of Jack's business.

"I'm surprised you took on Hamm as a client," Jack remarked.

"I accepted him on a limited basis, simply to investigate who was behind the chairlift sabotage and the poison dart. I want the answers to those questions myself and I might as well get paid for it. The Peak is my home turf, and I don't like people messing with chairlifts that I ride all the time."

"But who actually owns that mountain? It's federal land, right?"

"That's right. At least the northeast half of the mountain that isn't Indian land. Hamm owns about a hundred and fifty acres at the base area. But everything else, all the trails, the chairlifts—all of that is National Forest that's leased to the resort."

"So the feds could say no to the restaurant they're hoping to build at the top?"

"They could," said Howie. "But would they? Historically, they've supported the ski area. Money, money. They hold county meetings open to the public but after all the comments have been gathered, they've never said no."

"Is that necessarily a bad thing?" asked Jack. "Don't answer, I know what you'll say."

"We all need money to survive," Howie said anyway. "It's greed that's the problem. People who take so much more than they could possibly need. Have you ever spoken to Georgie about this?"

"I have," said Jack. "And I respect her opinions. We were all young once. I'm tolerant."

"Jack, you were never young. You were born an old grouch. In any case, I think we have this thing figured out, don't you? Hamm versus Captain Cosmo, battle of the Titans. Of course, they hired other people to do their dirty work. Hamm won, end of story. All we need now is to find the worker ants who have committed some very serious crimes and convince them that it's in their interest to squeal."

"Ants don't have hands, Howie. And I've never heard one squeal."

"I was speaking metaphorically."

Jack sighed. "You know, Howie, I'm not convinced this is quite that simple. Let's see what's on the flash drive that Danny gave me before we start popping champagne."

***

"Welcome home, Jack," Emma said when they entered the house. "I wasn't sure I'd ever see you again."

"I'm a hard guy to put down," he told her.

Howie was surprised to see Santo at the kitchen table with a glass of wine.

"I came by to see you," Santo said to Jack. "We need to talk."

Over the years, many cases had been discussed in the Wilder's old-fashioned ranch kitchen. The table was covered with a cream colored oil cloth that had a pattern of pink roses. There was a six-burner gas stove with two ovens, a walk-in pantry, dozens of cabinets and drawers, all painted a light green color that belonged to a different century, another time. It was the kind of kitchen where people spoke their minds on a winter's night, the windows black and frosty.

"Can I get you a glass of wine, Jack?" Santo offered, getting up from the table. He had made himself very much at home in the Wilder's kitchen.

"What are we drinking?"

"Chianti," said Emma who was stirring a large pot of chile at the stove.

"I'll have one of those," said Howie.

"Hold your horses, Howie," said Jack. "Let's go into my office a moment. I need to unpack."

Howie followed Jack's wheelchair down the hall into his office on the ground floor in what used to be the drawing room of the old Territorial house. Jack put down his overnight bag on the desk and wheeled around to face Howie.

"What's going on, Jack. You don't really need to unpack your toothbrush, do you?"

"It's not my toothbrush that worries me. I don't want Santo to know about the flash drive. Not yet anyway. Not until I have a chance to see what's on it. And we're not going to have a chance to do that until he leaves. So, I want you to stay afterwards, Howie. And don't say anything about the flash drive. That's what I wanted to tell you."

"Got it, Jack. Concealing evidence from the State Police is one of my specialties. Can we start on the chianti now? I've had a long day."

***

"So tell me about that rocket exploding down at the Spaceport," Santo said when they returned to the kitchen.

Sitting at the head of the table, Jack took a moment to sniff the glass of chianti he held to his nose. Jack considered himself a wine connoisseur.

"Rotgut," he concluded.

"Jack, it is not!" Emma objected. "That bottle cost $11 at Trader Joe's!"

"Emma, I'm sorry, dear, but you can't find a decent bottle of wine for $11."

"Well, I'm sorry, dear, too—but I refuse to pay a penny more just to be some kind of ridiculous wine snob. You can put an ice cube in it if you like."

"An ice cube!" he said darkly. "My God! In red wine!"

"Forget the chianti," said Santo. "I want to know about that rocket. Let's get our priorities straight. Six people died in that explosion."

"There isn't much to tell, Santo. The countdown was very exciting. A whole lot of tension in the observation building. You could smell the sweat. Five, four, three, two, one . . . the rocket lifted off and then about a minute later there was a big bang. The building shook like there was an earthquake. Then people started screaming and crying. That's all I can tell you."

"Was there anything suspicious about that explosion, Jack?"

"Suspicious? I can't say. There's going to be a lengthy investigation, of course. But it will be the scientists and engineers, not a detective like me, who will be able to answer that question. From what I've been told, they might never know for certain. There wasn't much left of the rocket to examine."

"Did you have a chance to speak with Gluck before he was killed?"

"He was busy with last minute preparations," Jack said evasively. "I was hoping to speak with him later but never got the chance."

"Well, our investigation is coming along a bit quicker up north," Santo said with some satisfaction. "We've identified the device on Tower 7 that crippled the chairlift and we know exactly when the explosion happened. 3:17. The device was very sophisticated, almost certainly triggered by remote control. I figure it was set off by someone on the ground. Which narrows the suspects considerably."

"There was a lot of traffic on the snow that afternoon," Howie said. "Skiers, boarders making their way down the Lift Line trail. It was cold and when people are covered up with helmets and goggles, balaclavas a lot of them, it's often hard to know who's a man or a woman, much less who they are. By the time Tomás arrived at Tower 7, almost twenty minutes had passed and whoever was on the slope at 3:17 would have been long gone."

"Maybe," said Santo. "We're checking all the security cameras of course, hoping to identify who was on the mountain then. There aren't any cameras near Tower 7 but there is one at the base of the Wolf Lift. All the chairs have numbers and that's how we found a skier on Chair 29 who heard a loud pop just before the lift came to a stop. He didn't think much of it at the time because there had been a lot of noise. Ski Patrol had been setting off charges on one of the chutes earlier in the afternoon and the wind had come up. The lift itself made noise. But when we questioned the man, he thought it could have been an explosion. We're still looking for more witnesses. Unfortunately, Howie, when you did that lift evacuation, none of you bothered to take names."

"That wasn't our concern just then," Howie answered defensively. "People were freezing and we were trying to get them down as fast as we could."

"I'm not criticizing you, Moon Deer. I'm just saying it would have been a help if you had taken witness statements."

"Witness statements! Santo, we didn't even know then that it was a crime scene! As far as we knew, it was only a mechanical malfunction."

"I'm just saying. Someone like you with a P.I. license, you should have been thinking ahead."

"Santo, you weren't there!"

With only some bickering back and forth, they drank wine, feasted on chile with grated cheese, minced onion, and cilantro and sat around the kitchen table talking until just after 10 o'clock.

When Santo was gone, Jack took Howie back into his office and gave him Gluck's flash drive. Howie sat down at the desktop computer with Jack in his wheelchair by his side. It took Howie a few minutes to figure out how to connect the flash drive. Nancy, as Jack called his iMac, was a complicated bit of electronics that combined an Apple mainframe with Kurzweil software for the blind. It had been designed by Buzzy Hurston, once Howie's Little Brother who had grown up to become a super-geek genius snatched up by the CIA after getting kicked out of Stanford for closing down BART, Bay Area Rapid Transit. He was on the run somewhere in South America after providing *The New York Times* with nearly a thousand pages of CIA secrets.

Howie found the right cord and the right place to plug in.

"Good evening, Howie," said Nancy in a pleasantly synthetic voice. She seemed authentically pleased to see him. As computers go, Nancy had tons of personality. "You have just connected an exterior hard drive from an unknown source. Do you want me to open it?"

"Nancy, open the damn flash drive!" Jack called from his wheelchair.

Almost immediately, the desktop filled with a picture of deep space. Moving slowly from the lower left to the upper right of the screen, a sleek spaceship came into view with the words GALACTIC EXPLORERS CLUB on the side.

The spaceship faded and was replaced with a closeup of Captain Cosmo himself, Daniel Gluck looking head-on into the camera. He was in an anonymous room that had no identifying objects on the walls. To Howie he looked crazy as a loon. He was several days unshaved. There were shadows under his eyes. His face was puffy, like he had just woken up. His eyes glowed.

"Hey, Jack, thanks for being there for me," said the Captain. "If you're playing this, it means I'm up in heaven looking down on you. But I have just a small surprise ending for my old friend, Hamm. Call it a farewell present from the grave. Here it is, pal—I know you'll make good use of it."

The message ended with a peal of stereophonic laughter that gradually faded. In its place, a single photograph filled the screen.

"Oh, no!" Howie cried. "No!"

"No *what*?" Jack demanded.

"This is awful!"

"Howie, for chrissake, *what* is awful?"

"It's a photograph, Jack. It's horrible!"

"For God's sake, Howie—tell me about the photo!"

"It's Leonard Hamm. It's from a few years ago. He's dressed in black. He's sitting on a chair and his pants are down to his ankles. His legs are hairy and pale, awful! There's a little girl on his lap facing him, her legs around his waist. She's nine or ten. Her skirt is up to her waist, and you can see she's not wearing underpants. It's Leilani, his goddaughter. She told me these people have made her their slave. A kind of pet. But it's more than that. He's abusing her. He's a pedophile!"

"Howie, calm down."

"I'm not going to calm down, Jack. I'm going to beat that creep to a pulp and rescue her!"

"Howie, don't. Let's just use the photograph to get him put away for a very long time."

But Howie had already stormed out of the room.

Chapter Thirteen

Jack spent the early part of Saturday morning outside on his back porch in the January sun, wrapped up in a wool hat and thick down jacket.

He listened as Gypsy nosed around in the snow and did her business. Jack didn't mind that. As he liked to tell anyone who would listen, he preferred dog shit to bullshit any day. Luckily, he had a year-round gardener who came once a week with a shovel.

The air temperature was 23 degrees but he had arranged his wheelchair so that he was in a perfect shaft of sunlight that warmed his face. Georgie had once told him a line from Samuel Beckett: "We spend our life trying to bring together in the same instant a ray of sunshine and a free bench." He liked that. In fact, he liked Georgie. Howie wouldn't recognize the person he became in her presence. She made him grouch-free.

Georgie had phoned earlier in the morning to say she had a terrible experience last night and she wondered if she could stop by to get his advice.

"Of course," Jack told her. "We'll have coffee together. You might bring us some bagels from Dos Flores Bakery."

As he waited for Georgie to arrive, he threw a slobbery old tennis ball into the bushes at the edge of the backyard for Gypsy to fetch. Gypsy loved chasing balls, as had Katya, his last guide dog. Katya's death had been shattering for Jack. He had been depressed for months. But Gypsy was here now and gradually he had come to accept her. Life goes on, he supposed—not entirely a happy thought, but one he accepted. In a different way, with a sorrow that had never entirely disappeared, he had come to love Gypsy as well.

Jack was throwing the tennis ball when he heard Georgie come into the house through the front door, stomping off snow in the entryway. He knew it was Georgie immediately from the rhythm of her footsteps.

"Jack? You there?" she called.

"Out back!" he called. "On the porch!"

Georgie came out onto the back patio noisily, shutting the sliding glass door behind her. To Jack, who moved much more slowly these days, she seemed almost like a hummingbird, moving at many times his speed. She seemed in a better mood than she had sounded earlier on the phone.

"I heard about that rocket exploding," she said, handing him a paper bag with his bagel, smoked salmon, red onion, and cream cheese. She had a vegan bagel for herself, avocado, tomato, and sprouts. "I hope you're okay?"

"I'm fine," he told her, though in fact he wasn't really fine. He was old and blind and ill, but he liked to keep that to himself. He wanted Georgie to think of him as a roguish fellow, still youthful.

Georgie kissed Jack on the cheek and stepped out into the snowy backyard to give Gypsy a hug. They ended up romping around in the snow together, both of them like puppies.

"Oh, I love you, Gypsy!" she cried. "I love, love, love you!"

Jack couldn't remember ever being so young. Howie had been right about him. He'd been born old.

"Okay, Georgie, pull up a seat—in the sun if you can manage. Tell me what's going on with you. And I want to know more about that group you're involved with at the Pueblo. The ones who are taking on Leonard Hamm."

"Forest Friends," she said. "Tell me, Jack, what do you think of John Concha, the War Chief?"

It was an unexpected question. "Well, he's quite a guy. Not somebody you want to cross. Why do you ask?"

"Like I said on the phone, I had a really bad experience last night. I'm trying to make sense of it."

"Go on," said Jack. "I'm listening."

Jack listened with growing alarm as Georgie described what had happened—getting stuck in the snow, how she was rescued by the War Chief, the odd men she had noticed at the meeting, the woman who called herself Julie North and claimed to be with CNN then admitted she was an FBI agent. And how two men with night vision goggles had appeared and shot her with silenced pistols.

"It was terrifying, Jack. I'm still getting over it. I was able to get away—I scampered off into a kind of gully and kept going. But it was the darkest night ever and by the time I dared to stand up and look around, I was totally lost. I couldn't see lights anywhere, I couldn't see a thing. I was starting to panic when out of nowhere the War Chief appeared and rescued me for the second time that night. It was embarrassing, to tell you the truth. Of course, I told him about the two men who had appeared out of nowhere and shot the FBI woman—if that's what she was. He had a torch and he wanted me to take him to the body. I was able to retrace my footsteps in the snow but when I got back to the place where she was killed, the body was gone. I don't think he believed me, but honestly, I wouldn't make up a story like that."

"There was no blood on the snow?"

"There wasn't. The snow was churned with so many footsteps it was impossible to tell what had happened there, but there was no sign of a body. The two men must have carried her away. You believe me, don't you?"

"Of course I do. Did Concha say what he was doing wandering around in the dark?"

"No, he didn't. I was so blown away by everything that I didn't think to ask him. John's not a very communicative sort of person. He's pretty intimidating."

Jack took note of Georgie calling the War Chief by his first name.

"So what do you think, Jack? I'm feeling better today but I'm still kind of freaked-out. I keep remembering those men with goggles and guns and the horrible wet gurgle that came from Julie's throat when she was shot. I can't get it out of my mind."

"That's only natural, Georgie. It's a good sign that you can talk about it. What you're experiencing is post-traumatic stress. It will fade in time, but you need to respect the fact that you had a very bad experience. Don't push it away, look it in the face. And from now on, you need to tread very carefully. I know you and your Forest Friends mean well, but I'm not sure you appreciate how dangerous it is to get in the way of really big money. There are hundreds of millions of dollars at stake with this gondola and revolving restaurant and believe me, people have been known to kill for a lot less. It would be a good idea for you to stay away from the Pueblo for a while and just lie low. I'm sure Howie has work you can do back at the office."

"Jack, I'm not going to be intimidated! This is important, it's something worth fighting for! If you were an Indian, you would understand. That restaurant is an obscenity!"

"I do understand, Georgie," he said gently. "But there are times when it's best to take a step back. Both Howie and I care very much about your safety."

"No, I'm not going to back down. I won't! I feel I have to make a difference in this world! Why am I alive if I'm going to stand aside and let bad guys win? A person has to stand up and fight!"

Jack sighed. He worried that she had put herself in a great deal more danger than she realized. He loved Georgie for her youth and idealism, but in this case youth and idealism could get her killed.

He knew he needed to speak carefully if she was going to listen. "All right, you're ready to do battle," he said. "I respect that. But a wise warrior takes careful stock of the situation. If you're going to be effective, you don't want to go off half-baked. So let's think this through a little. As it happens, I've been fighting bad guys all my life so why don't you let me help? If we work together, perhaps we can come up with a plan and put these people away. Okay?"

"Of course, Jack. I want your help."

"Good. Now, I have an idea how we can move forward but first I'd like you to take a look at a photograph. Will you do that for me?"

"A photo? Well, sure," she said doubtfully.

"It's a very unpleasant photograph," he warned. "It shows sexual abuse of a child. It's going to make you angry. Are you up for that?"

"If it will help, of course."

"Then follow me to my office. Howie brought the photo up on my computer and I printed it out."

Jack wheeled his chair inside the patio door and through the kitchen to his office with Georgie and Gypsy following behind.

"You'd better sit down for this," he said as he took the print from his desk and handed it to her.

"My God, that's Hamm!" she exclaimed. "What a sleaze bag! That poor girl!"

"Once we show this to Santo, I don't think Leonard Hamm will be building restaurants any time soon," Jack told her.

"Yes, but . . . wait a second. There's something odd about this photo. Do you have a magnifying glass?"

"There should be one in the left hand drawer of my desk. Howie uses it sometimes."

"Okay, let me look . . ."

Georgie took several minutes to examine the photograph.

"Damn!" she said after a while, as she put the picture and the magnifying glass back on the desk. "I think it's a fake."

"What do you mean? You're saying it's been photo shopped?"

"No, I'm not sure but I think it's AI. It's quite convincing but there's something off about it."

"Howie thought it was real."

"Aye, but Howie needs glasses. I've been telling him that for months, but he's in denial."

"So what makes you think it's AI?"

"Artificial Intelligence isn't perfect, thankfully," she said. "Not yet anyway—they keep improving it. But if you look closely, you'll notice small things that aren't right. In this case, it's the girl's left hand. It kind of melts into where she's holding it on her leg. It's subtle, but it's wrong. For some reason, AI has trouble with hands. Where did you get this?"

"Danny Gluck gave it to me. Before he went up in that rocket."

"Well, there you are. This is what made Gluck a billionaire, video games that stretch reality. He would be good at creating images like this. Lucky for Hamm, not quite good enough."

Jack sighed. "That's that, then. I thought we had Hamm locked up for the rest of his life, but I guess not. I'll still give it to Santo. He can send it to the forensics lab in Albuquerque just to be sure."

"I'm sorry, too. So what's next?"

Jack felt shaken. It wasn't only the photograph. If this photo had been faked, it threw suspicion on everything. As Georgie said, Captain Cosmo had become very rich by faking reality. In today's world, truth had no top or bottom to it. Reality was any lie you could get away with.

Meanwhile, Georgie was still waiting for an answer. What next?

"Let's drive to the Pueblo," he said. "I think we need to have a talk with John Concha to find out what he was doing wandering around in the dark."

"Jack, you should be taking it easy. I don't think I'm supposed to be driving you around places."

"Sure, you should. We're a team now, remember? Together we're going to get to the bottom of this!"

Chapter Fourteen

Georgie drove to the Pueblo on the main two-lane highway that the tourists used. No shortcuts this time. The road was plowed and there was asphalt showing. She had learned her lesson about driving in deep snow and wasn't taking any chances. Not with Jack riding next to her in the passenger seat. The snow had turned into grey mush along the sides of the road. The winter storm of two days ago had already lost its enchantment.

Jack was unusually quiet.

"Are you okay, Jack?" she asked. "You seem lost in thought."

"Not lost, my dear. But yes, thinking."

"About that photograph, I bet. Artificial intelligence."

"Well, it's true—I prefer real intelligence to the artificial kind. It's disturbing to watch the world slip into lies and fantasy. Virtual reality is an oxymoron, I'd say, with plenty of morons around, eager to gobble it up. Still, actual reality will have the final word. Bullets are real and they still kill people."

A chill ran up Georgie's spine as she relived, once again, the two men with their other-worldly night vision goggles coming out of the darkness. She worried it wasn't a good idea to be taking Jack to the Pueblo. Gypsy was in the back seat keeping an eye on him, but Jack seemed awfully old and vulnerable, his eyes hidden beneath his blindman's glasses.

He seemed to know what she was thinking.

"Georgie, relax. I'm not going to die on you, I promise. I just want to ask John Concha a thing or two, then we'll drive back home and I'll be a bored invalid for the rest of the day. Okay?"

"I just don't want Emma to be angry with me."

"Georgie, Emma gave up on me a long time ago."

"That's not true, Jack, and you know it!"

They drove the rest of the way in silence. The prospect of seeing the War Chief again gave Georgie an odd tingle of anticipation. Every time she had met him, she had made a total fool of herself and she was determined not to do so again. Not that it mattered, of course. Concha barely took any notice of her no matter what she did.

Georgie parked by the tribal government building, a modern structure of concrete and glass, funded by the BIA, the Bureau of Bashing Indians Around. The building was functional but lacking in personality. A sign by the front door said the public bathrooms were to the rear.

It was no problem getting Jack from the passenger seat into his chair. He had become stronger in the past year. He was able to stand by himself and even walk a dozen steps. The wheelchair was the portable one Jack kept for car travel, unmotorized. It was light and it folded in half for easy transport. Nevertheless, it always took some time to set Jack in his chair and Gypsy in her harness.

When they were ready, she wheeled Jack into the building. It had a spacious lobby with Pueblo art work and pottery on the walls and in glass cases. There was no one in the lobby except an elderly Native woman who was dusting one of the cases. Georgie approached, explained who they were and that they wished to see the War Chief.

The woman used her phone and a few moments later Concha appeared from a hallway. He was dressed in jeans and a checkered red and black flannel shirt that made him look like a lumberjack.

"Jack," he said respectfully, "Haven't seen you around lately."

"I was out of commission for a time. Had a damn stroke, John. But I'm back now. Back in the saddle. You've met Howie's daughter, Georgie, I understand."

The War Chief gave Georgie a cursory glance. "Yep," he said.

"She has her New Mexico State Private Investigator license," Jack made a point of saying. "She's become a valuable asset to our agency."

"Yep," he said again. "So, what can I do for you, Jack?"

"We need to talk about last night, John. About the body that vanished."

The War Chief hesitated. "Well, follow me," he said at last. "We'll talk in my office."

Concha led the way down a hallway with Georgie following behind, pushing Jack in his chair. Gypsy was on a leash whose end Jack held in his lap.

Georgie was thinking that John Concha looked good from the rear in his well worn jeans. It had been a while since she'd had a chance to study a strong, well-built man with a nice ass. Most of the guys she knew were more the arty/intellectual types.

Unfortunately, she wasn't paying attention. Concha had stopped to open his office door and she ran into him from behind, pushing Jack's wheelchair into the back of his legs. It wasn't a hard hit, but it was embarrassing. She backed off immediately.

"Oh, I'm so sorry!" she said.

"Georgie, watch where you're going!" said Jack.

John Concha gave Georgie a curious look, as though seeing her for the first time. His brief focus of attention made her feel almost naked. With a bravado that was all pretense, she looked right back at him.

The War Chief turned and led them into his office.

***

Georgie sat along the edge of the office and tried to make herself invisible.

The office was strictly utilitarian: a row of five metal chairs facing a metal desk. There were three flags on a stand behind the desk: the American flag, the New Mexico state flag, and the flag of the San Geronimo Pueblo. The Pueblo was by treaty a separate nation, not part of the United States. The only attractive part of the office was the large window with an immense view of San Geronimo Peak.

"A man who's had a stroke should be taking it easy," said the War Chief. "And yet here you are, nosing around."

Jack smiled. "Well, I've gotten old, John. I'll admit it. But that doesn't mean I'm ready to sit around every day with drool running down my chin."

Georgie felt the competitive energy between the two alpha males. They appeared to know each other well.

"So what do you want to know?"

"I want to know about last night, John. I understand you had some problems at the Community Center."

"Problems? Not really. I found the Moon Deer girl wandering around lost in the snow," Concha said without looking at her. "She told me a story about some woman she met who claimed to be an FBI agent getting killed, but when she took me to where she had left the body, there was no body there. No blood, no sign of violence, nothing."

Georgie, ignored on her metal chair in the corner, blushed.

"You think she imagined the whole thing?" Jack asked.

"I don't know. I'm just telling you what happened."

"All I can tell you is Georgie is an especially astute young woman. Not only does she have her P.I. license, she graduated with honors from Cambridge University. That's in England."

"I know where Cambridge University is," Concha said flatly. "In my experience, a college education doesn't make anyone less of a fool."

Georgie was about to make a loud objection, but Jack raised a hand to silence her.

"If I were you, John, I would regard Georgie's story with a good deal of confidence. She's not often wrong."

Georgie decided that it was time to speak up. "I promise, Mr. Concha, that I'm not making this up. She called herself Julie North. As I told you, we were standing together out in the snow, when out of nowhere two men appeared and took three shots at her and she fell down dead. Obviously, they carried the body away and cleaned up the ground where she fell while I was wandering around lost. It was at least fifteen minutes before you found me."

"Yes, and what exactly were you doing out there, John?" Jack pressed. "I don't believe you just happened to come across her."

"Well, I was looking for her, to be honest. She seemed the sort of girl who gets in trouble and I had a bad feeling last night that something was afoot. A girl like that needs looking after."

"What do you mean, a girl like that?" Georgie demanded, outraged. "And by the way, I'm not a girl, I'm a woman. Unless you want me to call you a boy, Indian boy!"

"Georgie, hold on," said Jack, quieting her. "Let's not get personal. There are some questions that need answering. Why did you have a feeling something was wrong?"

The War Chief gave Georgie a good long look before turning his attention back to Jack. At least, she had gotten his attention. Finally.

"Well, Jack," Concha said slowly, drawing out the words. "There were two suspicious guys hanging around in the Community Center. I didn't like them. I saw them deep in conversation with Ms. Moon Deer's friend, Pete Day Rise. I didn't like that either. Pete's a troublemaker. I've had to caution him a few times."

Georgie was seething with anger once again.

"Pete is just standing up for the Pueblo!" she said crisply. "I don't know why you're so against someone who's fighting this horrible plan to build a restaurant on top of the mountain. You just don't like Pete because he's young!"

"No, you're mistaken," he said solemnly, turning her way. "I want to stop that restaurant, too. But here on the Pueblo, the elders decide how to handle such things, not the children. We're a society that values the experience of grown-ups."

The children? The War Chief thought she was a child? Georgie was digesting this as Concha's phone rang. He put it to his ear and listened. "Yeah, yeah, I'll be right there," he said.

Concha stood up, signaling an end to their meeting.

He gave Georgie a stern look. "I'd appreciate it if you would have a word with Pete," he said to her. "I want to know who those outsiders were and what they were talking about."

"All right," she told him. "I'll do that. But there were a lot of different kinds of people there last night. Pete was spreading the word as best he could to anyone who would listen."

He nodded. "Ask anyway. I didn't like them and if you can find out what they were doing with Day Rise, I'd be grateful."

"Are you starting to believe me that there was a body on that snow last night?"

He hovered above her. He was a large man and he made her feel very slight.

"I'm not sure what to think, Georgina. But there are things happening that are starting to worry me, and I need to find out what's going on. I'm guessing that Day Rise will tell you things he won't tell me."

"Okay, I said I'll help and I will. If you give me your cell number, I'll call you if I come up with anything."

"I tell you what," he said. "Meet me for dinner tonight and we'll talk about it."

Georgie's mouth fell open. Was he asking her out?

"I have stuff to do early on, so it will be late," he added brusquely. "Let's make it 9 o'clock at La Rosa. All right?"

Perhaps it wasn't a date after all. La Rosa was the sleaziest diner in town, but it was open until one in the morning and served beer and cheap wine. The clientele was as rough as the underbelly of San Geronimo allowed.

Georgie's smile made her eyes glitter with amusement. Unexpectedly, a late-night dinner with the War Chief at the greasy La Rosa Diner seemed to her the most romantic invitation she'd had in a long time.

"Okay," she answered. "Yes!"

Chapter Fifteen

"I'm not sure it's a good idea for you to be having dinner with John Concha," Jack told Georgie when they were back in her old Subaru. "He's too old for you."

"He's not nearly as old as Santo and Santo has sure been giving me the eye!"

"Has he?" Jack asked sharply. "I hope he hasn't—"

"Oh, no, nothing like that. There's been nothing inappropriate. He's been the perfect gentleman. But it's something a woman feels when a man looks at her too long."

"Well, you tell me if that idiot gets out of hand and I'll deal with him, believe me! Santo's a fool where women are concerned. He refuses to accept that he's gotten old. The problem with old men, Georgie, is that deep inside they still think they're 20 year olds."

"You're not like that, Jack."

"No, I'm not," he said. "That's because I've learned the hard way to accept life as it is. Look, my dear, of course I'd like to be young again and have all the girls faint at the sight of me—"

"Women, Jack, not girls."

"See, there you have it. I wouldn't do well in today's world and I'm just as glad I don't have to try. Getting old is a pain the ass, Georgie. But I wouldn't want to be young again either. Now let's get back to John Concha. I'm not saying that John isn't a good man, but he's dangerous. When you're with him, it's like riding a bull with horns, you never know what he's going to do next. He's not safe."

Georgie wondered if Jack understood that riding a bull with horns had a certain appeal to a woman. A man who wasn't safe.

"Jack, honestly, I can take care of myself. And I might be able to find out what really happened last night. I think John knows more about this than he's letting on."

"Well, watch yourself, that's all I'm saying. Let's go see this friend of yours, Pete Day Rise."

"No, let me take you home first. Pete won't talk with you around. He trusts me. We've been working together. And I'm Native and you're not. People at the Pueblo don't open up to outsiders."

Jack saw the sense of this. Reluctantly, he allowed Georgie to drive him home.

"Just be careful, that's all I'm saying," he warned as she dropped him off.

"And you get some rest," she told him. "You've been doing too much running around."

Jack wheeled his way into his office and sat by his desk with an uneasy feeling. In truth, he had been uneasy ever since Georgie had told him that the photo of Leonard Hamm molesting a young girl had been generated by AI. You couldn't trust anything anymore. There was a game afoot, and it worried him that he didn't know what it was.

Then there was the question of Julie North whose body had vanished, the CNN reporter who had turned out probably to be an FBI agent. He had a slight acquaintance in Santa Fe who might be able to throw some light on the matter, FBI Special Agent Tony D'Angelo. They had met when Jack had been investigating a cold case murder of a young girl who had gone missing 27 years ago, and whose body had just been found buried in a backyard as a new owner of the house was putting in a swimming pool. As a general rule, Jack didn't like the FBI. But Tony was okay. He had shown Jack some respect as a retired police commander and had bent the rules for him, giving him access to an old file.

Jack phoned Tony in Santa Fe only to be told that he was unavailable. Jack was allowed to leave voicemail: "Hey, Tony, it's Jack Wilder up in San Geronimo. I'm working a case and I've come across something I thought you should know about. It concerns a woman by the name of Julie North who identified herself as a special agent just before she was shot—I'll explain the circumstances to you when we talk. I'm home now so give me a call back as soon as you get this. Hope you're doing well!" he added in his friendly voice.

Jack believed he had provided just enough detail to hook Tony's interest and he would get a quick response, but an hour later his phone still hadn't rung. Unfortunately, people no longer returned his calls as quickly as they used to. Sometimes they didn't get back at all.

He wished now that he hadn't let Georgie return to the Pueblo without him. All his instincts told him there was danger close at hand, but this was only a vague feeling that he couldn't pin down. His thoughts drifted in restless circles. At some point, he needed to check in with Santo. Plus, he should phone Howie and let him know that the photograph of Leonard Hamm molesting a child might be a fake.

There was so much to do. But for the moment, he felt a wave of exhaustion. The last few days were catching up with him. He could barely think, his eyelids began coming down like a curtain after the final act of a play.

He wondered what was wrong with him. He used to be able to work eighteen hours a day and stay up for days at a time, a mere forty years ago . . .

Jack thought he might close his eyes just for a minute or two, as sleep pulled at him with the profound weight of gravity.

***

Georgie stopped to fill her car with gas at the Speedway station near the turnoff to the Pueblo. Speedway seemed a funny name for a gas station but they had seven locations in San Geronimo, a near monopoly, and their price for a gallon was nearly 20 cents higher than gas in Santa Fe. There was a good deal of grumpiness about this fact in San Geronimo, along with conspiracy theories galore.

Not that gas stations would gouge people! Of course not!

She filled up on mid-grade. Howie told her the old Subaru needed high-grade, all the help it could get, but Georgie balked at the price. She refused to make the oil companies in Texas any richer than they already were. Somebody had etched FUCK YOU on the plastic screen on the pump that asked you if you had a reward card and if you wanted a car wash along with your gas.

When the tank was full, Georgie continued her drive onto Indian land. On Saturdays, Pete worked at his family's store in the historic part of the Pueblo, the ancient three-story condo-like adobe village, much photographed, that the tourists came to see. This old part of the Pueblo had been continuously occupied since the 13th century, long before Columbus. As far as Georgie knew, nobody lived in the warren of small rooms anymore. The population was spread out across the reservation in modern housing and prefab homes that resembled much of the impoverished rural Southwest. However, the historic buildings were meticulously maintained and the dusty plaza was still used for the religious rituals which—except for Christmas Eve and a few special occasions—outsiders were not allowed to attend.

Georgie parked and walked across the plaza to a small store on the ground level that sold Indian jewelry, postcards, and books on Native subjects. An old Pueblo woman sat stoically in a corner on a hard straight-back wooden chair while a middle-aged Anglo couple browsed the turquoise jewelry in a glass case.

"Oh, look at that necklace!" said the woman. "Isn't it darling? I could wear it with that green dress I bought in Lubbock last year!"

"I don't know, sweetheart," said the man. He had an expensive camera around his neck. "Might make you look too much like a Christmas tree."

Both the man and the woman wore brand new cowboy boots, getting into the Southwest spirit.

A small fire was burning in the kiva fireplace throwing out heat and the spicy scent of cedar. Georgie crossed the room to the old woman, Pete's grandmother, who sat with an expression of infinite patience on her deeply wrinkled face.

"Hi, I'm Georgie, Pete's friend," she said brightly. "Remember, we met last summer at the foot races?"

The old woman seemed to return to the 21st century from some time long ago. She looked up at Georgie as though she hoped a strong wind might come up and blow her away. Georgie didn't mind. She knew that for an old woman like this she was "that Lakota girl with a funny way of talking."

"Do you know where Pete is?" she persisted. "I thought he worked today."

"Didn't come in today," she answered reluctantly. "So I had to."

"Oh, really? Do you know where he went?"

"Don't know."

The Anglo man with the camera around his neck came over and began to bargain, hoping to bring down the price of the turquoise and silver necklace his wife wanted from $275 to $195. The old woman looked up at the man with almost sublime hatred. Luckily for him, he existed in such a profound cultural bubble he didn't notice.

Georgie knew she wasn't going to get any information about Pete so she said a cheery goodbye and left in order to look elsewhere.

For the next two hours, she wandered about the Pueblo searching for Pete, but no one knew where he was. He wasn't answering his phone, which wasn't like him. Generally, Pete never strayed more than a few inches from his greatly prized iPhone, the latest model.

She was about to give up when she saw one of the Forest Friends, Jerry Trujillo, the youngest member of the group. He was walking past the adobe church that the Spanish had built when they arrived in New Mexico in search of a rumored city of gold, forcing their religion on the Indians. Cultural imperialism was the way Georgie would describe it. The church was nearly 400 years old, fiercely Catholic in the northern New Mexican style, with gruesome paintings of Jesus on the cross, lots of blood. For many centuries, the northern mountains had been cut off from the more populated south and they had developed their own ideas of an unforgiving god.

Jerry was wearing a hoodie, walking with his head bowed. He was seventeen, small for his age, and the others barely tolerated him. Pete had made him his personal errand boy.

"Jerry!" she called, lowering her window and coming to a stop.

He came over obediently with a dejected hangdog expression on his face. He looked so cold she invited him into the passenger seat and turned up the heater.

"I'm looking for Pete—it's important I find him. Have you seen him, Jerry?"

"Well, no. Not since the meeting last night. But I haven't really been looking."

"So yesterday, at the meeting. Did you happen to see Pete with two white guys who looked out of place, not your usual arty environmentalist types. Ex-military maybe, that sort. One of them was an albino. Do you know what that is?"

"A kind of fish?"

"No, Jerry. It's a person with an absence of pigment in their skin. They're very pale and have white hair. There might have been a gringa with them—attractive, mid-thirties. When I met her she called herself Julie North."

Jerry looked away evasively and shook his head. "Georgie, there were a lot of people at the meeting. I didn't really notice anybody that much. Heya, look—could you give me a ride home?"

"Sure. But you need to tell me. You were with Pete most of the day, weren't you? Come on, Jerry—he kept you close to his side when there was stuff going on. Did you see him talking with two guys who looked kind of rough?"

"I don't think I should be talking about this, Georgie. Pete wouldn't like it."

Georgie was increasingly curious what Jerry was keeping back.

"Listen to me, Jerry. I'm secretary of the group, I'm involved in this up to my neck. So I need to know what's going on or I'm out. I'm serious. I'm not going to work with people who keep me in the dark. What about these guys, Jerry?"

"Georgie, don't quit Friends. We all like you and you're the only one of us who can do grant proposals."

"Then you need to tell me."

"Okay," said Jerry unhappily. "These two guys started coming around about a week ago. Pete had something going with them, but I don't know what. When I asked who they were, he said he was working on something to get the Friends some real money. But he said it was still 'in negotiation'—that's how he put it—and I was supposed to keep my mouth shut until the thing was firmed up."

"So you saw Pete meet with these guys?"

"Yeah, a few times. They got together at Pete's house when his parents were gone, but I didn't hear anything they said. Pete had me stand guard outside the house, to keep a lookout. He said it was because the negotiations were so sensitive, and he didn't want to jinx the deal by talking about it too soon."

"And the woman I mentioned? Julie North?"

"Yeah, sure. I saw her last night at the meeting. She was talking to one of the guys you're asking about, the one who was really pale. They were standing by themselves at the back of the room."

"Did you get his name?"

"I never heard any of their names, Georgie."

"Did you hear what they were talking about?"

"I didn't. And that's all I know, I swear. I have no idea where Pete is."

"Okay, Jerry, thanks," Georgie said thoughtfully, digesting this news. She didn't like what she was hearing. Sensitive negotiations to get money for Forest Friends? If this was true, he should have told her. She hoped he hadn't compromised the group in some way. Sometimes Pete was too slick for his own good.

"So look, how about going out with me sometime," Jerry asked, interrupting her thoughts. "You're a real babe, Georgie."

"What?"

"Next Saturday night, maybe? We could go to the new Star Wars movie in town."

"Jerry, no! You're seventeen, I'm not going out with you!"

"Seventeen's not so young. I mean, how old are you?"

"I am twenty-three," she told him in a voice of immense maturity. "Now, behave yourself!"

Chapter Sixteen

On Saturday morning, Howie woke up with a heavy weight on his chest.

Was he having a heart attack? He experienced a moment of panic. He was 43 years old, old enough for his body to quit on him. He should have been dieting!

But no, it wasn't heart failure—it was his cat, Orange, sitting on his chest, examining him dispassionately, hoping to be fed.

"Honestly!" he sputtered, managing with an effort to sit up in bed. She hopped off his chest with an angry meow. She was a cat certain of her own importance.

Howie looked at his bedside clock and saw it was 9:27. He had meant to get up earlier, but he hadn't slept well, wondering what he was going to do about Leilani and Leonard Hamm. After seeing the photograph, he had left Jack's house in an angry huff intending to beat Hamm to a pulp. But he hadn't gone more than a few miles before he realized that a more subtle approach was required. He had never beaten anyone to a pulp in his life, he wasn't even sure he knew how. Plus, practically speaking, Hamm had a dozen security guards and—according to Sean—guns hidden everywhere.

Yet Leilani had asked Howie to save her, and he was determined to do what he could. But he needed to think carefully about how to go about it.

He climbed down from his loft and considered his options while he refilled Orange's bowl of kibble and made coffee. Though Leilani had described herself as the Hamms' pet slave, she hadn't said anything about being sexually abused. Maybe she was embarrassed. Howie knew that children who were victims of sexual assault often felt guilty that they were somehow to blame.

It was a sensitive subject and Howie wasn't sure he knew enough about it to act in an appropriate way. He decided to ask Georgie's advice before he did anything. She would know more about this sort of thing than he did.

He got dressed, put his coffee in a thermos, and drove into town thinking he might pick up a bear claw on his way into the office.

Sadly, the Dos Flores Bakery was sold out of bear claws. Howie received the news stoically. He bought two plain croissants instead, one for Georgie, but she was not in the office when he arrived.

She had left a note on his desk: "Gone to see Jack. Take a look at email. There are two work requests. Not sure you'll be interested. See ya later! XXX, G."

He opened his office laptop and checked the agency email account. The first was from a local attorney he had worked for in the past who wanted him to investigate a woman who had slipped and fallen on the wet floor of a hardware store, the local branch of a national chain. It had been snowing the day of the accident and the floor was wet due to customers walking in. The woman's injury lawyer, a sleaze from Santa Fe, was suing the national chain for half a million dollars claiming the victim, a fitness instructor, would need major surgery and would never be able to work at her profession again.

Howie's job, should he accept, would be to sneak around and see if the woman was truly as injured as she claimed. He would also need to investigate if the hardware store had bothered to put the required yellow sign in a prominent place warning customers of the wet floor.

Howie groaned.

The second job offering was more interesting, but only slightly. A defense lawyer in a juvenile criminal case wanted Howie to prove his client was innocent, happily having sex with his girlfriend in the back seat of a car while a gas station in town was being robbed.

Howie groaned again. He wished he could refuse both jobs but he had decided to quit the case and return Hamm's bonus so he would need the work. Georgie kept the office books and he would need to consult her to see how much money they had in the bank.

At least he could put off a decision for a day or two.

He wrote Georgie a note: "I'm heading up to the Peak. No skiing today, I've decided to return Hamm's bonus and break the contract. Will explain when I see you. Love! XXXXX, me."

Since Georgie wasn't here, he quaffed the second croissant before he left the office. No sense in letting it get stale.

***

Howie was on the road, driving up the winding two-lane highway from the desert to San Geronimo Peak, at close to 12:30 p.m. The image of the photograph he had seen still burned in his mind, but he felt a killer calm.

The sky was blue, the snow was deep, and the line of cars snaking up the mountain moved slowly. Saturdays were always busy on the Peak and with the new snow the trails would be packed. As he climbed higher, the road became increasingly icy with patches of snow. The traffic crawled.

When at last he reached the parking lot, he had to drive around for twenty minutes before he was directed to a spot nearly half a mile away from the base area. He hopped onto a shuttle that was crowded with skiers and boarders with all their gear, everyone squeezed together. A woman dressed in a pink one-piece snow suit whacked him in the back with her skis as she climbed aboard.

"Oh, I'm so sorry!" she cried.

"It's nothing," said Howie, with almost maniacal patience.

It was nearly 2 o'clock by the time Howie reached the Hamm Haus. He walked through the lobby to the elevator but when he pressed the button for the sixth floor, the elevator refused to budge. He pressed the button a second time but again nothing happened.

He walked over to a young woman behind the reception desk. She was on the phone and ignored him.

"No, I'm sorry, we will be completely closed for a week," she was saying. "Yes, for repairs, I'm afraid . . . a water pipe has burst . . . we will be giving you a complete refund, yes, of course. And a 50 percent discount on your next stay with us . . . I know you made plans, and I'm so sorry, but it can't be helped. We can't stay open with no water . . . I really do apologize, goodbye." She put down the phone firmly on its cradle, an old-fashioned landline, and took a deep breath. She looked up at Howie with so much tension in her face that Howie was worried for her.

"You're closing for a week?" he enquired, trying to be friendly.

"Yes, yes," she said. She looked like one more question might do her in. "The heating . . . I mean, the water."

"I see," said Howie.

"How can I help you?" she asked sharply.

"Is there something wrong with the elevator? I'm trying to get to the sixth floor."

"That's the special access floor," she told him. "You can't go there without an appointment."

"I understand," said Howie. "Perhaps you can call upstairs to Leonard Hamm and tell him that Howard Moon Deer is here to see him."

"Do have an appointment with Mr. Hamm?"

"No, I'm afraid I don't."

"I'm afraid I have instructions not to allow any unauthorized person up to the sixth floor."

Howie wasn't sure he liked being an unauthorized person.

"Let me try Leilani, then. Could you give her a call? Leilani Kalawai'a. Tell her that Howard Moon Deer would like to see her."

"Do you have an appointment?" she asked again.

Howie sighed. "No. But you see, I'd like to talk with her to *make* an appointment."

"Yes, no, I mean." The woman was frazzled. "You absolutely can't phone her without an appointment!"

"Now, look," said Howie. "I understand I can't see her without an appointment. But I can phone her, can't I? To make an appointment."

She could only stare at him, breathing so hard he was afraid she was about to hyperventilate.

A man in a blue blazer appeared magically by Howie's side. He was large.

"May I help you?" said the man.

Howie looked up and recognized him from the airport. He was one of the security team who had arrived with Hamm on his private jet. He was clean-cut with short dark hair and a bland all-American face. He could have been a high school basketball coach from Iowa. There was an earpiece in his left ear with a coiled wire snaking down into the collar of his blazer. His eyes were icy.

Howie was polite. "Yes, I'm sure you can. You were at the airport so you know who I am. I don't have an appointment, but I need to see Mr. Hamm about something that's work related. I'm sure he'll want to see me."

The man in the blue blazer was equally polite. "I'm sorry, Mr. Moon Deer, but Mr. Hamm isn't available. Of course, you can leave him a message. That wouldn't be a problem."

"I see," said Howie. "Well, perhaps I can see Leilani. I would be happy to leave my message with her."

He shook his head. "I'm sorry, but that's not possible either. I have instructions to allow no one up to the 6th floor."

"If I can use the house phone—"

"No, that's not possible, I'm afraid." His eyes narrowed dangerously. The nice Iowa basketball coach had vanished. This was more a Stasi agent from East Germany back in the bad days.

"Okay, fine," said Howie, deciding it was time to leave.

He wandered out into the sunlit plaza. People were starting to come down from the mountain, everyone in a festive mood talking about the turns they'd made and the spills they narrowly avoided. With the blue sky and the snow, the world was lit in blazing Technicolor.

Something strange was going on at the Hamm Haus. He walked around to the front of the building and saw that the bar and restaurant were closed, the door locked. Of course, you can't open a restaurant without water. Yet it seemed odd.

He shrugged, not knowing quite what to do with himself. A cup of coffee, he decided. He stood in line at the Black Bean, an outside kiosk, ordered a double Americano, and took it to a free bench next to Magic Mountain, a cute shop that sold ski gear at twice their usual cost.

His Americano was just getting cool enough to drink when he saw Sean Basset walking by in jeans and a fleece jacket. Sean noticed Howie and came over.

"Moon Deer! How's private eyeing?"

"In a muddle, actually. How about you? Looks like you're off work today."

"I'm not working period. I just came up to clear out my locker."

Howie gave him a questioning look. "Really?"

Sean sat down on the bench beside him. "I got fired last night. After I dropped you off at the airport I drove home and found an email from HR informing me that my services were no longer required, effective immediately."

Howie was shocked. Sean had been a mainstay of San Geronimo Peak for many years.

"You're kidding?"

"Nope, I kid you not."

"Did they say why?"

"No, they don't give reasons. Everybody who works up here has to sign an agreement that they serve at the pleasure of the corporation. Which means they can fire us any time with no warning for any reason they like. I phoned the new boss of Human Resources this morning—she's one of Hamm's handpicked people from New York—and she wouldn't even talk to me."

"That's incredible!"

"Well, I've had trouble with the new management before. None of them know anything about running a ski mountain. All they care about is selling real estate. Plus, I'm not sure they really want me to find out what happened at Tower 7."

"But why? That doesn't make sense!"

Sean shrugged. "I don't know. These people are weird. They smile a lot, but they walk right over you if you get in their way."

"This is awful, Sean. You must be pissed off."

"Not really. I had a kind of epiphany as I was getting drunk last night. What's the old saying? Don't get mad, get even. I've arranged a little surprise for Hamm that he's not going to like."

Howie waited. "Yes?"

"Howie, all of us on Patrol are tight friends. We have to be. The way we work, our lives are often on the line. We need to rely on one another completely, without question. So we're sticking together. We're going to finish work today because there are guests on the mountain who need to be kept safe. We don't want anyone to get hurt. But that's it. After today, we're walking off the job. We're on strike until they meet a whole bunch of demands that have been building up for a few years. They're going to discover very quickly that they can't keep this mountain open without Ski Patrol. As of tomorrow, the Peak will be closed."

"This is a shocker!" said Howie.

"So you'd better get your skiing in today. I'm sorry for the people like you who really love this mountain. But we've had it with the way they've been screwing us around. We're just not going to take it any more."

"I get it, Sean. I do. My God, Hamm's going to be losing tens of thousands of dollars a day!"

"More like a hundred thousand dollars a day, Howie. Of course, that's a drop in the bucket for someone like Hamm. But we'll see how long he holds out."

Howie sensed this new twist was going to complicate the Tower 7 investigation, though it was hard to say how. Meanwhile, he could only shake his head in amazement.

"Listen, I'm looking for Leilani, Hamm's so-called goddaughter. Do you have any idea where I might find her?"

"You have a thing about this girl, don't you?"

"Not really. Not the way you're thinking. But I'm worried about her. I'm not sure she's safe."

"Well, I don't know the girl, but I've heard people talking about her. Supposedly Leilani does the 4:30 yoga class every day in the rec room so you might find her there. Some of the guys are saying she looks pretty good in a leotard."

"Thanks," said Howie. "I'll give that a try. One more question. Do you know what's happening at the Hamm Haus?"

"What do you mean?"

"They're giving guests refunds and turning them away. The bar and restaurant are closed up tight. I heard a woman at the reception desk say they don't have water."

Sean shook his head. "I have no idea. Sounds like the usual cockups with these people. The rest of the village has water, as far as I know. Well, I gotta go," he said, rising to his feet.

"Good luck, with the strike," Howie told him.

Despite the Technicolor day and skiers and boarders milling about, it was clear to Howie that trouble was simmering on San Geronimo Peak.

***

Howie had an hour and a half to kill before the 4:30 yoga class where he hoped to find Leilani. The Peak offered free yoga classes twice a day to their staff, once in the morning at 7:30 and again after the lifts closed in the afternoon.

On the surface, this appeared to be an example of enlightened employment, the new model pioneered by companies like Google. But in fact, Howie suspected it was a cost saving measure to minimize injuries, especially for departments such as ski school and Patrol whose work took them onto the snow. Management wanted to keep their workers athletic and supple because injuries on the clock cost money.

Howie knew he was being cynical. Maybe Hamm paid for yoga classes because he was a closet Buddhist who wished love and compassion upon the world.

But probably not.

With time to kill, Howie considered getting his skis and doing a few runs. If Patrol managed to close down the mountain, this might be his last chance for a while. But he wasn't up for it. Today he found the crowds of skiers and boarders in their festive outfits grating on his nerves. There wasn't a black or brown face anywhere to be seen. Yes, there were a small number of Chinese. For Chinese expats who worked high-tech jobs in Texas, skiing was big status. But in general, this was a sport for the upscale White Man and his fluffy White Woman. He could tell by looking at the faces that nobody was thinking about the war in Ukraine or climate change or racism. Everyone was having fun.

"Fun!" he said to himself darkly.

In fact not everyone was having fun. A woman sitting nearby was shouting at her two small children playing in the snow.

"Stevie, stop throwing snowballs at your sister!" The woman was overweight, red in the face, looking like her children were driving her over the edge.

"Some vacation this is!" she complained, turning to Howie. She sensed a receptive ear and for the next fifteen minutes he listened to what a miserable creep her husband was. For the past two days, Tom—the husband—had been off skiing leaving her to take care of two unhappy children who never stopped fighting. She had tried to put them in kiddie ski school but they refused to go. They hated school of any kind. And except for bombing each other with snowballs, they hated snow as well, which they found cold and nasty. Meanwhile the family was spending a mint—$700 a night for a cramped room at the Hamm Haus, and God only knew what their credit card bills were going to be after all the restaurants. $26 for a hamburger, could you believe it? The woman was contemplating divorce.

"I hate him!" she confided to Howie. "I hate his stinking guts!"

Oddly enough, listening to the woman put Howie in a better mood. He found he could smile again.

At 4 o'clock the lifts closed, and the sun had disappeared behind the mountains casting long shadows. There was a fading gray sky overhead. The temperature was dropping quickly, and Howie was thinking he might need another Americano when he saw Leilani walking across the plaza toward the staff meeting room where the yoga class would be held. She had a mat rolled up in a sling across her back.

"Howard!" she said when she saw him. Her eyes showed some alarm.

"We need to talk, Leilani. I've been waiting to see you."

"Well, yes, of course . . . but you see, I have a class."

"This is more important. Can we go somewhere inside, I'm starting to freeze out here. Someplace private."

"Okay, yes." She smiled with some effort. "I'm always glad to see you, Howard. Let's go up to my room."

Howie wasn't sure her room was the safest place to be.

"I heard the hotel was closed. Isn't there a problem with the water?"

"Where did you hear that? Everything's fine, honestly. Let's go."

After the incident in the bathroom, Howie was reluctant. But he had been waiting for hours and he didn't want her to get away. He followed her into the Hamm Haus then up the elevator.

"Have you been skiing?" she asked him brightly, making a stab at conversation.

"Not today. And after today, I don't think anyone will be skiing for a while."

"Really?"

He left that hanging as he followed her down the hall. Leilani had a suite with a small kitchen and a separate bedroom. It was nice but impersonal. It had the sterile feel of a hotel, and it was on the third floor rather than the sixth. The windows faced the ticket office across the plaza. Howie sat on an armchair that was so comfortable it seemed to float somewhere between the floor and the ceiling. The chair told him how tired he was.

He got to the point right away.

"Look, Leilani, I'm here to help you. I know this is a difficult subject, but I want to know if Leonard Hamm has been abusing you. Sexually, I mean. If this has been going on, I can make it stop."

She looked away. "Oh, Howard! . . . I don't know what to say!"

"This isn't your fault, Leilani. You don't need to be ashamed. You were his victim. Now, you asked for my help, and that's what I'm going to do. I'm going to help you. But I need to know exactly what's been going on."

"But it's so embarrassing! I'm not sure I can talk about it."

"If you like, I can phone my daughter, Georgie. She's twenty-three, a very nice person, and she might be easier to talk to than me. Would you prefer that?"

"No, I want you to help me. It's just very difficult."

"I can see that. Take your time."

She turned to him at last with a bright smile. "I tell you what, let's have a drink. I'll make us mai-tais! It will make me feel relaxed!"

"Leilani, I don't really want a drink. But if you want one for yourself . . ."

"No, please, I make very good mai-tais, I have a special recipe. A bad mai-tai is too sweet, but the way I make them is just right. Please, it will make it so much easier for me to talk!"

Put like that, it was hard to say no. He watched from the living area as she stood in the kitchen with her back to him pouring from various bottles into two tall glasses full of ice. When she brought his glass, he saw there was dark rum floating on the top with a sliver of pineapple sticking up from the ice and a bright red cherry.

He took a sip. It was delicious, a drink from the Polynesian heavens. It was like drinking ambrosia. He took another sip.

Howie made a point of sitting up. He didn't want to get too comfortable. "Let's ease into this. Why don't you tell me about your childhood," he began.

She laughed self-consciously. "My childhood? After my mother died, Leo adopted me and I'm not sure I had much of a childhood at all."

"I understand that your mother was killed on his estate?"

"Yes. It was terrible. I've always been afraid of crocodiles. But I don't really remember it all that well. I was only 8 years old. I remember my mother, of course, and I think about her sometimes. What that was like for her, bleeding to death, dying in a car on the way to the hospital." Leilani shivered. "My poor mother!"

"I'm so sorry. So what was it like growing up with the Hamms?"

"Oh, they spoiled me. They didn't have children of their own, you see. But it was very strange. We travelled a great deal from one big house to another. They hired tutors for me, but they kept me to themselves. I didn't have friends. I liked all the things they gave me but I was lonely."

"That doesn't sound good," said Howie.

"No, it wasn't. When I was fourteen, they finally let me go to a real school and things got better then. We were in Singapore at the time. They sent me to a very posh international school, and after that a school in Switzerland. We kept moving from one place to another and they kept a very close watch on me. Chauffeurs took me to school and then drove me back to wherever home was then. School was my only real escape and I studied very hard. I got my masters in statistical biochemistry in Argentina, at the University of Buenos Aires."

"Congratulations!" Howie was impressed, even though he had no idea what statistical biochemistry was. "Tell me, why do you call Leonard Hamm your godfather, not your adoptive father?"

"That's how he wants me to present myself to people we meet, and I go along."

"I understand you came to San Geronimo before him on your own, so you must have at least some independence."

"Well, yes, he wanted me to get his office ready here. He had to stay in Singapore to finish up a business deal. In the last year he's let me off the leash a little. I'm well trained, you see, and I'm the only person he really trusts. He worries about people he doesn't know. He's certain there are plots to kill him. He even has someone tasting his food before he eats anything. He's afraid of being poisoned."

"A food taster? Really?"

"He's a very unhappy man, Howard. All that money, it's only made him afraid."

"Let's talk about how he's abused you, Leilani. I know how difficult this is, but it's very wrong, and I want to help."

"Oh, Howard! You make me feel so safe!"

"Good, I'm glad to help you feel safe. But I need to know exactly what he's done. Maybe you'd feel better writing this down instead of talking about it. Would that be better?"

Better better butter batter . . .

Howie felt suddenly very strange. Words had begun to lose their meaning.

"What . . . what did you say?"

The room itself had gone wonky on him. Howie was starting to feel like he had fallen down a rabbit hole.

She came over to where he was sitting and knelt on the floor in front of him.

"No, Leo never abused me. I don't know where you got that idea. You see, Leo doesn't care about sex. He doesn't really have a body. It's like he's a disembodied brain. It's only money that he cares about."

"Moomy?" he managed, barely able to speak.

"No, money. That's what the game is all about. Numbers. It has nothing to do with anything real. It's all in the mind."

"Mind mooney?"

"You must try to relax, Howard. I'm so sorry about this, really I am. You're such a nice man and you're very sexy in a funny way. I mean, you're not ordinary sexy. But my goodness, when I was sitting in your lap with my legs around you, I almost came. You see, I'm a bad girl. I'm bad, bad, bad."

"Wha wha?"

"I wanted you to save me, I really did. I thought if anyone was ever going to save me it would be you. But then I said to myself, do I really *want* to be saved? And the answer was no, I don't. Have you ever experienced something like that? Wanting to be saved, but knowing that if you were saved you couldn't have fun anymore? The thing is, it's so boring to be good."

He could only stare at her agog, google eyed.

"I was tempted. I want you to know that. But you don't have any money, and I couldn't live like that. I bet you don't even have a new car. I'm actually very spoiled. I like being rich. I'll miss you, I really will. But a girl like me needs to be realistic. You see, the Hamms don't have children, they only have me. I'll inherit everything one day. I can't turn my back on that. You see that, don't you?"

Howie was fading fast.

"Oh, Howard!" she said gazing at him with concern. "I hope you don't hate me. I like you so much! I think I even love you a little. But you're in the way. I don't have a choice."

That was the last semi-coherent thing Howie heard. Leilani's words drifted into space. She faded into a mist.

Howie fell back into the chair, whose arms encircled him, hugging him tightly. The last thing he remembered, Leilani was on her knees holding his hands. He tried to talk but all he could say was mai-tai, mai-tai, again and again. Her eyes were sympathetic.

Then there was nothing. What happened after that, Howie didn't know. He fell into a black hole.

Chapter Seventeen

On Saturday afternoon, Jack was in his wheelchair in his downstairs home office with his head bowed, snoring loudly. Emma was at the library. Gypsy snored at his feet. They were making quite a symphony together when the sound of a helicopter woke him up.

With a final snort, Jack came to life reluctantly, irritated by the disturbance.

Helicopters overhead had become a nuisance in recent years, along with private jets. The county hospital was less than a mile away and helicopters were often needed to ferry medical emergencies to Albuquerque. Jack understood that. He was willing to make allowances for heart attacks and skiers who had crashed head first into a tree. But this particular chopper was hovering over his house and the noise was growing to a crescendo rather than fading into the distance. The wind from the rotor blade rattled his windows and shook the huge old cottonwood tree outside. It was like being in a hurricane.

"Don't land in my backyard, you idiot!" Jack cried.

Obediently, the chopper moved off down the street and landed in the vacant lot three houses away. A few minutes later, Jack's doorbell rang.

"For God's sake!" he complained to Gypsy. "This is starting to feel like the L.A. rush hour!"

Grumping every inch of the way, Jack powered his chair from the office down the hall to the front door.

"Yes, yes, I'm coming, goddammit!"

He opened the door with deadly intent. There were two people outside.

"Jack, it's Tony D'Angelo," said a friendly voice. "You left a voicemail, so I thought I'd stop by in person to say hello. This is Special Agent Martha Chomsky. May we come in?"

Jack smiled.

"You flew here in a chopper, did you?"

"Hey, it's the only way to go. There's less traffic in the sky. How's life, Jack?"

"Life is life," he answered. "Better than death, I suppose. But just barely."

Tony chuckled dutifully. Jack turned his chair and led them into the kitchen.

***

"Have a seat," Jack told them. "But let's not have any more nonsense about less traffic in the sky. You didn't come here in a chopper just to bullshit. What's this all about?"

"Julie North," he answered. "That's not her real name, of course. But it's a name not many people know. So I need to know how you know it."

"Let's say I have a source," said Jack.

"Don't fuck with us," said the woman, Special Agent Chomsky. "This is a serious matter. You need to answer our questions."

Jack smiled. "You know, you've just reminded me why I don't like Feds." He turned to Tony. "So this Julie North woman who doesn't have a real name—she's one of yours?"

"That's not the sort of information we generally give out," said Tony. "But I'll make an exception in your case. Yes, she's a special agent working undercover and she's gone missing the last two days. We're concerned about her."

Tony D'Angelo had a tenor voice with a cadence of the streets in it. The woman agent's voice was lower than his. Special Agent Martha Chomsky was from back East, he guessed. She spoke the trans-Atlantic English that was current with the professional classes. And she was young. Her voice had the kind of frisson that the young women liked— even Georgie spoke that way sometimes—as though they were either too lazy or saturated with sex to take the effort to articulate.

"Tell me about this Julie North," said Jack. "What was she doing in San Geronimo?"

"Now, listen up, Jack," said Tony. "Before I answer questions, I need to know your involvement in this case. This is Bureau business and I gotta know if I need to worry about you staying clear of something that's very sensitive."

"Tony, I'm retired! I don't have any involvement with anything! Look at me, I'm an old man in a wheelchair!"

"That didn't stop you from flying down to the Spaceport courtesy of Daniel Gluck," said Special Agent Chomsky.

"What? You're keeping tabs on me?"

"Jack, we're investigating that rocket explosion," said Tony. "Not me personally, but the Bureau has a large presence down there. So yes, we have a list of everyone who was at the launch. The point is, you're not the invalid you pretend to be. So tell me, who's your client?"

"I don't have a client. I didn't even know that there's a case. That's what I'm trying to tell you, Tony. I'm retired."

"Yeah, yeah, sure you are. Now let's get real. You left a message that Julie North got shot. Either you start telling us what you know or you and I aren't going to be friends any more."

"Okay, Tony, calm down. What I know is all second-hand. It's my granddaughter, Georgie, who's involved. She had an odd experience Friday night at the Pueblo."

"I didn't know you had a granddaughter, Jack."

"Well, she's my honorary granddaughter. She's the daughter of my partner, Howie Moon Deer. She's 23 years old, a very smart girl and I'm fond of her. If I had an actual granddaughter, she'd be the one."

"Okay, go on."

Jack told Tony and Martha Chomsky the full story, as he knew it. How Georgie, the secretary of Forest Friends, had organized a meeting Friday night at the Pueblo Community Center to raise money to fight the expansion of the ski resort, and the woman who had approached her claiming at first to be a journalist from CNN.

"So, this woman, who called herself Julie North, convinced Georgie to follow her outside the community building in order to do an interview. She said her cameraman was waiting outside. Georgie followed the woman off a little ways into the night. It was dark, there was several inches of snow on the ground, and Georgie was starting to wonder where the cameraman was. That's when Julie admitted she wasn't from CNN, she was a Fed. But before she could say anything more, two men with night vision goggles appeared out of the dark and shot Julie. She collapsed dead onto the snow and Georgie dove into the sagebrush and crawled away. She was wandering around half-lost when she ran into John Concha, the War Chief. When she told him about the woman getting shot, they circled back to where it happened but there was no sign of the body. It was gone."

"So maybe she wasn't dead after all," Tony suggested.

"Maybe. What do I know? But I can imagine a very good scenario for why professional killers happened to be at that meeting. This group, Forest Friends, aren't much more than a few hipster Indians who probably smoke a lot of weed. But being Indians gives them a megaphone with people who have a romantic notion of Indian causes. See what I'm saying? What they're doing endangers some powerful people with very big money at stake. That's where I would start looking, the big money crowd—that is, if I weren't a blind old cop who's supposed to be retired. What do you think, Tony?"

"I'd say it's an idea that we've already considered. Now what about this honorary granddaughter of yours? I'm going to need to see her."

"Good idea. But what you need to do, Tony, is *listen* to her. You can try calling her at the Wilder & Associate office downtown. Georgie's the office manager. Better yet just stop by. She's been living in the office. She calls it her *pied-à-terre*. She's always there during office hours," Jack told them.

In fact, he knew very well that Georgie wasn't at the office. She was at the Pueblo. But he wanted a chance to coach her before the Feds had a go at her.

"What's her father's name again? Your partner?"

"Howard Moon Deer," said Jack.

"And what's he up to?"

"Up to? I don't know. He runs the agency now, not me. He doesn't always fill me in on the cases."

"Want me to tell you what he's doing?" said Chomsky. "He's been poking his nose into the Tower 7 homicide on San Geronimo Peak. We have an interest here. We want to know who his client is."

Jack made a helpless gesture. "How would I know? The last I heard, he wasn't working for anyone. You appear to know a lot more than I do."

"Jack, what happened at the Spaceport and what happened at Tower 7 are both part of an active FBI investigation," said Tony. "This is official and we need to know what you know."

"So, you're saying the two events are connected?"

"Oh, come on Jack, don't play dumb! You know as well as I do that the two things are connected. So I want to know what you and Moon Deer and this Georgie girl have been doing."

"Okay, I see that. I understand completely," said Jack. "And every good deed deserves a little favor in return. So let me ask you something, as simple as simple can be. What was Julie North doing at the meeting?"

"You expect me to answer that?"

"Listen, I know how to keep my mouth shut. But I have to know. My granddaughter was two feet from that woman when she was shot, and I don't like that."

"Right, your granddaughter!" Tony said with a sigh. "Okay, okay. Let's not play games. Martha, tell him."

Special Agent Chomsky shifted in her chair. "Julie was looking at the Indian angle. We think there's a possibility that these Forest Friends, as they call themselves, have been keeping some bad company. But you need to promise you won't repeat what we're about to tell you to anyone. I'm not kidding. Don't tell this to Moon Deer, don't tell it to your honorary granddaughter. Okay?"

Jack wasn't pleased, but he promised. He often played loose with law enforcement, but being old school, a promise to another cop was a promise.

"Okay, you have my word. I'll keep this to myself."

"All right. So here's the deal. This is about a security outfit. A very unique high-end security company based in L.A. that calls itself Deep Vigilance. You ever hear of them?"

"No," said Jack.

"I wouldn't think you would. They're ex-military, special ops. They got used to breaking laws in Iraq and Afghanistan and when they got back to America, they didn't see why they should stop. Deep Vigilance has a legitimate business supplying security to high end celebrities and politicians. But underneath that cover, there's a small group that does murders, kidnapping, whatever the client wants—and the only clients they take are very wealthy."

Jack was starting to understand. "So, these are the people who sabotaged that chairlift?"

"We believe so."

"So the question is, who hired them?"

"That's what we want to know. The logical answer is they were hired by Daniel Gluck to ruin Leonard Hamm, but it may be more complicated than that. We've been investigating this group for nearly two years. They've done a lot of nasty stuff you don't need to know about. They've always covered their tracks, but if we can nail them in just one of their exploits, they're finished."

"But what's their interest in the Pueblo?"

"That's easy. Indian land would give them easy access to the ski resort. They could have hiked up the mountain from Pueblo land in order to get to Tower 7 on the other side."

"That would be quite a hike, Tony. From what I've been told, that's a steep mountain. Plus, they would be climbing in the snow."

"Like I said, these are ex-military, special ops. They're trained to do stuff like that. But they would need help from the Indians. That's what Julie was doing at the Pueblo Friday night, trying to find their contact. We're thinking it's the head of this Forest Friends group, a guy by the name of Pete Day Rise. He's been seen talking with Dwayne Bellman, one of the Deep Vigilance operatives. He goes by the name Skull and he's an ex-Navy Seal, a very dangerous individual. Unfortunately, the guy is Teflon coated. We haven't been able to pin anything on him."

Jack didn't mention Howie's theory that the person who planted the explosive device was from Ski Patrol. He was happy to cooperate with the Feds, but there was no sense in overdoing it.

"Now from what I'm hearing, Forest Friends have no love for the ski resort," Tony continued. "They wouldn't mind sabotaging a chairlift. Especially if there was enough money involved. This is where your honorary granddaughter comes in. She would know something about this, don't you think?"

"Tony, Georgie would never have anything to do with a stunt like that. She's the most honest, idealistic person I know."

"Yeah, but idealism can lead to some bad stuff."

"Not with Georgie." Jack spoke with certainty, though in fact he wasn't a hundred percent certain. This wasn't the first time he worried that she was in way over her head.

"Now it's your turn to talk, Jack," said Tony. "You seem tight with this granddaughter of yours. So, what else has she told you?"

"Tony, I've told you everything I know. People don't keep me in the loop anymore. In any case, I don't understand why your ex-military goons should have been hanging around the Pueblo Friday night. If they blew up that chairlift, their job was finished. You'd think they would be eager to disappear."

"Perhaps their job isn't finished," Tony suggested. "Perhaps there's more to come."

Jack sighed. This was exactly what worried him. More to come. With Georgie a possible target.

"I tell you what, Tony. Let's take a drive down to the office and see what Georgie can tell us."

"I'll talk to that girl on my own, Jack. You're not going anywhere."

Jack put on his most helpful expression. "Without me, she won't tell you a thing. Georgie's a tough young lady. Grew up on the streets of Glasgow. I can vouch for you and encourage her to talk."

Which was true. Except he knew Georgie was safely gone from the office. Jack was determined to keep Special Agents D'Angelo and Chomsky as far away from her as possible.

***

"Well, damn—Georgie's not here!" said Jack when they reached the office. "Sorry about that, Tony. I bet she's gone off to Howie's place. He built her a cabin and she likes to go there when she's feeling stressed. It's very peaceful. Untouched forest, a mountain stream, a meadow."

"That's swell, Jack," said Tony. His irritation was beginning to show. "You'll save me time if you just give me Moon Deer's address."

"I'm afraid there isn't an actual address. I mean, there *is* an address in the county records somewhere, but we had a kid working here a while back who was a serious computer whiz, and he was able to make sure Howie's spread never showed up on Google maps. But it's easy enough to get there. Here, I'll describe it to you . . ."

Jack's directions included driving 10 miles north on the main highway, turning right at a faded red barn where there was a black horse in a corral, another 10 miles on a twisty country road, past a cluster of run-down trailers, turn left onto the dirt road at the blue mailbox, and it was only two or three miles after that.

"You can't miss it," said Jack.

Special Agent D'Angelo didn't speak for a moment. "You think it's funny giving us the run around, don't you, Jack. Except it's not funny at all, my friend. Not one bit."

"Well, I guess no one will hire me as a stand-up comic. But honestly, Tony, I hope you get the bastards who are causing all this trouble. We need to put billionaires back in their box."

"So you're a Marxist now?"

"I'm not any kind of ist. I'm just an old man who doesn't like assholes with a lot of money running things. Most of the good people I know are just getting by."

Tony and his partner departed with a frosty goodbye. When they were gone, Jack sat behind his old desk and tried to phone Georgie but she didn't answer. He left a voicemail.

"Georgie, I was hoping to reach you. I've just learned some things that are worrisome. So I'd like you to leave the Pueblo as soon as possible and go somewhere safe until we have a chance to talk. Don't return to the office. I want you to stay out of sight for a few hours. Maybe go to the library or some café you've never been before. I'll explain when I see you."

Jack put down the phone and sat for a few minutes deep in thought. He enjoyed being in his old chair behind his big old-fashioned desk. It made him feel almost like himself again. A real person with a real job. But he was worried about Georgie.

"So what are we going to do about this?" he said aloud to Gypsy. "We need wheels, we need help. Any help at all, really. As long as it's not the damn FBI . . ."

Gypsy snuggled her nose into his lap.

"You know what I hate most about being blind?" he confided, man to dog. "I have to rely on other people to drive me around! Did I ever tell you about the '65 Mustang convertible I had in California? Me and Emma used to drive down the Coast highway to Big Sur, the wind in our hair. We'd stop at a little place south of Half Moon Bay for abalone sandwiches. Those were the days, I tell you! Back when we were young . . ."

With nostalgia biting at his heels, Jack was tempted to find his way to the liquor cabinet and pour himself a shot of single malt. But he doubted if Howie kept a bottle there anymore. Most likely single malt had gone the way of abalone sandwiches that cost $3.95.

"I guess we have to bite the bullet," he told her. "Santo is our best hope. He's a cop, of course, but he has wheels with a siren and roof lights. Better than a taxi. What do you say?"

Gypsy wagged her tail enthusiastically. Which in doggie language meant, "Sounds swell, Jack. But please, no siren!"

***

"Okay, I'm here," said Santo, as he sat in the client chair facing Jack and his oversized desk. Everything about Jack was oversized, including his ego. "Now what's the emergency?"

"I'm worried about Georgie." Jack paused to let that sink in.

"What about Georgie?"

"I just had two FBI agents here. They have a wild theory that whoever sabotaged that ski lift is in cahoots with the Indian kids Georgie's been hanging out with. They think a couple of hit men hiked up from the Pueblo side of the mountain at night and got down to the lift from there."

"Come on! In the winter?" Santo objected. "At night? Impossible!"

"Maybe not." Jack didn't want to break his promise of silence to Tony, but he had to tell Santo something. It was a matter of threading the needle, leaving out any mention of a certain security outfit in L.A. "They're thinking it was done by ex-Navy Seals who did special ops stuff in Afghanistan. Those guys are beyond fit, they're monsters. Some of them never adjust to civilian life so they go freelance when they're back in the States. Have gun will travel sort of thing."

"Paladin? Yeah, sure, the philosophical gun slinger with a code of honor. Total fantasy, but what the hell. You used to watch that show?"

"I did," said Jack. "Howie has another theory. He thinks it was a Ski Patroller who disappeared afterwards. Howie's idea is the Patroller planted the device while on his rounds at the end of the day. This makes more sense to me, but we don't know for certain. Then there's the question of who shot Tomás with that poison dart. Howie likes to imagine it as some kind of exotic Amazon blow gun, but it could be much simpler than that. You can buy dart guns on the Internet these days."

"Okay, but let's get back to Georgie. Why is she in danger?"

"Because she's the secretary of Forest Friends, the group that's fighting the ski resort's plan to build a restaurant on top of the mountain. The problem is these kids have no money and so they're looking for funding. There's no real leader of Forest Friends, but Georgie tells me that the alpha male—that's her description—is a guy by the name of Pete Day Rise. Tony D'Angelo, the special agent I know, thinks the special ops people offered him money in exchange for access to Indian land. Like I said, this is total supposition. But if it's true, they may have killed Tomás Romero and they're not going to want to leave any witnesses behind when they've finished with whatever they've been doing."

"Okay, a few theoretical ex-military types who were theoretically hired to sabotage a chair lift and ended up killing the head of lift ops—no evidence for any of it. Sure, it's possible. But it's a little thin, Jack. Who hired them?"

"Captain Cosmo, of course. The billionaire formerly known as Daniel Gluck. Meanwhile, Georgie is at the Pueblo looking for Pete to see if there's any truth to this theory. I let her go before I understood the danger she might be in. I tried to call her just now but she's not answering. I think you and I need to drive to the Pueblo and find her."

"Jack, I can't go onto Pueblo land! I don't have any authority there. And there's no you-and-I here!"

"Santo, you need me. And Georgie needs both of us to get her out of harm's way. There's no time to lose."

"Jack—" Santo was about to object but just then his phone chirped. "Excuse me a second," taking the phone from his coat pocket. "Yeah? . . . where? . . . for chrissake, Rachel, slow down. Okay, set up a perimeter . . . okay, I'll be right there."

Jack had good hearing, so he knew what Santo was going to tell him."

"We got a body, Jack. It was dumped in the sagebrush a few miles west of town. Two people were cross-country skiing out there and found him. The ID in his wallet says it's Pete Day Rise. I gotta go."

"I'm coming with you."

"I'm sorry, but no, you aren't."

"Yes, I am," said Jack.

Chapter Eighteen

Georgie didn't realize her phone was dead until she had returned to the office from the Pueblo and tried to call Howie.

This was irritating. Her phone was four years old, but she didn't feel the need to upgrade every year when it did everything she needed a phone to do and it worked just fine. But the battery didn't hold a charge the way it used to and this had become a problem, especially since she often forgot to put it on the charger at night.

Some days Georgie wanted to throw all her electronics into the trash, walk off into the mountains, and never come back. Other days she longed to fly to Paris and sit drinking wine in some stylish Left Bank café dressed in Dolce & Gabbana. It wasn't easy to be culturally schizophrenic.

It was nearly 5 o'clock by the time she parked in the alley behind the Wilder & Associate building and came in the back door through Jack's old office. She was hungry and had stopped on the drive home for a falafel wrap at The Enchanted Carrot, the vegan café on the north side of town.

She plugged in her phone and saw immediately that Jack had been in the office, come and gone. There was a bowl of water left on the floor for Gypsy that hadn't been there earlier. She wondered who he had cadged to chauffeur him around. Jack was a con artist, really. But she liked the old rascal.

She walked through the building to the reception area in the front room and sat down at the big desktop computer to check for messages. Outside on Calle Dos Flores there were sounds of tourists roaming the historic district in search of New Mexico atmosphere and Happy Hour deals on margaritas. It was Saturday night, and the town was revving up. And she had a date!

Sort of a date, anyway. She wasn't really sure. Probably not.

John Concha had asked her to find out what she could about Pete and the two men he had been talking with on Friday night. But she wasn't sure she had learned anything important. The main reason for the meeting had been to raise money, so of course Pete would be chatting up potential donors. Pete was an extrovert. He was a good front man because he liked talking to people. She only wished he hadn't been so secretive about those two guys. Apparently he had spoken to them several times. She was the group's secretary, after all. She needed to be included in any discussions about fund raising.

Georgie wished she had unearthed tantalizing facts to dazzle John Concha with her brilliant detective work. But she hadn't.

He must think I'm a total idiot, Georgie told herself miserably. She had made a fool of herself every time she'd been with him, and she was determined never to do that again. Tonight, she wanted to be prepared. She wanted to show him that she wasn't a silly girl.

The big question was what she was going to wear to the La Rosa Café. She wanted an outfit that would accomplish a number of things. For a sleazy diner, she needed to dress down, while at the same time hint at a sophisticated knowledge of fashion that suggested a woman of the world. *Haute grunge* was what she was looking for. Her look had to convey that though she wasn't the sort of person who cared about clothes, she was sexy and smart, a woman desired by men so he'd better pay attention. She was not to be trifled with!

What she wanted most of all was respect. It maddened Georgie that he had written her off as an airhead. Though, of course, since she had acted like an airhead every time she had been with him, it wasn't a stretch for Concha to take her for one. Tonight, she needed to be smart.

"Smart and cool," she told herself. With an outfit to match. "I'm going to dazzle that fucker!"

Unfortunately, she didn't have clothes that would dazzle anyone. The fault was hers. Georgie hated shopping. Her wardrobe was minimal, a few pairs of jeans, a single dress, some snuggly sweaters, tatty underwear, and little else.

She ended up wearing jeans and her favorite black turtleneck sweater. Glasgow *louche*, she hoped. The jeans were tight, the sweater showed her figure. She didn't wear any makeup.

Georgie set forth to La Rosa at a few minutes before nine. The night was breathlessly cold with a black sky full of stars that glittered and winked with laughter at the small creature, so full of hopes and worries, so far below.

***

The La Rosa Café was in a strip mall on the south side of town. It was barely noticeable from the highway, with only a simple handpainted sign that was half-hidden beneath an awning. In a tourist town where every restaurant had tons of atmosphere, La Rosa had no atmosphere at all.

The tables were Formica top, the chairs tattered. Many of the customers looked like they had just arrived from prison by long-distance bus.

The room was crowded and steamy hot. Every table was taken, every booth. There were a few arty Anglos, but mostly this was the Spanish side of town.

She spotted John Concha in a booth by the window. He was seated drinking coffee while an old Indian man stood by his table speaking to him in urgent tones. As she watched, John shook his head without looking up. It was clear that he had not asked the old man to join him in the booth.

Georgie passed through the room, aware of male eyes sizing her up. She didn't like that, but she was used to it. She kept her head high, eyes straight ahead, and pretended a half dozen men weren't undressing her in their minds. However, the moment she slid into the booth across from John Concha, all the male eyes turned away and minded their own business. The War Chief inspired respect, if not downright fear.

The old Indian standing by the table was speaking Tiwa so Georgie didn't understand a word. John looked up at her and said something to the old man that made him nod and walk away.

Georgie gave Concha a questioning look. "What was that about?"

"I told him he could come speak to me tomorrow during office hours but not now. He wants me to take his side in a feud he has with his brother. It's been going on for thirty years, about a tractor they once shared. I've told him over and over again to let go of the damn tractor. Don't waste your life in small arguments over nothing. Put your mind on the bigger picture."

Georgie had never heard such a long speech from John Concha. She looked at him in some amazement.

"So what's the bigger picture?" she asked.

He smiled, the second amazing thing he'd done since she sat down. "Oh, that's for you to decide, young lady. I hear you went to college over there in England. People say you're smart."

Georgie wasn't sure what she thought about him calling her a young lady. It tingled with condescension. John Concha was old-fashioned, but she was willing to let it go. Old-fashioned suited him. She was glad that he knew she was smart.

"I believe in the cosmos," she told him. "There are more than 100 billion stars in our galaxy alone, and hundreds of billions of galaxies in the universe, beyond our ability to count. That, I think, is the bigger picture."

His eyes were grave as he studied her. Georgie felt herself flush. She was glad when the waitress came over to take their order. Concha said he would have chicken enchiladas, Christmas—both red and green chile—and Georgie said she would have the same. She didn't want to take the time to study the menu with John watching. Georgie ordered a Modelo Negra, John said he would stick with coffee.

"Don't you drink?" she asked him when the waitress moved away.

"I do not. Indians shouldn't drink, Georgina. We don't do well with alcohol."

"I understand that," she said defensively. "But I grew up in Scotland and my mother was Anglo, so sometimes I have a glass or two. It would be heresy in Glasgow not to drink. I don't overdo it, though," she added.

"So, Scotland. Then Cambridge University, I understand . . . what are you doing in New Mexico?"

The honest answer would have been I don't really know, I'm still finding out. But she said, "My da is here. I wanted to get to know him." Which was true also.

"All right, have yourself a beer, you might need it," he said. "I have something to tell you that you're not going to like."

"What?" she asked, suddenly alert.

But the waitress interrupted them again. She came to the table with the coffee carafe and Georgie's beer—in a bottle, no glass, with a wedge of lime in the neck.

"What aren't I going to like?" she repeated once the waitress was gone.

He hesitated.

"Tell me," she insisted.

"It's your friend Pete Day Rise. He's dead. His body was found by two cross-country skiers off in the desert west of town. He was shot in the back of the head."

Georgie's mouth fell open. She couldn't speak.

John was watching her carefully. "I'm sorry," he said.

"When?" she managed.

"When was he shot? I don't know. His body was found this afternoon. Jack and Lieutenant Ruben are out there now with the crime scene unit so we should have more details soon."

"How . . . how do you know about this?" Her voice broke. It was hard to get words out.

"I got a phone call. I have friends in the State Police."

Georgie's eyes filled suddenly with tears. With a gasp, she began to sob. She couldn't help herself. The tears flowed like a flood let loose. John watched her solemnly without a word.

"Sorry . . . I'm sorry . . . oh, God!" she managed.

She couldn't stop crying. She and Pete hadn't been particularly close, but they had worked together and she had liked him. His death overwhelmed her in a way she couldn't explain. It was the shock that someone she had known had been shot in the back of his head. She kept picturing it, and it was awful. It brought back the memory of the nightmare figures with goggles and guns coming at her from the dark. She could very well be dead now, too.

Gradually, Georgie got hold of herself until she was making little hiccoughing sounds, trying to breathe and wiping her nose with the tissues the waitress had brought. The first coherent thought she had was that she must look awful. The sophisticated woman of the world had turned into a blubbering child. She had done it again, making a fool of herself in front of John Concha.

"Lucinda, maybe hold the food," John said to the waitress who was hovering uncertainly by the table. "Can you get her some more tissues. Maybe coffee with something strong in it."

"You know we only have a beer and wine license, John," she told him. "But I got some Johnny Walker in the office."

The drink when it came was in a mug and it was strong. It made Georgie's cheeks glow red and now she knew she was several steps beyond unattractive. She looked up at the War Chief wondering what he could be thinking.

"Take your time," he told her quietly. "There's no hurry."

"I just feel so awful! Poor Pete! He was kind of an asshole, really, but it's hard for me to take in that he's dead."

"Just sit for a spell, Georgina. I shouldn't have sprung this on you so suddenly."

"No, it's me. You probably think I'm a real cry baby . . . I'm awfully embarrassed!"

Whatever he thought of her, he kept to himself. He continued to study her while she ignored the beer and sipped the spiked coffee.

"Are you feeling better now?" he asked.

She nodded.

"Do you feel up to answering a few questions?"

She nodded again.

"Tell me what happened this afternoon when you went to the Pueblo looking for Pete. Were you able to find out anything?"

Georgie took a deep breath. "Not much," she admitted. "I went around to some of the Forest Friends guys asking for him, but nobody knew where he was. I phoned Pete three times, but his voice mail was full and he didn't answer. Then just as I was leaving, I ran into Jerry Trujillo by the church. He's Pete's messenger boy and he always stayed pretty close to Pete's side. I drove Jerry home—he started coming on to me, which was a drag, but I got him to tell me some interesting stuff."

"What do you mean, he came on to you?" Concha asked.

"It was a childish sort of pass, not a big thing," she told him.

"Okay, that's good. Now let's hear your interesting stuff."

"Jerry saw Pete with the two guys you asked me about. Apparently, they had some kind of deal going on with Pete. They came to his house to meet with him a few different times. But Jerry was told to wait outside, and he never heard what they were saying. Pete told him it was about getting funding for Forest Friends, but that he didn't want to talk about it too soon and bring bad luck. Jerry said the guy who seemed to be in charge was the albino and he looked pretty tough."

"Did he say how much money Pete was hoping to get?"

"No. Jerry said he didn't know anything more. And that's all I was able to get out of him."

John nodded solemnly. "Well, all right. Thank you, Georgina. I'll have a talk with Jerry myself."

Georgie found it funny that he called her Georgina. It was very formal. He was a mountain of a man and she was afraid of him a little. But she had been afraid many times in her Glasgow childhood and had learned how to pretend to be bold.

She sniffed back the last of her tears. "So, now how about telling me something in return? What is it about those two guys that worries you?"

Concha shook his head sadly and didn't answer.

"And by the way," said Georgie. "Jerry *did* see Julie North with those guys Friday night. I know you don't believe me, but that woman was real. And I saw her get shot."

"Perhaps you did," Concha agreed. "But there's nothing much I can tell you, except I recognized one of the men, the albino. I don't know what he's up to but he's bad news."

"How do you know him?"

Concha regarded her. "I knew him in Afghanistan," he said finally. "He was Special Forces."

"That means you were Special Forces, too," Georgie told him. "Is that what you did over there?"

"It was," he answered. "I was a teenage kid from the Pueblo who wanted to travel and the military was my ticket to the wide world. I learned a lot over there, but none of it was good. I saw and did things I will never talk about. But such has been my journey, and I won't apologize."

"You became disillusioned with the war?" As soon as she asked it, she sensed it was a stupid question.

He smiled slightly. "Disillusioned? Pray to whatever gods you worship that you never see war, Georgina. It's not clean. It's ugly. It reeks of butchered bodies and lies. It was the lies I hated most. They wanted to keep me there, they offered me a promotion, but the second my tour was over, I got myself back to San Geronimo. This is my land, and these are my people. There is no honor in the white man's world. So this is where I will remain. This land is where I find the meaning of life."

Georgie couldn't think of anything to say that wouldn't sound stupid. John Concha had found the meaning of life. His life, at least. She wondered if she would ever find that for herself.

The dinner came finally when John nodded to the waitress that they were ready. The enchiladas were very good, real northern New Mexico cooking, and they were spicy hot. They ate mostly in silence and when they were finished, Concha paid at the counter, though Georgie offered to pay her share. She didn't want to presume. They filed outside into the freezing night, Concha holding the door for her. The moon had just risen over the mountains. The traffic on the highway swished by in a flash of headlights and snatches of rap music that were heavy on the bass.

He walked her to her car.

"So do you believe me now?" she asked as she stood with her keys in hand. "About Julie North and me seeing her fall down dead?"

"I believe you are a truthful person," he replied. "However, not everything you see is as it really is."

"You think there was some kind of hocus pocus that night?"

"Perhaps," he said. "Goodnight, Georgina."

She looked up into his eyes. He was nearly half a foot taller and they were standing close. She had the oddest premonition that he was about to swoop down and kiss her.

But he didn't. He turned away and headed toward his huge white pickup truck that you just about needed a ladder to climb up into.

John, take one more look at me! she thought intensely, sending it over airwaves. She believed in telepathy if you gave it enough zap.

He walked a few feet, then stopped, and turned to face her.

"Watch yourself, Georgina. You're far too pretty for your own good. And you're not as tough as you think you are. That worries me. There are dangers in this world and you need to take care."

"Yes, sir," she said, trying to sound slightly mocking, but not succeeding.

She watched as he climbed into his huge manly truck and drove away.

Was she too pretty for her own good?

Georgie was left to wonder if this was a compliment. Or just the opposite.

Chapter Nineteen

The temperature was frosty in Lieutenant Santo Ruben's State Police Explorer as they sped into the open desert west of town. Jack rode in the passenger seat with Gypsy in the back. His traveling wheelchair was collapsed in the cargo section.

Santo had his roof flashers on and they were going fast. A lot faster than Jack liked. He felt the speed. The wind was buffeting the vehicle. Every now and then Santo touched the siren in order to pass a car.

"Santo, slow down. "I'd prefer to get there alive."

"I'm worried, Jack. I don't like it one bit that Georgie went to the Pueblo to see a guy who's in the desert with the back of his head blown away."

"I don't like it either. But let's not panic. The chances are she didn't find Pete and she's on her way back to the office."

"Then why isn't she answering her phone?"

"I don't know. Maybe she forgot to bring it with her."

"Jack, people her age *never* forget their phones. They're attached with an umbilical cord. Look, why don't you try calling her again."

"Santo, I tried to get her five minutes ago."

"Well, try again."

Dutifully, Jack told his phone to call Georgie. An irritating voice told him that the number he was trying to reach was unavailable.

"Damn!" said Santo.

The SUV hit a bump and they were going so fast they became airborne for a dozen feet. The highways of rural New Mexico were far from smooth.

"For chrissake, slow down, Santo!"

"I can't slow down, Jack. I'm too stressed . . . hold on, I'm going to pass an RV . . . get out of the way, asshole!"

Santo floored the Explorer. He swerved into the next lane to pass the RV with his siren screaming as Gypsy in the back seat began to howl.

"God save me!" cried Jack.

***

Twenty minutes later, they turned off onto what passed as a road in this part of the high desert. A sign said Dry Rock Creek was 13.5 miles and the Santa Jacinta Wilderness Area 34.7 miles. The road was barely two parallel tire tracks through the snow and frozen earth with sagebrush between them. The sage scratched the bottom of the State Police Explorer as they bounced over the uneven land. The sun was low in the west and night wasn't far away.

Santo parked behind a black State Police pickup truck that had arrived earlier. The crime scene was a few hundred yards off into the sagebrush, accessible only by foot. Santo left Jack and Gypsy in the SUV and followed a trail of footsteps in the snow into a steep arroyo and up the other side to a rocky landscape strewn with large boulders.

It was a vast land with a huge horizon of forbidding mountains and sky. To the east, there was a hint of human habitation, houses small in the distance. But to the west, there was nothing but the fantastical geography of the Southwest. To Santo, a Chicano who had grown up in Chicago, the high desert looked like his idea of death. It frightened him a little. Santo often wondered why he had stayed in New Mexico so many years. It was no wonder he was in need of female comfort! The loneliness here was profound.

For Santo, the women came and went. There were wonderful romantic beginnings, nights of wine and roses that always arrived at a bitter end. He truly didn't understand why Jack—that grumpy old geezer—had managed to find a lifelong companion while he, with his matinee idol looks, had not.

I'm going to turn my life around before it's too late, Santo promised himself as he approached two state troopers who stood by the body.

"Sergeant," he said in greeting to Rachel Kronin. "Ted," he said to the new recruit who stood next to her. He gave each of them only a cursory glance. It was the body on the snow that had his full attention.

The body was frozen solid in a grotesque position, encased in a thin sheet of ice. Pete Day Rise lay halfway on his side with his arms and legs splayed open. He looked like a four-legged animal that had fallen over. The back of his head was a mess of frozen red goo. Santo had seen worse, but his stomach lurched and he felt an overwhelming sense of unease. He had been thinking of death too much lately. He had to take a deep breath.

"Damn, when will people stop killing each other?" said Santo doing his best to throw off his unease. "So where are the two skiers who found him?"

"I took their statements and let them go," said Rachel. "They were freezing out here and I didn't see why I should detain them. The man's a doctor in town and the woman teaches 5th grade at the charter school. Luke and Carmelita Richardson. We know where to find them."

Santo nodded, but he wasn't pleased. He should have been the one to decide whether to let them go.

"Do people really ski out here in the sagebrush?"

"Some do. There's not enough snow most winters, but when there is, it's a wide-open playground. You can go forever."

"Great," said Santo, in a tone that said he didn't think it was great in the least.

Sergeant Rachel Kronin had been sent to him from Santa Fe two years ago. She did a good job but they had never become close. Santo knew that she didn't like him. She seemed to know instinctively that he was a womanizer and borderline alcoholic. She let him know without the need for words that he'd better not try anything with her. He didn't. The Sergeant worked out in a gym and at the slightest hint of flirtation she would probably have knocked him flat.

"Have you called the M.E.?"

"He's on his way along with the crime scene folks."

Santo studied the snow around the body. There were two tracks made by narrow cross-country skis that came from the direction of the road. Close to the body the snow was too churned up with footprints to make much sense of what had happened here.

"The Richardson's took off their skis to give the body a better look," Rachel told him. "Like I said, the guy's a doctor and he was curious to know the cause of death. They walked around a little."

"I can see that," said Santo. "I hope they didn't touch anything. Well, let's back out of here and wait by the road for CSU and the M.E. Single file, please. Let's not mess up this scene any more than we have to."

In silence, the three of them walked back toward where they had left their vehicles. Santo took up the rear, imagining different narratives for Pete Day Rise's death. His best guess was Pete had been killed somewhere else and his body dumped far out in the desert where it wasn't likely it would ever be found. A month from now, they might have dug a shallow grave to get rid of the body with more certainty, but the ground was frozen now. It was their bad luck that two cross-country skiers had chanced to come this way.

As Santo walked, he scanned the snow for the footsteps the killers must have made. He imagined two people, but there might have been just one if he was strong enough. He would have dragged the body from the road as far off into the sagebrush as time allowed. But if that was what happened, Santo could see no sign of it.

As he was crossing the arroyo to the other side, he thought he saw something odd in the snow a hundred feet off to his left. He wasn't sure. From a distance, the deepening shadows cast from a sagebrush can take on strange shapes.

"You two go on up ahead," he told Rachel and Ted. "I want to check something out. Until we get set up better, I want you two to keep watch. Make sure no more skiers get in. I won't be long."

Rachel stopped to give Santo an evaluating look. She was doing that a lot recently. Santo was aware that she disagreed with every decision he made. She kept it to herself, but it was written on her face.

He didn't care, not really. He knew he couldn't get rid of her without a very good reason so he did his best just to ignore her.

The snow was deep in places, causing Santo to stumble as he crossed over a depression and headed uphill toward where he was sure he had seen something that was man made.

When he came closer, Santo saw the disturbance in the snow was a dozen feet of snowmobile track. The slice of track must have been made at some time after the Thursday storm, either Friday night after the meeting or earlier today. It disappeared on both ends where it had been covered by blowing snow.

Santo kept looking. He climbed up a short hill hoping for another sighting of the track. Luckily, there were sunny places where the snow had mostly melted that showed broken sections of tracks moving in a westward direction. He imagined this was how the body had been brought to this distant stretch of high desert, by snowmobile. But the snowmobile couldn't get here by itself. It must have been brought on a trailer pulled by a car or a truck.

Santo paused for a few minutes to study the geography of the land. If he continued in the direction of the snowmobile tracks he was certain he would come to the continuation of the road where he had left Jack, though farther to the west.

But why were they heading west toward the mountains? There was nothing out there but more mountains and desert. As far as he knew, every road in this direction reached a dead end. People camped out here and dumped trash but none of these four-wheel drive tracks connected with a paved highway that would take them back into civilization.

Then Santo remembered that there *was* such a road, though it was seldom used. The killers probably weren't locals. According to Jack they were hired thugs from out of town. So where were they staying while they did their job? They would need a place to camp.

Santo didn't know this land well but he had an idea of where they might have gone. He retraced his steps to the path that Rachel and Ted had taken. He was out of breath when he returned to where the vehicles were parked. Sergeant Kronin and Ted were in their police pickup with the motor running getting warm. Santo waved to show them he was okay and headed to his SUV where he had left Jack.

"Brr!" he said, climbing into the driver's seat. "Days like this, I start fantasizing about moving to Florida where winters are warm."

"Sure, Santo. Now tell me what's going on."

"You know, Jack, you're not the only decent detective around here. What's going on is I'm pretty sure I figured out how the killers got the body out here. Better yet, I believe I know where they went afterward. They might still be there so I'm going to pay them a visit. This could prove dangerous. So maybe I should leave you with Rachel and Ted. It'll be safer for you."

"Oh, for chrissake, Santo—let's just go!"

Chapter Twenty

The winter evening faded quickly into night. Santo switched on his headlights as they drove toward the mountains on the frozen desert track.

"Here's what I'm thinking," Santo said to Jack. "The road we're on now probably isn't on any map. I've never been here before but I'm betting from the direction we're going that it's going to connect at some point to County Road B969. That's a gravel road, just wide enough for two cars to pass. But if I'm right, it'll connect with a paved highway at a small community on a tributary of the Chama River that calls itself Vallecitos. I've never been there but I've heard there's nothing except a small RV park that hunters sometimes use and a store that has a one-pump gas station outside. A friend of mine in the Sheriff's Department told me about it. He likes to hunt elk. I'm thinking a little out of the way place like that would be a good hideout for someone who wants to stay out of sight."

"That's quite a stretch, Santo."

"Is it? The tracks I found pointed more or less in this direction and Vallecitos is the only destination I can think of out here. The way I see it, if these are pros who came to San Geronimo to do a job, they'd need a base. They'd have to spend some time in the county getting the lay of the land and working out what they were going to do. But they wouldn't want to stay at a motel or any place that would attract attention. Two hunters hauling a trailer would fit right in without much notice in an off-the-map sort of place that few people know about. Meanwhile, the Pueblo and the ski resort are only a bit more than an hour away."

"You think they'd dump Pete's body so close to where they were staying?"

"I think they believed they were perfectly safe. Those two cross-country skiers stumbled on that body by an unlikely chance."

"Maybe," said Jack.

"I bet I'm right."

"I bet you're not."

Before they had gone another mile, Jack and Santo had a bet going, a bottle of Glenlivet to whoever was right. They had made bets like this before, it was almost a ritual. Nobody lost because they generally shared the bottle together nights in front of the kiva fireplace in Jack's office telling cop stories, past adventures that grew more outrageous as the level of the bottle went down.

The faint desert road meandered for a number of miles and it was slow going in the dark. But there were tire marks in the snow from a vehicle that had passed this way recently and Santo was confident he was on the right track. Without warning, they came over a rise onto a gravel road. There was barely any snow on it, only occasional patches, but the snow reappeared and deepened as they turned southwest and climbed toward the mountains.

"This has to be the road I was telling you about. B969," said Santo.

"See any signs telling you that?"

"No, but what else could it be?"

"The yellow brick road to Oz?"

"For chrissake, Jack!"

They kept driving for a long twenty minutes and Santo was starting to get discouraged. If he was right, they might find the hitmen who had dumped the body in the desert. But if he was wrong, this trip would be a waste of time when there was no time to lose.

Finally, they came to a paved two-lane highway and Santo felt his shoulders relax. Half a mile later there was a small store with an old-fashioned gas pump standing in a circle of yellowish light cast by a single bulb hanging from a utility pole. The sign above the door said Vallecitos Mercantile, which seemed grand for what was hardly more than a wooden shack. A faded poster taped to a window said you could buy a 24-pack of Bud Light for $16.95 as well as a fishing license and ice. But not tonight. The store was closed and there was no one around.

"Vallecitos!" Santo announced. "You owe me a bottle of Glenlivet, Jack."

"You win," said Jack, in fact relieved they had not been wasting time.

Santo pulled over into the gravel parking area and let the engine idle.

"As dumpy little places go, this is about as depressing as they come," said Santo. "God knows, there are plenty of forgotten places like this in New Mexico, way off the beaten track, probably two or three families, everybody related by incest. You'd be surprised how many homicides occur in tiny places like this."

"Where's the RV park?"

"Across the highway, there's a driveway that crosses a wooden bridge onto the other side of the river. There isn't any traffic. There's only one light shining from a pole by the RV office. Otherwise, everything's dark. It looks like about the loneliest RV park you've ever seen, Jack. There are three old houses lined up along the highway that are barely standing. There's nothing but the store, the RV park, and the river. It's kind of spooky. You can almost imagine some zombie with a hatchet coming at you from the dark."

"Don't imagine it, Santo."

"I'm not. I'm just saying."

"Okay, remember, you have a shotgun. If any zombie appears, you can shoot the son of a bitch—"

"Jack, I get it. Let's check out the RV park."

Santo put the SUV in gear, crossed the highway, and turned onto the wooden bridge that crossed the river.

"Uh-hah!" said Santo thoughtfully.

"Uh-hah what?"

"There's a strange looking RV at the far end of the park. It's one of those off-road monsters with big tires. Otherwise the place is empty. It's just what I was picturing, the kind of vehicle the guys who killed Pete might have."

"Yes, but ordinary hunters might have an outfit like that."

"I don't know, Jack. It doesn't look so ordinary."

"Any sign of life?"

"No, it's dark. No sign of anybody. I think I need to check it out. But first I'm calling for backup. These people could be dangerous."

"Normally I'd say that's a good idea. But how long do you think it'll take for backup to get here?"

"Forty-five minutes, maybe. But look, if anybody's inside that RV, they're not going anywhere. I'm blocking the bridge, the only way out of here."

Jack thought about this for a minute. "Here's another idea. Put your roof flashers on and shine your spotlight on them. Let's put the fear of God in them and see if we can flush them out."

"I don't think that's a good idea. If this is what I think it is, these guys are well armed. It'll give them time to grab their weapons."

"Santo, if this is what you think it is, these guys already know we're here. They're professionals, remember. And if Georgie is right, they have night vision equipment. They're probably studying us right now."

"Okay, that's possible," said Santo. "They could be sitting in the dark waiting for us to make the first move. You know, my first idea is best. I'm going to call for backup before we make any move at all."

Santo's SUV had a satellite radio. He was reaching for the microphone when the side door of the RV burst open and someone ran out. It was a girl and she was running fast toward a stand of trees by the river. A moment later a man somersaulted out after her like a circus acrobat. He rolled on the ground and came up in a squatting position with a gun in his hand.

"Down, Jack!" Santo cried.

A shot was fired and the windshield of the Explorer broke into a spider web of cracks. Jack had ducked just in time. The bullet barely missed his head. He heard the whoosh of air as it passed.

"Stay down!" Santo told him, grabbing the shotgun from the dashboard. He rolled out the door onto the bridge and came up firing. There were two loud shots one immediately after the other.

"Damn, I got him, Jack! He's on the ground!"

Jack had a .38 revolver in his hand that he had pulled out of an ankle holster as Santo was reloading. In the back seat, Gypsy was barking with excitement. With difficulty, Jack opened his door and slid out onto the ground. He closed the passenger door as quietly as he could.

"Santo, Don't let Gypsy out!" he whispered. "Close your door!"

"Jack, what the hell are you doing? For chrissake, where did that gun come from?"

"I may be blind but my hearing is excellent. Believe me, I'm a better shot than you are in the dark. Careful, Santo—he's down but still alive!"

"No, he's —"

Santo was certain the guy was dead. The shotgun blast had thrown him backward with great force. But Jack had heard him move and suddenly the man from the RV began firing again in Santo's direction. Two bullets zinged into the front of the Ford Explorer and continued spraying the ground.

"Ahhh, fuck!" Santo cried in shock and pain. "Oh, goddamn!"

Santo had been hit. Jack didn't make a sound, resisting the urge to call out to him. The gunman hadn't seen Jack on the other side of the SUV. He sensed the location of the gunman with bat-like certainty. He knew he had one chance and one chance only. He had been a very good marksman in his day, but this was going to be tricky. As soon as he fired, his own position would be revealed.

He raised his .38, rotated the cylinder past the empty chamber, paused to take a final reading, then began firing.

He fired all five shells in rapid succession, sweeping slightly from side to side. The silence that followed was electric. Jack didn't move. If he had missed, there would be a barrage of fire coming his way any second. But the silence held. Jack was listening so intensely for gunfire he didn't realize at first that Gypsy was barking from inside the Explorer. He was relieved to know she was okay.

"Holy shit!" Santo cried from the other side of the vehicle. "Did you get him?!"

"Careful, Santo," Jack called to him. "I don't know. How badly are you hurt?"

"Took one in my leg, lower down. Hurts like a son of a bitch! I don't know how bad it is yet."

"Hold on, don't move. I'm going to crawl your way. Can you cover me?"

"Yep. Still got my shotgun. Wish Gypsy would be quiet—I can't hear if he's moving."

Jack got on his hands and knees and crawled around the rear of the Explorer. It wasn't easy, his arms and legs weren't strong. He had to stop once when his legs started to cramp. He reached Santo after what felt like a marathon.

"Okay," said Jack, staying low. He was exhausted. "Which leg is it? Let me feel around a little, see if I can tell how bad it is."

"Left leg," Santo said tightly, gritting his teeth. "Oh, man, it hurts!"

Jack felt his way downward from Santo's thigh. When his hand moved below Santo's left kneecap, Santo cried out in pain. Jack took his hand away. He had felt splintered bone and blood. A lot of blood.

"How bad is it, Jack?"

"It's not good, but you're going to be okay. We just have to stop the bleeding. Give me your belt. I'll do a tourniquet."

"Can't move . . . too much pain . . . feel sick."

"Hang in there, Santo. I'll use my own belt."

Jack pulled his belt loose and wrapped it several times as tightly as he could get it around the fleshy part of Santo's leg a few inches above the knee. It was a leather belt and the holes didn't extend far beyond Jack's Santa Claus belly.

"You're going to have to hold the end of the belt, Santo. Okay? Hold it as tight as you can. But we have to get you to a doctor. I'm going to radio for help."

"What about the son of a bitch with the gun?"

"I think we can assume he's a goner. He would be taking shots at us if he was still alive."

In fact, Jack didn't assume that in the least. But there wasn't time for caution. He used the door handle to pull himself up into a standing position. As soon as he opened the car door, Gypsy came bounding out onto the ground.

"Good girl!" he told her. "Go sniff that guy on the ground. If he moves, bite the hell out of him!"

It was impossible to say how much Gypsy understood. But she bounded off toward the RV as Jack pulled himself up into the driver's seat.

"Hey, Jack," said Santo. "I got a bottle of Jameson's stashed under the front seat. Think you could hand it down to me? I sure as hell could use a drink about now."

Jack suppressed a sigh. It wasn't good that Santo was drinking on the job. But this wasn't the time to worry about that. He found the bottle and lowered it down from the window into Santo's waiting hands. For Irish whiskey, Santo managed to sit up.

"Just drop it, I got it," said Santo.

Jack hoped the Jameson's would knock him out. He used the police channel to radio the San Geronimo station to say there was an officer down and they needed to get a medical chopper to him as soon as possible.

***

Santo was too weak to climb up into the warmth of the SUV and Jack was too weak to help him. Fortunately, the night had warmed so it was just above freezing. Drops of wet snow were dripping from the trees.

There was a stack of emergency thermal blankets in the cargo area of the SUV and Jack got two of them to wrap around Santo as he lay on the ground.

"How you holding up?" Jack asked.

"Better with the whiskey. Want a slug?"

"Not now. But you go ahead. The chopper should be here soon."

"Yeah," said Santo vaguely. "Look, Jack, if I don't make it, I want you to call Estelle, my last wife —"

"No, don't go there, Santo. I mean it. You're in a lot of pain, I know that, but you're going to be okay. Now, I need your help so don't get soft on me. I need to know about the person you saw run out of the camper. Where did he go?"

"It's a she. I guess she's in the woods somewhere. She was running like hell. Maybe she was a hostage, I don't know."

"Okay, she probably hasn't gone far. I'm going to give her a shout and tell her it's safe to come out."

Sitting on the ground next to Santo and Gypsy, Jack cupped his hands and shouted, "Hello, this is the New Mexico State Police! I'm sure you heard the gunfire, but it's over now. That guy's not going to bother you anymore. Are you okay?"

There was no answer.

Jack shouted again. "My name is Commander Jack Wilder, I'm a retired cop from California. My friend here is Lieutenant Santo Ruben. He's the chief of the State Police in San Geronimo. He's wounded but he's going to be okay. You're safe now, you can come in!"

There was a pause, then a girl shouted back. "How do I know you're really cops?" She sounded young.

"Hold on a second and I'll show you."

With an effort, Jack climbed back into the driver's seat and turned on the roof lights. Bright flashes of red and blue lit up the night.

"See that?" he shouted. "We're for real and we're here to help you. Now you need to tell me—are there any more of them around?"

"No, there was just that one. The other two left this afternoon and they haven't returned."

"Other two? Okay, now come on in and we'll talk."

"I don't know," said the girl sullenly. "I don't trust nobody."

"I understand why you're cautious. How old are you?"

"Fifteen," she said.

"What's your name?"

"Dakota," she replied. "My pa owns the trailer park."

"Where's your pa now?"

"Don't know," she answered. "He's off on one of his drunks. Haven't seen him for a week."

Jack had pretty much figured out her position from the sound of her voice. She wasn't far away. If her father owned the RV park, she would know places she could hide.

"Dakota, nobody's going to hurt you any longer. So why don't you come out and tell us what's been going on here."

"Okay, I guess." She stepped out cautiously behind a stand of trees that followed the bank of the river. She hesitated, standing in the snow barefoot with her arms across her chest.

"Christ, Jack, she's naked!" said Santo through gritted teeth.

"You must be freezing," Jack called. "Look, Dakota, I'm blind so it doesn't matter if you don't have any clothes on. As for the lieutenant here, he's seen everything. I'm going to send my guide dog to you. Give her a call and she'll come to you. Her name is Gypsy and she's really sweet . . . go, girl!" he said to Gypsy.

Gypsy bounded over the snow to the girl.

"Come here, doggie," he heard the girl say.

"You can put your arms around her neck, it'll warm you up a little. Now hurry, you need to get some clothes on."

Jack got two more thermal blankets from the back of the SUV. He handed them to her as she arrived. "Good, wrap them around you. There's a helicopter on its way to help us but before we get warm, I need your help to get Santo up into the back seat. He's in a lot of pain but we can do this if we work together. You sound like a good strong girl."

"You bet I am!" she told him.

"Great," he said.

And she was strong. Together, they got Santo onto his feet. He helped as well, hobbling onto his good leg. With a final push, they managed to hoist him up into the back seat. Gypsy jumped into the rear after him. Jack climbed once more into the driver's seat and Dakota got in on the front passenger side. The engine wouldn't start. One of the bullets must have hit some vital part of the engine. But the heater worked. Jack turned it on full blast hoping the battery would hold out until the helicopter arrived.

Jack sat back, numb with exhaustion. Santo was in a daze in the back seat clutching the bottle of Jameson's. The heat washed over them and put them in a stupor. None of them spoke for a minute. The windows were soon fogged up with all their deep breathing.

"Hey, I could use a hit of that bottle," Dakota said.

"You're not old enough to drink," Santo managed, still a cop.

"For chrissake, Santo—give her the damn bottle," Jack told him. "What does that matter now? I think I'll have a hit of that whiskey, too."

"If there's any left," said the girl.

Jack snorted and shook his head.

"Okay, Dakota," he said. "Let's hear your story."

***

She was a large girl with a freckly face and watchful eyes. She was chubby, the kind of fat that came from junk food and empty calories.

Dakota had been "home schooled," she said, but Jack could only wonder what that meant. Her mother had run off when she was three, leaving her with a drunken father and a ramshackle RV park. But she was tough, tough as any girl growing up in the badlands of New Mexico might be. And she wasn't stupid. Jack was willing to bet that she was the one who ran the household, such as it was.

"There were three men," she said. "They showed up two weeks ago with that funny looking RV and a big pickup with a camper shell that was pulling a trailer with two fancy snowmobiles on it. Said they were hunters, but I didn't believe them."

"Why not?" asked Jack.

"Don't know, just something about them wasn't right. They had too much money. I thought they were cops at first. But they weren't that either."

"Describe them, please."

"They were big guys, real strong, the sort who work out. In their thirties, maybe. They were polite but not friendly. One of 'em was real pale and hardly had any eyebrows. He was the worst, I didn't like him at all. They had guns, but they sure weren't hunting rifles. One of them had a MK18."

"You know enough about guns to recognize a MK18?"

"Sure, I do. Pa gets all the gun magazines. You don't hunt elk with an assault rifle. Those guys scared me!"

"They registered for their stay, I presume?"

"Well, sure. But we're kind of casual here. We only have six sites and this time of year, we hadn't had anybody for nearly a month before those three showed up. Only one of 'em registered, the real pale guy, and he didn't fill out everything. The other two, I never got their names."

"What name did the pale guy give you?"

"He said he was David McCauley, but I didn't believe him. From Tulsa, Oklahoma. Maybe that part was true."

"Did you ask to see an ID?"

"Naw. I mean, we don't hassle people like that. Fuck rules and regulations, that's what my daddy says. He's an anachranist, or what ever they call it."

"Anarchist?"

"Yeah, that's it. Want me to get the registration book? It's in the office."

"We'll get it later. Let's just stay warm in here now. How did they pay?" Jack asked.

"Cash. I could tell they had money, so I charged 'em $60 a night, the high season rate. It didn't bother them. They gave me hundred-dollar bills."

Jack doubted there was a high season at the Vallecitos RV Park, but he only nodded. "So how was it that you ended up in their RV?"

Dakota told her story in a straight-forward manner, no frills, no detours. Jack was inclined to like her.

For the first week, the three men parked at the far end of the compound and kept to themselves. Dakota didn't see much of them. They were often gone, sometimes with their snowmobiles, sometimes leaving the snowmobiles behind. It might have continued this way except for the fact that with pa gone on an extended drunk, Dakota was bored. It wasn't that she was nosey, but she didn't know what to do with herself. So, one afternoon when the men were off in their pickup, she wandered over to the trailer with the snowmobiles in order to have a closer look.

The two Polaris snowmobiles on the flatbed trailer were high end and Dakota knew they cost more than $20,000 each. She couldn't resist climbing on the seat of one of them and playing with the throttle.

"Vroom!" she said, imagining herself speeding over a snowy meadow with a wake of snow flying up behind her. She liked the idea of making a lot of noise on a hushed winter day. The Polaris was fancy with a number of mysterious dials and switches that she could only guess at.

She was having so much fun that she didn't see the white pickup truck as it came over the rise toward the RV park. She climbed off quickly, but they had seen her. As she jumped down off the trailer she slipped on a patch of ice onto her butt and from where she sat she could see there was something strapped to the underside of the trailer.

It was a big gun of some kind. A huge motherfucker, was how she put it. At first she thought it was a shoulder missile launcher because she had seen such things in the gun magazines her pa kept alongside his pornography collection. He liked photos of semi-naked women straddling big guns. Dakota had studied the magazines with interest since there were a number of things she wouldn't mind blowing to smithereens. But she didn't recognize the big gun that was strapped securely beneath the trailer. Maybe it was some sort of super bazooka, she imagined. Or a cannon.

Whatever it was, she was smart enough to know that she had better get the hell out of there fast.

She jumped to her feet and took off running into the woods. She followed a fisherman's path she knew that ran upstream along the Rio Vallecitos. The trail was covered with unbroken snow, but Dakota knew it well. The river itself was only a dozen feet across this time of year and the surface was mostly frozen.

Dakota was fast, but not fast enough. She heard truck doors slam and feet running behind her. As she ran, she knew she was leaving a clear trail to follow in the snow. Her only chance was to cross the frozen river and perhaps escape to the other side. But she would leave tracks there also. The three men were strong and well-trained and they were coming for her. There was no way she could escape them.

She didn't give up easily. She ran with all her might, faster than she had ever run before. But they caught her at a spot where there was a rocky beach. One of the men tackled her from behind, while another took her by the shoulders and pressed the barrel of a gun against the back of her head.

Dakota thought she was about to die.

"Don't!" she pleaded. Every cell of her body called out for life.

The men hesitated long enough to argue among themselves whether to kill her right there and then. Held tightly, Dakota couldn't see their faces, she only heard voices. The decision was a toss up. They couldn't leave behind a witness. But caution won out. A teenage girl could be a useful pawn, a hostage if they had trouble making their escape.

They decided to let her live, at least for the moment. They bound her up with rope and one of the men tossed her over his shoulder and carried her back along the path to their RV as though she weighed nothing. Once she was inside, she was tied to a metal bar, her butt on the floor, her back against a wall. A gag was duct taped to her mouth. Dakota struggled but there was nothing she could do.

The next three days were hell. She was given water once a day, but no food. Twice a day, morning and night, she was untied and allowed to use the small bathroom, heavily guarded and the bathroom door left open. Dakota knew that this wasn't due to kindness but to the fact they didn't want to stink up their RV. On day two, her gag was taken off, but she was warned that it would return the minute she tried to talk.

On day three, the pickup with the trailer and two snowmobiles drove off leaving one man behind to guard Dakota. She knew they were going to kill her in the end but with two of them gone she had a glimmer of hope. Dakota knew what men were like.

It was her only hope. A man, a girl—the two of them alone in a camper far from other people. But she was weak and cramped and she didn't feel well. She hadn't had anything to eat for three days, and she wasn't sure she could pull it off.

Her chance came that evening when he untied her so she could use the bathroom. There wasn't much to evacuate after three days but it felt good to stand and stretch. She didn't know the man's name. In all this time, they had never addressed each other by name. He was clearly the youngest of the three, still in his twenties. Like the others, he was large and monstrously fit. He had a dull face that showed nothing about himself.

As usual, the door was left open as she used the bathroom, but he looked away uninterested.

"I'm hungry," she said, coming out of the bathroom. "I mean, I'm really, *really* hungry."

He glanced at her but didn't answer.

"If you give me a sandwich, I'll give you a blow job," she offered.

He glanced at her with a flicker of interest but still didn't answer.

"Hey, there's just you and me here, nobody has to know," she went on. "All I want is a sandwich—I'll do anything for it, anything you want."

"Shut up," he said.

But Dakota knew she had him. There was a thickness in the air, a heat. She went on describing things she had seen in magazines but never done. In truth, she'd had only one experience with sex with a 14-year-old boy who had camped here with his family last summer. From the one time, she had concluded that sex was overrated, but this didn't stop her from describing in detail what she would do in exchange for something to eat.

Jack listened without judgement, understanding the lengths people would go to in order to survive. Dakota was candid, almost matter of fact, as she told him what happened next.

She was a clever girl, no schooling but country smart. Her plan wasn't very complicated.

After some preliminaries, she got down on her knees and smiled up at him enticingly. She opened her mouth and pretended she was enjoying herself too. She wanted him to relax. Then she bit down hard.

He screamed in pain and outrage as she grabbed his ankles and yanked his legs out from under him. Strong as he was, he was unprepared for her assault. He fell backward onto the floor, hitting his head against the edge of a table.

Dakota didn't waste time. She jumped over his body and bounded for the door. The door was locked and it took a second to find the right latch to get it open. The man was stunned but already rising unsteadily to his feet.

Dakota escaped the trailer just in time. She ran naked into the winter night, barefoot on the snow, determined to escape. She ran so hard she didn't even feel the cold.

She didn't realize at first that he wasn't following her. As he came raging out the door with a gun in hand, he saw the New Mexico State Police vehicle on the creaky bridge that crossed the river. The girl would have to wait.

***

"What do you think, Santo?" Jack asked, hoping to distract him from his pain.

Santo didn't answer. He was slumped in the back seat against the car door, passed out. Jack didn't know if it was because of the loss of blood or the Irish whiskey, but he was worried.

He changed places with Gypsy, putting her into the front and taking her place in the back next to Santo. He didn't want the tourniquet to loosen. He held the belt tight, using both hands. Without his belt, he nearly lost his pants getting out and then back in the Explorer.

He hoped the helicopter would get here soon. Already it seemed like they had been waiting a long time.

Holding onto the tourniquet, he kept questioning the girl, addressing the back of her head in the front. Not that he much cared about her answers. It was more habit than anything else. At the moment, he was much more concerned about Santo.

"Nice dog," she said. Gypsy had managed to put her head in Dakota's lap, always up for more love. "I like dogs. They're nicer than people."

"That's often true," said Jack. "Though occasionally there are mean dogs and decent people."

"So what's it like being blind?" she asked.

Jack smiled thinly. "It wasn't my first choice, Dakota. But you have to take what you get. Now, tell me everything you can about the men. You were with them for three days, you must have heard them talking to each other."

"Not really. Not in front of me, anyway."

"Could you tell who was in charge?"

"I dunno. Probably it was the real pale guy. I don't think it was the one they left to guard me. Whenever there was crappy stuff to do like wash dishes, he was the one who did it."

"Did they have accents of any kind?"

"Accents?"

"You know—Texas accents, for example. Like saying 'ah-cy' instead of 'icy.'"

"No, not like that. But they didn't talk like people around here. I guess they sounded sort of like city folks."

"Okay, that's good," he said encouragingly. "Did the two who left in the pickup say where they were going?"

"Naw."

"Not even a hint?"

"No, not a thing. Like I said, they were real quiet. Didn't talk hardly at all."

Jack didn't like that. It implied serious discipline on their part for Dakota to spend three days with these people and know so little about them. They were clearly very good at what they did.

He took a breath and continued, "Now, I'm sure you understand, Dakota, what I'm worried about is the large gun you saw beneath the trailer. Can you describe it to me again, please."

"I told you, I was on my back, looking up at it from the ground. It was bolted to the underside of the trailer."

"How long was it?"

"Maybe seven or eight feet. I dunno. There was some sort of tripod folded up alongside it. It looked like it would take a few guys to handle it."

"How wide across the barrel?"

"You sure ask a lot of questions!"

"I do because I have to, Dakota. Now, tell me about the barrel."

"It was maybe six or seven inches. I don't know. I mean, I didn't have a lot of time. I was on my back, worried they'd seen me."

"Did you hear any hint—anything at all—about what they planned to do with it?"

"No, I keep telling you—they didn't say nothing at all."

Dakota was losing patience with all the questions, but Jack kept prodding, hoping she had noticed some small thing. If the two key men had driven off with the snowmobiles and a very large gun of some sort bolted to the bottom of the trailer, it meant something bad was in play. He had to know what they were up to.

"Did they say anything about San Geronimo Peak? The ski resort."

"No. How many times do I have to tell you? They didn't say anything!"

"Okay, okay, I get it," Jack told her. "You've done a good job, Dakota. I'm glad you got away."

"Hey, you know, there is one thing. I mean, it's nothing they talked about. But now that you mention the ski resort, one time when they let me go to the bathroom, I saw a map spread out on the table. It was kind of pretty. It showed the mountain all white with snow and all the trails marked with their names and everything. There was also a brochure for a hotel up there. It had a funny name. The Hog House."

"The Hamm Haus?"

"Yeah, that's it. When the pale guy saw me looking at it, he picked it up off the table and put it away."

"Really?" said Jack. "That's great, Dakota. That's just the sort of small thing I'm looking for."

He kept at her, asking more questions. Sometimes the same question again and again. But he couldn't get anything more from her.

At long last, he heard sirens in the distance and a few minutes later, two police cars and an ambulance drove onto the rickety wooden bridge. There was no helicopter but at least this was something.

Sergeant Rachel Kronin was the first to arrive and Jack did his best to explain what had happened as concisely as possible.

"Look, Sergeant, I'll be glad to answer all your questions. But first you've got to get Santo to the hospital. And I need somebody to drive me up to the ski resort. I don't know exactly what's going on, but I'm certain something very serious is about to happen up there."

"You must be kidding!" said the Sergeant. "What? You think I'm going to be your private chauffeur? What's going to happen is this, Mr. Wilder. You're going to come back to the station with me and we're going to go through your statement in a whole lot more detail than you've done so far."

"Sergeant—"

"No, you need to shut up, Mr. Wilder, and let me do my job. I want you to stay in the car while I look around and we'll talk later."

Jack couldn't get anywhere with her. She was a tough cookie.

Luckily Santo regained consciousness while two ER medics were lifting him from the back seat and getting him onto a stretcher.

"Santo, listen closely," Jack said before they could carry him away. "I need to get up to the Peak. Those men have a damn missile launcher and something very bad is about to happen. I'm seriously worried about Georgie. If she's not on the Peak I'll look for her at the Pueblo. But I need wheels and a driver. You're the boss. You've got to speak to Sergeant Kronin and order her to do what I'm asking."

Santo grunted and didn't reply. But while Santo was being transferred to the ambulance, the Sergeant walked alongside his gurney and spoke with him.

A few minutes later, she returned to the Explorer. "Okay," she said reluctantly. "You've got your wheels and Ted will drive you. I sure could have used him here, so I hope you're pleased with yourself for fucking up my investigation!"

Jack *was* pleased. But not overly so. There were too many things to worry about and he knew he was miles behind and time was running out.

Chapter Twenty-One

Howie opened his eyes emerging from darkness into an equally dark room. He had no idea where he was or how he got here. He hardly knew who he himself was.

As he came awake slowly, he discovered that he was in a large luxurious bed that wasn't his own. He was naked. There was a subtle smell of femininity in the room, a hint of a flowery perfume. But he was alone in bed, there was no female anywhere. The sheets were smooth and satiny.

His memory returned in pieces. He was in the Hamm Haus, on the third floor, Leilani's suite. The last thing he remembered was Leilani making her "special recipe" mai tai and handing him the glass. There had been a slice of pineapple in it and a maraschino cherry. He remembered touching glasses with her. He remembered thinking how pretty she was. She had smiled seductively, like he was her favorite person on the planet. It seemed to him that they had talked some more, but like a dream half-remembered after waking, he couldn't remember what they had said. Then there was nothing.

Leilani!

She'd given him a knock-out drug! It was unbelievable! He was starting to believe that rescuing damsels in distress wasn't such a good idea after all.

But did they have sex? That was the question. To all appearances, it looked that way, but he couldn't remember a thing about it.

He gathered his senses slowly and got out of bed. A narrow edge of moonlight came in from the curtain. He could just make out a lamp on the bedside table. He found the switch but no light came on. In hotels, you sometimes didn't know if the bedside table lamp didn't work because a switch by the door wasn't on.

As his eyes became accustomed to the dark, he was able to move around well enough without bumping into furniture. The first thing he needed to do was find his clothes. He looked around the bedroom, but they weren't anywhere to be seen. Howie wandered naked through the suite in a daze but they weren't on the floor, where he might have shed them in wild passion. Nor were they on any of the chairs or sofas. There was no sign of Leilani.

He pulled open the edge of a curtain and saw it was night. The ski resort sat in mute darkness, dream-like in the mountain valley, not a light showing anywhere. This was worrisome. Something very wrong was happening here.

There was a three-quarter moon in the sky with clouds floating past, alternating light and shadow, barely illuminating the outline of the mountains. He could just make out the lower station of the bunny lift that ran up the easy little slope where first timers learned how awkward it was to get around with boards attached to their feet.

Howie made his way to the door that led to the hallway. It was locked. At first, this didn't seem to be a problem. The lock looked like standard hotel ware, designed to keep people out, accessed by a card. From the inside, hotel locks were generally fairly easy to work. Hotels didn't want to keep people from going downstairs to spend money in the bar. Nevertheless, Howie fiddled and tried different options, but the door refused to open. Finally, he rattled the door in frustration. He was locked inside the suite.

Next he tried the phone in the sitting room. He would call downstairs for help. But the phone was dead. No matter which buttons he pushed, nothing happened. He walked into the bedroom where there was a second phone by the bed. That was dead as well.

He sat down on the edge of the bed and pondered his situation. He had no clothes, no shoes, the hotel phones didn't work, and all his personal belongings were gone as well—his wallet, his phone, his car keys, everything. He had been stripped bare and he was starting to get angry.

Howie strode over to the bedroom windows and with a great yank pulled down the scarlet colored curtain and wrapped it around his shoulders like a toga. At least he wasn't buck naked now.

He walked back to the front door to the hall and tried it again, but no matter how he fiddled with the lock, it still didn't open. He tried the phones again, but they were as dead as they had been before. He looked closer and saw why they weren't working. The cords had been cut with a knife.

"Leilani! Goddamn it!"

Howie was getting angrier and angrier. Clearly Leilani was in league with Hamm, her so-called godfather, intent on keeping him locked in this suite. But why? Something must be happening or about to happen that they didn't want him to interfere with.

Meanwhile, this was an embarrassing situation. Jack was going to laugh his head off. Nor would it be easy to explain to Claire. Howie felt an increasing urgency to escape.

He stood by the bedroom window that looked down from the third floor at the ticket office and a slice of the driveway that came up from the parking lot to the hotel. The snow glistened with a strange phosphorescence. The stillness was eerie. Not a creature was moving, not even a mouse.

But then he saw a solitary figure, a man dressed in heavy winter clothing running up the driveway towards the hotel. He looked like he might be a hotel worker or a security guard. Howie pounded on the window trying to get his attention, but the man didn't look up.

In desperation, Howie shed the curtain he had wrapped around his body and stood naked banging on the window with his fists, hoping the solitary figure would see a madman on the third floor and call the police. But he still didn't look up. He ran purposely up the road unaware of the naked man in the third-floor window. Howie watched as he turned a corner and disappeared from view.

Howie collapsed back onto the bed, discouraged to the point of exhaustion. Fortunately, desperate thoughts lead to desperate actions. There was a wide strip of undisturbed snow beneath the window that was deep and soft.

All he needed to do was break the window, tie a few sheets together, and he could get out of here.

***

The window was inoperable, a solid piece of glass approximately four feet high and six feet wide. The suite was climate controlled. There were thermostats but guests were not allowed to breathe the fresh mountain air.

Howie looked around for something heavy. He thought an armchair that sat by the dresser might do. It was well-padded and solid. He couldn't tell its color in the dark. With some effort he picked it up, stood a few feet back, raised the chair above his head, and threw it hard against the window. But the glass refused to break. The chair bounced back into the room.

Howie had to pause for a few minutes breathing hard. The dim reflection from the unbroken glass showed a prehistoric creature standing naked in the room, more ape than human. He was beyond caring.

He saw a floor lamp by the sofa with a heavy metal base that looked promising. He picked it up by its neck, pulled the electric cord free with a violent jerk, and wrapped the cord around the stand. The lamp was heavy. He raised it above his head and swung it in a circle, spinning with his body, like a discus thrower gathering speed and momentum. With a grunt of effort, he let go and smashed the heavy end of the base into the glass.

That did the trick. The glass shattered and the shards flew out into the night, followed by the floor lamp itself which tumbled end over end and fell into a heap of snow by the side of the hotel. Cold air rushed into the room.

Howie grinned with satisfaction. Now he needed to tie the two sheets from the king size bed together, anchor the hotel end to something stable, climb out the window without cutting himself on the broken glass, and lower himself to the ground without breaking his neck. This was easier said than done but he was on a roll.

After tying the sheets together, he pushed a writing desk against the wall next to the window and tied the end of the sheet around a solid wooden leg. Now that the two sheets were anchored, he used a blanket to clear as much glass as he could from the window frame then tossed the remaining length of sheet out the window. Unfortunately, the two sheets didn't go very far. If they didn't tear apart, they would take him down a single floor which would leave him with a drop of at least two stories to reach the ground. But there was no other option. With luck, the snow on the ground would break his fall.

He wrapped the curtain around his shoulder and tied it in a loose knot that left the lower half of his body naked. The arrangement was awkward but he wanted something to wear when (and if) he reached the ground.

"This is crazy!" he said aloud to the room. But he couldn't turn back now. He climbed up on the desk so that he was even with the window frame, took hold of the sheet, and stepped into the night.

The sheet held.

He used his feet to leverage himself against the building and lowered himself down, one hand at a time. He barely felt the cold. It was going well.

He was parallel to the window on the floor beneath him, starting to relax, when the sheet abruptly gave way. With a cry, he plummeted to the ground and sank into the snow bank up to his chest. The snow broke his fall as he had hoped, but the cold was unbearable.

He knew he had to move quickly before he got hypothermia. It was a struggle to get free of the snow. He thrashed with all his strength and managed a kind of icy swim upward, far enough so that he was able to grab hold of a decorative iron fence and pull himself out the rest of the way. He hadn't seen the fence from the third-floor window, and it was pure luck he didn't land on it.

The curtain had fallen free during his fall, but he managed to wrap it around his body and run as fast as his frozen feet would take him around to the front end of the hotel. He didn't stop, he kept going across the plaza toward the locker room where he stored his gear. As he sprinted across the plaza he caught sight of a huge snow cat lumbering down the mountain, its headlights shooting beams of light into the trees. The sight wasn't unusual. The grooming of trails took place in these wee hours. He was glad to see some semblance of normality on the mountain.

He reached the door of the locker room. His hands were so numb he had trouble punching in the code that opened the lock, but he got it after several tries. The locker room was heated but dark. He slammed the door shut after himself and tried to catch his breath. The sudden rush of heat was painful and prickly.

He made his way cautiously into the darkness, arms forward feeling for obstacles. From the wet slap on the floor, he knew his left foot was bleeding. Every step he took hurt as he made his way down the row of lockers. His locker was number A24, four lockers down from the end of the row. He felt with his hands, one locker at a time.

The locker room wasn't fancy, nothing more than long wooden benches, a cement floor, and metal lockers side by side. The locker cost $1175 for the season, which was more than Howie paid for his pass. It was worth it for locals like himself who didn't want to haul heavy skis, boots, and gear every time they drove up the mountain for a few hours of skiing.

At the start of the season, Howie had bought a high-tech lock that opened with the touch of his right index finger pressed against a small square on the side. He was glad for this tonight since he wouldn't have been able to open a regular combination lock in the dark. He almost wept with joy when the lock opened and he felt his way inside to find his long underwear, ski socks, ski pants, a down vest, a heavy sweater, neck warmer and helmet. His boots were on a rack at the end of the locker room.

"Never again!" Howie swore vaguely as he let the scarlet curtain fall off his shoulders and dressed himself in every warm piece of clothing the locker held.

He was finally warm, feeling almost human again, when he heard footsteps coming from the adjoining room where skis and snowboards were stored.

The door opened and the light of a flashlight scanned the room, stopping on Howie as it caught him in its beam. He felt woefully exposed.

The light came closer. In the reflection from the lockers and walls, Howie saw it was a man with a pair of skis over his shoulder. He wore a shoulder holster with the butt of a gun showing from beneath his unzipped parka.

It was Sean Basset.

They looked at each other in surprise.

"Howie," he said. "What the hell are you doing here at this hour?"

"I could ask you the same question, Sean."

Sean lowered his skis so that the ends rested on the cement floor.

"You know, you really shouldn't be here, Howie," he said wearily. "Not tonight."

Oddly, Howie was having exactly the same thought.

Chapter Twenty-Two

State Police Patrolman Ted Hirsch was a decent driver.

He drove fast. Jack was aware of the wind rushing past, the powerful engine of the patrol car slicing its way forward through the volume of air. But unlike Santo, there was something calm and steady about the way Ted drove that made Jack feel he was in safe hands.

"So you were a police commander in California," Ted said after several miles of silence. There was a question mark of disbelief in his voice.

"I was," Jack told him. "In San Francisco, the rank of commander is just below the deputy chief. But in my time, the deputy chief was a hack who was always off playing golf with some big shot. So, I did his job basically. It was an office job, mostly, and I missed being on the streets. There was always a lot of pressure from the mayor and the D.A., lots of politics. They usually tried to make me the fall guy when they were the ones who fucked up. But that's the way it is on a big city police force."

"Sounds pretty hairy," said Ted.

"It was," said Jack. "A real juggling act. Until I lost my eyesight. To be honest, I wanted to keep on going. I could have done that job with my eyes closed. But there were rules about things like that. They medically retired me and I moved to San Geronimo."

"But then you opened a detective agency. So you *did* keep on going."

"Yep. So what made you decide to become a cop, Ted?"

"I ask myself that sometimes. Honestly, I think it's because my parents were so dead set against it. We moved here to New Mexico from Santa Barbara when I was ten because my mother was certain a big earthquake was coming, and the California coast would fall into the ocean. She saw it in the Tarot cards. My mom and dad are New Agey, I guess. Nice people but my home life was pretty chaotic. No set meal times, nothing like that. Most nights I had to forage in the fridge for my own dinner. I think I wanted more order somehow . . . sorry, I guess I'm boring you with all this."

"Not at all."

Ted seemed anxious to talk, not yet accustomed to firefights and dead bodies in the snow. Jack let him ramble.

"So, you think the Lieutenant is going to make it?" Ted asked.

"I sure hope so," Jack told him.

"Me too. The Loo is a good guy. He's tough, but fair. This is my first assignment, you know. I only graduated from the Academy six months ago and I know I have a lot to learn. He's been really patient the times I've screwed up. But, man, his leg sure looked bad! That bullet totally shattered the bone!"

"He's in a lot of pain right now, but he should be okay, Ted. Doctors are pretty good these days with wounds like that."

"I sure hope the Loo isn't going to have to face an internal investigation for shooting that guy. I mean, after getting shot himself, it seems pretty obvious he was defending himself."

"There's always an investigation after an officer involved shooting," said Jack. "There has to be transparency. But Santo isn't going to have a problem. He didn't kill that man. I did."

"What? You're kidding!"

"I am not kidding, Ted. This isn't something I would ever joke about."

"But you're . . . I mean, you're—"

"Yes, I'm blind. But I have exceptionally good hearing and I'm a very good shot. Luckily, I was carrying a small snub-nosed revolver. After Santo got wounded, I slipped out of the Explorer onto the ground and the gunman didn't see me. I fired in his direction and I guess I got lucky. Forensics will find it was my .38 that killed that man, not Santo's 9 mil."

"Jesus!" said Ted. "Does Sergeant Kronin know about this? She didn't say anything!"

Jack smiled. "Neither did I. She wouldn't have let me go if I told her the truth, and there wasn't time for that. She'll find out soon enough and we need to get up to the Peak as quickly as we can."

"Look, Mr. Wilder, I'm sure you were justified to do what you did, but I don't want to get into trouble here."

"You won't, Ted, I promise. Santo is going to be okay, and he knows exactly what happened. He'll cover for you. So let's keep going. As fast as you can, please. As long as we get there in one piece."

"Jesus!" Ted muttered again. "Shot by a blind man!"

"Blind luck," said Jack. "Now, let's hurry."

As they drove, Jack tried to phone Georgie several times. The first two times he tried they were too far from town and there was no cell service. The third time, he got her voicemail but she still didn't answer.

"Damn!" said Jack in frustration. "Why the hell doesn't that girl answer?"

***

How Georgie ended up in bed that night with John Concha—after saying goodbye to him at La Rosa Café—was something she later pondered.

Was it the spin of the roulette wheel? The toss of the dice? Or had the gods sent Cupid her way with an arrow in his bow?

In Georgie's case, it wasn't an arrow that did the mischief but a rusty nail that punctured her front right tire as she was driving from the La Rosa café toward the office in town.

The nail and her front right tire found each other as she was passing the Dollar Store next to the Holiday Inn. Georgie felt the sudden wobble, but she didn't know what it indicated. She wasn't good with cars. Automobiles weren't in her DNA. She drove another two blocks before the tire shredded and the metal rim began clanging on the pavement. Too late, after the damage was done, she understood she'd better pull over and stop.

"Honestly!" she cried with a groan of irritation. Outside it was dark and cold, ten o'clock on a January night.

For the second time in days, she called Triple-A to come rescue her. To her annoyance, she was told to expect a wait of an hour and a half before a tow truck could arrive.

"Fuck!" she said profanely. This was the last straw. Everything had gone wrong. Pete was dead. Murdered! And she had embarrassed herself in front of the War Chief yet again. He didn't like her. She was far too pretty, whatever that meant—but she knew it wasn't good.

And now she was stuck, stuck, stuck in a dead Subaru on a lonely winter night under a black sky near a strip mall where every store was closed. She banged the steering wheel with her fist. "Ow!" she cried. She knew she was being silly, but honestly, this was unbelievable. It couldn't be happening, but it was.

In her misery, she hadn't noticed that an oversized white pickup truck had pulled up behind her, its fierce headlights blazing through her rear window. The headlights switched off and a large man lumbered her way and knocked on her window.

She looked up with a start. It was John Concha.

"Oh, no!" she cried, hugely embarrassed. She lowered the driver's side window with a hopeless expression on her face. Here she was once again in need of being rescued!

"There's something wrong with my car!" she told him unhappily. "The front began to wobble and I had to pull over. Something must be broken. But look, it's okay, I can take care of it. I called Triple-A. I'm sure you have more important things to do."

"Let me take a look."

He walked around to the front and returned to her window a moment later. "You have a flat tire and you shouldn't have driven on it. The tire is all sliced up. The rim looks okay, but I'm not sure."

"You can't drive on a flat tire?"

"No, Georgina, you can't. But never mind, I'll change it for you and we'll just have to see if the rim's okay. Let's take a look at your spare."

Georgie didn't know what to say. This was getting more and more embarrassing. "Well, you see, I had a flat a few months ago—I had it changed, and I always meant to take the old tire to get patched, but somehow I never got around to it."

"So, you don't have a spare?"

"Oh, I hate cars! I wish I had my old bicycle! That's how I used to get around before Da insisted I needed to learn to drive if I was going to live in New Mexico! God, I miss my bicycle! I was fine without a car. I was happy! Well, I guess I'll just have to buy a new tire."

"Georgina, you're going to need *four* new tires because your Subaru is all-wheel drive, and the tires need to match."

The look on Georgie's face was pitiful. "Come on, we can wait in my truck," he told her gently. "I have a friend with a tow truck. He can be here in ten minutes."

***

The inside of John's truck was intimate. To Georgie, the cab was so high off the ground it felt like being in a treehouse.

They sat in the dark with the engine and heater purring softly. She could see John's eyes in the reflection of headlights from the cars whizzing past on the highway. He was regarding her with interest. The air felt electric between them, but probably that was only Georgie's imagination. It seemed to her that he was about to say something personal, maybe open his reserved manly heart an inch or two.

"I think I can get you a discount on the tires," was what he said. "I have a cousin who has a tire shop who owes me a favor."

"Great," Georgie managed.

"You'll want to get good snow tires," he cautioned. "I should warn you, four tires are going to cost a lot."

Georgie sighed. "This old car eats up money. Da gave it to me. I really appreciate that, I do. But it's sort of like trying to kick a donkey to get going. What I don't like about Subarus is just about every arty Anglo in San Geronimo has one. I mean, it's like having an ID that says you're a certain kind of person who votes a certain way and probably does yoga."

He actually laughed. "Those are the newcomers, all right."

"To you everyone's a newcomer, aren't they?"

"Well, sure, my people have been here a long time. But even us, long ago we were migrants too. My ancestors came here from Chaco when the earth went dry there and could no longer sustain us. Long before that, the people came to the New World over the Bering Straits. That's what they say anyway. In the end, all of us are migrants. We're only passing through."

"Well, I'm probably the most hopeless newcomer you've ever met," she said with an attempt at a smile. "This is the third time you've had to rescue me. I feel like such a fool. And honestly, I'm a very competent person. You wouldn't know it, but generally I don't expect men to save me."

John's smile had a sadness to it. "Listen, Georgina, I know all about you. I know the work you did with Murdered and Missing Indigenous Women and how you found Susan Bright Water. You have my respect as a serious person. Susan is my niece, and I'm grateful."

"It's very nice of you to say that. Thank you! I *am* serious, I'm good at what I do. So, I don't know why I fall apart somehow when I'm with you."

"I think I know why," he told her quietly. In the darkness of the cab he leaned her way and Georgie had a luxuriant feeling that she was about to be kissed.

But it didn't happen. Just as he was beginning to swoop, a truck with flashing yellow lights pulled onto the shoulder in front of them.

It was John's cousin with the tow truck.

***

The cousin was a round friendly middle-aged man. His name was Ray and he enjoyed talking about tires. He and John spent quite some time considering the best tires for Georgie's Subaru, and what they would cost. She had an old Outback, the new models had larger tires, so Ray would have to think of what he had in stock.

It wasn't that tires didn't interest Georgie. Safe tires for winter driving were a requirement if you wanted to survive until spring. But she was impatient with them now.

She listened quietly as Concha horse traded with his cousin and got the price of four new tires down to $650. John assured her that this was at least 20 percent off.

"Great," she told him. "I mean, thank you. Really. I mean it."

They followed the tow truck to a garage/tire outlet on a side street north of town. It was arranged that Georgie would leave her car there and Ray would change the tires tomorrow. She could pick up her Subaru in the late afternoon. If she paid cash, they could forget the tax.

"I'll bring cash," she told Ray with a pleasant smile.

Once this was settled, Georgie sat next to John in the darkened cab. He didn't start the engine immediately.

"So, where do you want me to take you?" he asked.

"Where do you want to go?" she asked in return.

"You know where I want to go, Georgina."

"Do I?"

"I think you do."

She had to take a breath, because suddenly it was hard to breathe.

"Then take me there," she said.

And he did.

Which was when Georgie turned off her phone so that the night would belong to them alone.

***

John's house was neat and attractive. It was an old adobe with thick walls and low ceilings, but he had fixed it up nicely. For a bachelor he lived well. There were interesting paintings on the walls by Native artists—John said they'd been given to him by friends.

But they didn't stop long enough to admire the artwork.

Within seconds of walking in the door, she was in his arms, standing in the living room kissing passionately. For Georgie it had been a long while since she had been with a man, and she could tell that John hadn't been with a woman for some time either.

For a big man, he was tender and considerate. They stood kissing for what seemed a small slice of eternity. After a few minutes, his hand found its way under her sweater and shirt until it came to her breasts.

Georgie hated bras and she wasn't wearing one. She slipped her own hand down into the front of his jeans.

It went quickly after that. He picked her up and carried her into the bedroom as though she didn't weigh a thing. In fact, she felt weightless, no gravity at all. They fell onto the bed laughing and kissing, both of them ridiculously horny.

"Hold on just a second!" she told him as she straddled him. "I need to use the bathroom."

Georgie wasn't on the pill. She had sworn off sex some months before, believing—at the time—that men always ended up being a disappointment and she was through with the entire comedy. But she wasn't through. She moved quickly, slipping her diaphragm inside her, not wanting to break the mood, and walked naked into the bedroom where he was waiting on the bed. He was naked too and he looked very good, lean and strong, not an ounce of fat on him. Georgie thought he might be the sexiest man she had ever seen.

"Come here," he said. "I want you badly, Georgina."

"I want you, too, John."

She was walking toward him when Concha's phone on his bedside table began to chime.

They both looked at the ringing phone as though a turd had appeared on the table.

He groaned. "Damnation! That's my hot line. I've got to answer it," he told her. "That's one ring I can't ignore. Gimme a second."

The room was so quiet that Georgie was able to hear the voice from the phone.

"John, two white men in a big pickup just drove into the Pueblo on the old Black Canyon Road. It looks like they're heading up the mountain. Antonio saw them. He was out in his sweat lodge. They're pulling a trailer with two snowmobiles. They had to stop to do something underneath the trailer. They needed to use flashlights, which was how Antonio saw one of the men was the albino fellow you told us to be looking out for."

"Okay, okay," said John reluctantly. "Meet me at the bottom on the canyon road by the bridge. I'll be there in ten minutes."

John disconnected as he turned her way. "Well, that's bad timing, Georgina. I'm so sorry but I've got to go. This is serious. Those men are back and they're up to something. But look, we have days and nights before us, and we'll find another time."

"I see that, of course, I do. It's okay, John. I understand. But take me along."

"Georgina, I can't!"

"Yes, you can. Pete was my friend and this is my case. I've been looking for those people, too. I'm a professional just like you are, and I can take care of myself. Forest Friends is *my* organization—I'm their secretary, John. So I need to know what's going on and if Pete compromised the organization in any way. I'm involved in this, like it or not."

For Georgie, this was a key moment. Either John Concha was going to show respect and treat her as an equal, or she was just some girlie he wanted in bed.

He looked at her, shook his head, and smiled.

"Okay," he said. "You're something else, girl, you really are. And you look damn good just the way you are, I gotta tell you that. But you'd better get some clothes on. It's cold outside."

Georgie had just fallen in love with John Concha.

Chapter Twenty-Three

"Hold on, Mr. Wilder!" cried State Police Patrolman Ted Hirsch as he slammed on his brakes.

Jack had been dozing on the drive back across the high desert from the RV Park. He came fully awake as he jerked forward in his seat harness. With a yelp, Gypsy was thrown from the back seat over Jack's left shoulder, ending up in his lap.

A Rocky Mountain bighorn sheep had wandered onto the two-lane highway a few miles from town. Because of the dark, Patrolman Hirsch hadn't seen him until the last minute. The ram stood defiantly in the middle of the two-lane highway gazing at the police car without much interest. He was a huge animal with curved horns and a massive chest. He ambled off slowly into the sagebrush at the side of the road. Bighorn sheep had been reintroduced in New Mexico in the 1930s. After nearly dying off several times, there were now nearly two thousand of them in the northern regions of the state and they were often seen.

"I'm so sorry, Mr. Wilder. That was damn close!" Ted apologized. "He just appeared out of nowhere."

"It's okay, Ted. Danger often comes unexpectedly."

Jack had been thinking about Tomás Romero before he had dozed off. Tomás certainly hadn't foreseen a poisoned dart out of nowhere when he climbed Tower 7 to investigate why the lift had stopped.

For Jack, there was something about that incident that didn't seem right. On one hand, death by a poisoned dart was just the sort of thing that Danny Gluck might dream up. It was straight out of a comic book. But why kill Tomás?

Jack let Gypsy remain in his lap even though it was uncomfortable. He stroked her head as he tried to pinpoint what was bothering him.

"Tell me, Ted, are you a skier?"

"I'm a snowboarder."

"Do you go up to the Peak often?"

"Sure, when I can. But I wouldn't say often. It's expensive and I don't have much time off. I've had a few days up there this season, but that's all."

"Okay, tell me something. Have they put you on the Tomás Romero homicide?"

"Well, sure. All of us at the station are working that investigation in one way or another. There's been a lot of overtime. The Lieutenant assigned me to do a background check on the victim. I also did searches on everyone we could find who was on the snow below Tower 7 that afternoon. I didn't come up with anything much but I like that sort of work. I'm hoping to make detective some day. It would be a whole lot more interesting than arresting drunk drivers at two in the morning . . . not that getting drunk drivers off the roads isn't important," he added quickly.

"So, what did you find out about Tomás?"

"Only that he was a good family man and everybody liked him. He had seven grandchildren and eight great-grandchildren. He'd been working on the Peak since he was a teenager. He didn't have any enemies that I could find. Everyone I spoke to had enormous respect for him."

"What did you learn about the people on the snow by Tower 7?"

"Well, that was frustrating because Lift Line is a busy run, especially late in the day. Skiers and boarders often use it to make their last run down the mountain. So there was a lot of traffic that we can't account for. We have no idea who many of these people were."

"But there are cameras on the mountain, aren't there?"

"Sure, but only in a few places. On the Wolf Lift, there's a camera where people get on at the bottom and another where they get off at the top, but nothing in between."

"Have you checked the video tapes?"

"Not me personally. But the Loo gave me the job of typing the murder book into the computer, so I pretty much know where the investigation stands so far."

"No kidding? You transcribed the murder book?" said Jack. With every homicide, there was a murder book—a daily journal that kept track of every detail of the investigation. This put Ted Hirsch very much in the know. "Do you have a good memory?"

"Yeah, I do."

"Okay, then let's back up. I think we're missing something, so let's go over it again. What time did the Wolf Lift stop running?"

"At 3:17 exactly."

"And when did Tomás get involved?"

"Okay, the lifties were the first ones who tried to figure out why the lift had stopped. Usually this is a fairly routine procedure. Skiers getting off the chairs can trip the emergency bar that stops the lift if they don't get off in time. If they come around all the way and they're starting to head downhill again, their feet will hit a bar and the lift stops. The bar needs to be reset and this takes a few minutes. The Wolf Lift stretches 3,545 feet from the bottom to the top and a number of people are involved in the running on both ends."

"You've done your homework, Ted."

"Well, yes, I try. To answer your question, over ten minutes passed before the lifties on the scene realized that they had no idea what was going on. That's when they radioed Tomás, the head of lift ops. It was 16 degrees and the people on those chairs were starting to get very cold. This had become an emergency. We don't have the exact time that

Tomás set off on a snowmobile with two more snowmobiles following behind him, but they were at Tower 7 by 3:45. By that time Ski Patrol was involved as well. Sean Basset, the head of Patrol was there on the snow with three of his crew to meet Tomás when he arrived. According to Sean, Tomás saw something he didn't like and he climbed Tower 7 at approximately 3:50. These times are approximate because nobody was keeping exact account."

"Okay. How long was Tomás up on the tower?"

"About five minutes, according to Basset. He climbed all the way up to the top. That's when he saw that the cable was off the runners and there was some sort of device up there. At 3:57 Tomás grabbed his side as though he was in pain, and he tumbled backward from the tower. He was held by safety ropes from falling all the way to the ground, so he ended up just hanging in the air."

"How do you know the exact time he was shot?"

"Sean recorded the time in his notebook. He didn't realize a crime had been committed. He thought Tomás might have had a heart attack. But at this point Basset knew that there would be questions asked and a workplace investigation, so he started paying closer attention."

"Did he see anybody who might have fired the dart?"

"He didn't. He said there were about twenty people standing around in the snow, but he never got their names. Along with the possible heart attack, there was a growing emergency with people freezing on the lift. That was his focus, the guests dangling on the chairs."

Jack was silent as he digested this information. He had heard all of it before, but he was hoping something would click that hadn't clicked earlier. It didn't.

"What is it that worries you, Mr. Wilder?"

"It's the fact that if the bomb had already done its job, the lift wouldn't be running any time soon. So why did Tomás have to die?"

"Maybe it was just the icing on the cake. A kind of exclamation mark, you might say."

Jack shook his head. "I don't think so. That was a crowded scene and the killer was taking a big chance of getting caught. Tomás had to die for some very good reason. Either he knew something, or he saw something that was a threat to whoever killed him. I don't know what exactly, but I think that's what you need to find out. Now tell me again about the people on the snow at Tower 7. The killer had to be in that group. I understand that you don't know everyone who was there. But let's go over the ones you know."

"There were some gawkers, of course. We've interviewed five of them and there's not much to tell you. None of them had any connection with the resort or any reason to kill Romero. Then there were the three Ski Patrollers and Sean Basset, as well as the two lift ops guys who had come up on snowmobiles with Romero. But they were there to help."

"Have you done background checks on these people?"

"Again, not me personally. But it's being done. It's a big job and I don't know if they've covered everyone yet."

"And nothing came out so far of any real interest?"

"As I say, not really. The only thing we learned is kind of sad. It's Sean Bassett. His 11-year-old son, Luke, has been diagnosed with leukemia. They've had to fly him down to Dallas a few times for treatment. He's very sick, unfortunately."

"I'm sorry to hear that," said Jack. "My partner Howie is a friend of Sean's. I'm surprised he hasn't mentioned it to me."

"He probably doesn't know about it. Not many people do. Apparently, Sean's the sort of person who keeps stuff like this to himself. We only found out about it by checking his credit card activity, which showed him paying for the flights to Dallas and the motels there. All three of his cards are maxed out. It must be terrible for the family—not only the emotional rollercoaster but the money. A disease like leukemia can send people into bankruptcy."

Jack nodded. "I imagine Sean has good medical insurance after working at the Peak so many years. He's one of their key employees."

"I don't think anyone's looked into that, but I'm sure you're right," said Ted. "Especially with the new owner. I mean, Leonard Hamm's a billionaire. A smart guy like that would want to take good care of the people who work for him."

"You'd think so, wouldn't you?" said Jack thoughtfully.

Chapter Twenty-Four

Sean grabbed Howie's arm as they were coming out of the locker room.

"Hold on," he whispered. "Let's wait for these people to pass. It would be better if they didn't see us."

Six men in identical white snowsuits had just appeared around the corner from the ticket office building. They marched with military precision in single file across the deserted plaza. They each carried guns in holsters that were strapped to their thighs. They were a sinister sight.

The only light came from the snow cat that was lumbering down the last hundred yards of the Red Fox trail toward the base. The multiple headlights made the snow cat look like an alien spacecraft. The lights briefly caught the face of the white-suited figure at the head of the armed men crossing the plaza. It was the man in the blue blazer who had escorted Howie from the Hamm Haus earlier in the day. Howie remained as still as possible in the shadows of the locker room building hoping to avoid a second encounter. He watched as the single file crossed the plaza without a word and disappeared around the bend of the Mountain Lodge Restaurant.

"What was that about?" Howie whispered to Sean.

"I'm not sure. Hamm's been going crazy with security the last few days. Maybe it has to do with the electricity being off."

"Who was the guy at the head of the line?"

"His name is Blake Townsend. He's the head of Hamm's private army. Come on, Howie, let's move. We don't want to be here when those guys come back."

Howie was dressed warmly in ski clothes from his locker, which was an improvement from his earlier situation. Sean had loaned him a pair of

Sorrels from his own locker, calf-high boots with fake fur trimming around the top. The boots were slightly small for Howie, but not by enough to be a problem. At four in the morning, it was still as dark as midnight and bitterly cold, no hint yet of dawn. In place of a hat, Howie wore his ski helmet with his goggles resting on top. He was dressed for a high mountain expedition on a winter's night.

With Sean leading the way, they hurried across the plaza to where the snow cat had just stopped by the Rabbit Lift that serviced beginners on the bunny slope.

Sean said he needed to make a trip up the mountain to Patrol Headquarters in order to get some important files he didn't want Hamm to have, as well as a number of personal items including several pairs of skis. He didn't know how long the strike would last and tonight would probably be his last chance to access his office. He asked Howie to come with him and help with the files.

The snow cat was a huge machine with a cabin perched high above the massive treads. There were attachments on the front and back—the blade in front, a curved piece of metal that pushed snow, and the tiller at the rear that had a spinning cutter bar with spikes. Following close behind the cutter bar there was a comb that groomed the snow into a soft corduroy pattern. It was a fine art to groom a slope correctly without leaving "whales" (mounds of snow) or dangerous breaks and irregularities on the trail. The groomers spent the entire night getting the slopes ready for the morning crowd. To Howie, the machine looked like a giant crab.

"You ever ride in one of these monsters?" Sean asked.

"Never," said Howie. "But why don't we just take snowmobiles?"

"Howie, leave this to me. This is what we need to get up-mountain tonight."

Howie was dubious. He wasn't sure it was a good idea for him to be part of this expedition, but at the same time he didn't want to be left behind.

"Where is Hamm, by the way?" he asked.

"I don't know. I haven't seen him in a few days."

"Have you seen Leilani?"

"There you go again, Moon Deer. Do you have the hots for that girl?"

"I do not, Sean. Believe me."

"Anyway, I haven't seen either one of them. The only contact I have with Hamm these days is by text, which suits me fine. He's not going to be happy when he finds out I've closed down his mountain."

"He doesn't know yet?"

"He will first thing this morning. I wanted it to be a surprise."

"Sean, are you sure you're doing the right thing?" Howie asked. "And where are the other Patrollers? I thought you said you were all in this together?"

"We are, Moon Deer. But getting the files is something I have to do by myself. There's some incriminating stuff in those files that Hamm will destroy if he gets his hands on them. I can't let that happen. The others will be along by first light."

"What do you mean, incriminating stuff?"

"Hamm's been cutting corners ever since he took over. That's what these hedge fund people do. They buy up something, fire most of the employees, and tear the business apart. All they care about is profit. This mountain isn't safe anymore for anybody."

"Okay, but tell me why you're packing a gun, Sean."

Sean sighed in exasperation. "Howie, Tomás was murdered and his killer hasn't been caught. I'm just not taking any chances. Now, let's get going. We don't have a lot of time."

***

A man dressed in jeans and a beat-up black parka climbed down from the cat and handed Sean a set of keys. The driver had a grizzly dark beard and the parka had oil stains on the front. Howie had never seen him before. He didn't know the night crew, who inhabited a different universe from the fun-seeking ski world of the day.

"Thanks, bro," said Sean. "I won't forget this."

"No problem," said the man. "She has half a tank which is enough to get you up and down a few times. But keep your eye on the gauge. These babies suck up fuel."

"I'll do that," said Sean.

The man said good luck and headed off toward the locker room. Sean hadn't bothered to introduce Howie. Sean led the way across the snow to where the giant snow cat was waiting.

"You really know how to drive these things?" Howie asked.

"I do, Moon Deer. My first job up here was making snow, then I got into grooming for a while before I joined Patrol. Here, let me show you where to climb up."

From the rear of the cat, Sean climbed first onto the platform above the treads and from there went up a short ladder into the cab. Howie followed and settled into the front passenger seat. The cab would seat four people, high above the ground, two in front and two on a bench in back. It was quite comfortable. There was glass on all four sides providing a panoramic view of the surrounding terrain.

Sean fired up the engine. Instead of a steering wheel, there were two metal arms and a number of foot pedals that controlled the speed and direction. Other levers and buttons operated the blade in front and the grooming equipment in back. The cab itself could pivot around so that the cat could go forward or back with equal ease. It was a sophisticated piece of machinery.

Sean took hold of the controls and the crab-like monster lumbered up the Red Fox trail at its top speed, 14 mph. Howie had never been on the mountain at night and it was eerie. The headlights lit the snowy landscape ahead with a strange white clarity. At one point an animal scurried across the trail moving so quickly Howie wasn't certain if it was a bobcat or a fox.

They did little talking on the way up. Sean was focused on keeping the cat on a safe course and Howie didn't want to disturb his concentration. Whenever trails converged, Sean took the easiest trail upward. The snow cat had a wide base but it could tip over if the driver wasn't careful. Many of the runs had a double fall line, downhill but also a sideways slant from one side of the slope to the other. Snow cat drivers had to keep this in mind. A screen on the dashboard showed a cartoon image of the cat at the gradient degree it was traveling. 90 degrees was the maximum a snow cat could manage without tipping over. Beyond 90 degrees, a winch was needed with the cable anchored to some secure place above in order to groom the steep expert slopes. Sean explained this to Howie as they climbed upward. He kept to the easy trails that had gradients no steeper than 20 degrees.

It took nearly forty minutes to reach the Patrol Headquarters on top. Howie climbed down from the cab after Sean and followed him into the darkened building.

"Home sweet home!" said Sean as he flipped a light switch. Nothing happened. "Damn, no electricity here either!" he said. "Well, we'll just have to work by flashlight."

They went to Sean's small cubicle of an office in the rear of the building and took two flashlights from a drawer. Sean sat down on his swivel chair, pulled open a drawer of a metal filing cabinet, and began leafing through the papers there.

"You know what?" he said after a moment. "I don't have time to go through all this stuff right now to find what I'm looking for, so let's just take the whole cabinet. It won't be too heavy with both of us carrying it."

"Sean, are you sure this is okay? Legally speaking, those files belong to the company, not to you personally."

"Maybe, but morally they're mine. A lot of this is my work over twenty years."

"It doesn't seem like you expect to be coming back here any time soon. Don't you think you're going to win this strike?"

Sean paused and regarded him. "I don't really know, Howie. Maybe yes, maybe no. All I know is I'm finished. I've spent too many years on this mountain and I'm starting to think I'm ready for a change. Look, I'll take responsibility for what I'm doing. All I need is a helping hand."

"But I'm not sure I want to get in the middle of your fight with management, Sean. It's really not my place. Like it or not, I'm still working for Hamm. I've decided to give his money back and break my contract, but I haven't had a chance to do that yet."

"I get it, you have legal obligations. But you only agreed to find out who messed with Tower 7 and killed Tomás. I think I can give you some answers about that. But first let's load this file cabinet onto the cat."

"You know who killed Tomás?"

"Not for certain, but I have a pretty good idea. Look, there really isn't time for this conversation now. So please, Howie, do it for old time's sake—help me load the file cabinet onto the cat and we'll talk on the way down."

Howie had a nagging feeling that he shouldn't get involved with this escapade, but Sean was his friend and it was too late to back out now.

Nevertheless, he was starting to feel jerked around and if Sean knew who killed Tomás, he was going to get that out of him on the way down the mountain, no matter what.

Howie took the front of the file cabinet and Sean the rear and they managed to carry it out of the building and load it into a storage area on the front deck of the cat.

Just as they finished, Howie heard the thwap of a helicopter coming their way. He looked up into the starry sky but could see nothing. Gradually, as the sound came closer, Howie could just make out the shape of the helicopter. It was flying without its running lights. It was so dark its black body seemed to melt into the night.

"Now, that's strange . . ." he began, but broke off.

Sean had his gun out with the barrel pointing his way.

"I'm sorry I have to do this," Sean said. "I've always liked you, Howie."

"I liked you, too," Howie answered. "Until this minute."

Chapter Twenty-Five

Riding in the dark along the back roads of Indian land in the late-night intimacy of John Concha's monster pickup felt entirely different than being in John's truck had felt before. There was an electric current between them, an unspoken force.

Georgie didn't entirely mind that they had been interrupted. At this point, even being in the cab together was foreplay. She was glad they didn't need to talk about snow tires anymore.

"So, Black Canyon," she said gently. "Where does it go?"

"It's a gravel road, pretty steep and rough in places. It snakes up the mountain almost all the way to the top. It's not a road many outsiders know about. Someone must have told these men about it."

"Pete, you're saying."

"Yes, it almost certainly had to be Pete Day Rise. I'm sorry, Georgina. I know he was your friend."

She sighed. "It's so strange! I thought I knew him, but I guess I didn't."

"It's not always easy to know another human being."

She looked at him, trying to decipher any hidden meaning in his words.

"Don't you think lovers can know one another completely?" she asked, knowing immediately after the words were out that it wasn't true. She thought of Ashton Woolridge the Third, her elegant, wealthy Cambridge lover who had gotten her pregnant and whom she had found in bed with her best friend.

"I think in the end we're always a mystery to one another," he said. "But that's part of the magic."

"Aye, the magic," she replied. Or the sorrow, she said to herself. "So, when you say the road climbs nearly to the top, you mean it goes up to where Pueblo land meets the ski resort?"

"Almost all the way, yes. In the summer you'd need to climb the rest of the way on foot. In the winter, you could do it in a snowmobile if you knew exactly where the trail was."

"And you think that's where the two outsiders are going?"

"I think so. But of course I don't know for certain."

"The albino man, the one you knew in Afghanistan, you've never told me his name," Georgie said.

John hesitated. "He called himself Skull," he said distastefully. "The people in that special group never used their real names."

"Were there women in the group?"

"Yes, a few. In my experience, women sometimes make the most ruthless warriors." He glanced her way and half-smiled. "So, tell me, Georgina, do you know how to use a gun?"

"I do."

His eyes showed some surprise. "Did your father teach you?"

She laughed. "Howie? No, he doesn't like guns. I mean, he has one, he's used it once or twice. But it's not his thing at all."

"Then who taught you?"

"Jack."

Concha laughed with astonishment. "*Jack?* You must be kidding! He's blind!"

"You'd be surprised at what Jack can do. He has amazing hearing, a kind of radar. And smell. It's uncanny, really. He knows exactly where people are. He's very protective of me. I'm sort of his honorary granddaughter. Last spring, he insisted that if I'm going to be a detective, I needed to learn how to protect myself. So he gave me a Glock and we spent two afternoons a week all summer long out on the police range by the landfill showing me how to shoot."

"Really? A blind man giving shooting lessons. Incredible!"

"Well, it was. He talked me through it. A few times he stood behind me holding my arms to make sure I was in the right position. He was very thorough. We used paper targets starting at 7 feet away and gradually worked our way up to 25 feet. He wasn't satisfied until I could consistently hit the two inner circles, preferably the bullseye. I learned how to take the Glock apart and clean it, how to load the magazines properly, the works."

"Very good. But have you ever used your gun for real?"

She shook her head. "No, I'm happy to say I haven't. I've only shot at paper targets. And I don't have my gun with me tonight. I didn't think I'd need it."

He smiled. "You think I'm safe?"

"No, John, I don't think you're even slightly safe. But somehow I feel safe when I'm with you."

"Good," he said. "I very much want you to be safe. That's why I want you to have a gun tonight. I don't think you'll need it, but it doesn't hurt to be careful. There's a 9mm Glock in the glove compartment. I'd like you to take it out and familiarize yourself with it."

Georgie opened the glove compartment and took out the gun. It looked very much like hers.

"Take out the magazine and tell me how many rounds it holds."

She did as he told her. "Fifteen rounds," she answered. "That's what my gun holds."

"Then you probably have a Glock 19. The gun in your hand is a 19X and there are seventeen rounds. Give it a good looking over then put it back in the glove compartment for now. If we meet up with Skull and his partner I want you to have it with you at all times. Is that clear?"

"Yes, sir," she answered, with only the slightest touch of irony.

"You're very important to me, Georgina," he told her. "I'm going to take care of you, but if we run into trouble, I need to know that you'll do exactly what I say."

"Yes," she told him. And she would. She believed in her feminist soul that she could trust John Concha with her life.

***

The road that climbed Black Canyon was at the northern edge of Pueblo land. John and Georgie came over a rise and found two San Geronimo Tribal Police pickup trucks waiting for them by a one-lane wooden bridge that crossed a frozen stream.

"Stay here," Concha said to Georgie. He stepped from the cab leaving the engine running and walked over to the tribal cops. There were four cops in dark blue uniforms with pistols on their hips and rifles in their arms. They stood in a circle with John and conferred in Tiwa. After a few minutes the cops got back in their vehicles and John returned to where Georgie was waiting in the cab.

"Okay," he said, "we're ready to roll."

John led the convoy up into the foothills on a rough road at 20 mph in second gear. At first the climb was gradual, but after a mile they came to a switchback that zig-zagged up the mountain in a steep ascent. John downshifted into the lowest gear. The road had been roughly plowed, but it was only a single lane with mounds of snow pushed to the sides.

There were no guard rails and as they climbed higher, there were dangerous places, long drops from the cliffs to the valley below. John drove with calm authority and she trusted his driving. He knew this land well. Still, it was impossible not to be nervous, especially as they came around the hairpin turns.

John kept his attention on the road ahead that was lit garishly by the high beams of his headlights. He didn't try to make conversation. Georgie hoped there would be daylight when they descended, better visibility. Of course, then she would be able to see the jaw-dropping cliffs more clearly.

As they climbed higher the snow grew deeper and the vegetation changed from piñon to Douglas fir and white pine. After a few miles, the zig-zag climb leveled off and passed through a heavily forested grotto where the tall trees formed a tunnel overhead hiding the night sky.

John came around a corner and lurched to an abrupt stop. A tree had fallen across the road blocking the way.

"Stay here," he told her, which was starting to sound like a refrain. He grabbed his rifle from the rack and bounded out onto the road. The four tribal cops joined him and together they inspected the tree that was blocking their way.

John climbed back into the cab a few minutes later.

"Well, it wasn't the wind that brought that tree down," he told her. "Someone felled it with a chainsaw. Roy was up here yesterday cutting firewood and he says the tree wasn't down then. It's Skull who did it. He brought down that tree to stop anyone from coming after them."

"Can you drag it clear of the road?"

"That would be difficult. It's a big tree. But Roy has a chainsaw in his truck, and we'll be able to cut it up. It'll take a little time."

"So, Skull deliberately cut off his own retreat. Is there any other way for him to get down the mountain once he's finished with what he's come to do?"

"There are a few horse trails, but nothing you could drive a pickup down. Not even a snowmobile would make it."

"Then they're not planning to come back this way. They're going up and over and down into the ski resort. They'll leave that way."

"Yep!" John agreed with a sigh. "Son of a bitch! Well, I'd better make a call and let them know they have trespassers."

"Is there anyone there to answer at this time of night?"

"The village has a small four-person police department. They should answer."

John found his phone and pressed the screen with his finger. He had the Peak's police department on fast dial.

He listened, disconnected, then tried another number, the main switchboard at the resort. After a moment, he put down his phone and gave Georgie a strange look.

"Nothing," he said. "The phones at the resort don't even ring. I'm starting to think we need to get up this mountain fast and see what the hell is going on over there!"

Chapter Twenty-Six

Jack and Ted pulled into the parking area of San Geronimo Peak at 4:28 AM.

"Now that's strange!" said Ted.

"What's strange?" asked Jack.

"The whole place is dark."

"Well, it's night," Jack said with a yawn. "That's usually what happens at night. It's dark."

"No, it's more than that. All the lights are off. There should be outside utility lights left on, but there's nothing. The whole village is dark. It's eerie. I can just make out the shapes of the buildings against the snow. But it all looks . . . haunted. That's the only way I can describe it. It's like everything is under a spell."

"I get it, Ted. But don't let your imagination carry you away."

Ted drove cautiously up the huge parking area to the road where skiers and boarders were required to leave their cars and continue on foot to the ticket office and the slopes. There was nobody around. A second road further along was posted with a sign, NO ENTRY! HAMM HAUS GUESTS ONLY! Ted flicked on his roof flashers and continued toward the hotel.

"Now, that's *very* strange!" said Ted, coming to a stop. He switched on the spotlight on the driver's side of his vehicle and swiveled it toward the hotel. "There's a broken window on the third floor. The whole window is busted open. There's glass on the ground. The hotel itself looks deserted, no guests in sight, nobody. Something very weird has been happening here."

Ted continued more slowly than before until he came around a corner into the open plaza that led to the chairlifts. Without warning, a huge search light was turned on by the edge of the snow sending a white beam high into the night. It was as though there was about to be a Hollywood premiere or a sale at a car lot. The glare was so sudden, Ted had to shield his eyes. Even Jack felt it.

That was when Ted saw the men in white. There were three of them standing near the search light, all dressed in white military snow uniforms with rifles slung over their shoulders.

"Jesus!" said Ted. "There's a few heavily armed guys in uniform standing on the plaza by the snow."

"Security?"

"I guess so, but they look more military than that."

"Have they seen us?"

"I'm afraid so. Three more of them are coming up the road behind us. They have assault rifles pointed at us. I'm afraid we're in trouble, Mr. Wilder."

"Ted, under the circumstances you need to stop being so formal. I'm Jack. Now be careful. Don't do anything sudden."

"I get that. But I'm not going to let these people intimidate me!"

Ted stepped out of the Explorer and faced the three men who were coming his way.

"Stop right there!" Ted commanded. "This is the New Mexico State Police and I want to know what's going on here!"

Without a word, one of the men in white stepped forward and hit Ted across the side of the head with the butt of his rifle, sending him sprawling onto the ground.

Jack was able to piece together what was happening from the sounds outside the car. Gypsy was barking loudly. He took hold of her collar, told her to shush, and lowered his window. He listened as footsteps came his way.

"Good morning," he said calmly. "Would you please send word to Leonard Hamm that Commander Jack Wilder would like to have a word with him. I have information that he needs to hear. Please inform Mr. Hamm that it's possible I might be able to save his life."

***

The three men in Arctic white conferred among themselves in a language that sounded to Jack like Albanian. Long ago, Jack had arrested a gang of Albanians who ran a prostitution ring in San Francisco, and he thought he recognized a few words, but he wasn't sure.

Several phone calls were made and eventually Jack was helped into his wheelchair and pushed through a side door into the Hamm House. Gypsy and Ted followed close behind. Ted was wobbly after being smacked in the head, but he insisted he was fine. Both Ted and Jack had been searched with professional thoroughness and relieved of their weapons and phones. At first, the men in white had insisted that Gypsy remain in the patrol car, but Jack insisted that he would go nowhere without her and after another phone call, she was allowed to accompany them.

"I need your eyes, Ted," Jack said as he was wheeled through a long corridor. "Where are we?"

"We're in a service area of the hotel. They're taking us into an industrial sized elevator. I'm afraid this isn't looking good. These guys are armed for battle."

"It's going to be okay, Ted. They might have the guns, but we have the brains."

"Sure," said Ted. "To tell you the truth, my brains are feeling just a little scrambled right now."

The elevator had padded sides and looked as though it was used to move heavy furniture. They dropped downward with a sickening speed that left Jack's stomach behind. The elevator kept descending further into the depths of the mountain.

"We must be hundreds of feet underground!" Ted said when they finally came to a stop.

The door whooshed open, and they were led into a concrete corridor lit by harsh overhead bulbs.

"This is weird, Jack. It seems to be a bunker of some sort."

"The dog and the cop will remain here," said one of the men as they reached a cavernous reception area. "Mr. Hamm will see no one except Mr. Wilder."

I'm afraid not," said Jack. "We're all going to stay together, thank you very much."

"That is not allowed," said the man. He raised his assault rifle.

"Says who? Give Hamm a buzz, why don't you? Tell him if he wants to hear what I have to say, it will be on my terms."

There was a good deal more conversation in what sounded like Albanian. After five minutes, a metal door opened with a hiss and Jack, Gypsy, and Ted were led into a room that felt cavernous and damp. Jack didn't like the claustrophobic feeling of being so far underground, the oppressive weight of the mountain above him. There was a metallic smell of processed air. He sensed the presence of at least three more people in the room.

"So, Mr. Jack Wilder, of course I know who you are," said a raspy voice. "Your partner is in my employ and you've roused my curiosity. But health first, Mr. Wilder. Body and mind—you can't have one without the other. I'm about to enjoy my morning cocktail. Leilani, why don't you pour these people a glass of carrot juice."

"No, thank you," said Jack. "Carrot juice isn't really my cup of tea."

"Oh, you're making a great mistake. I drink a large glass of freshly pulped carrot juice three times a day. It's the secret of my success, Mr. Wilder. Carrot juice has given me great vigor and brain power."

"It's made his pee-pee turn orange," said the voice of a middle-aged woman with a faint Brooklyn accent.

"Gloria, *please*!" said Hamm with irritation. "You must excuse my wife, Mr. Wilder. She doesn't understand the benefits of *daucus carota sativa*. This is the gods gift to mankind."

"Sure, as long as you like orange pee-pee," said Mrs. Hamm. "Personally, if I want fruit juice I'll take champagne."

"The carrot is *not* a fruit," Hamm said sternly. "Have a seat, Mr. Wilder. Leilani, please see if Mr. Wilder and his police friend would like a different beverage."

Ted led Jack to a sofa and sat down beside him. Gypsy made herself comfortable at their feet.

"Would you care for coffee?" asked a sweet young voice. "Perhaps a cup of herbal tea?"

"I'm fine," said Jack. "And so is Patrolman Hirsch. We're not here to socialize. Now, before I tell you what I know, I need to know what you're up to. Why are you hiding out in this underground bunker, Mr. Hamm? The electricity is off, you have armed soldiers roaming around, it seems like your ski resort has been closed down—what is it that you're so afraid of?"

"I think you know the answer to that very well, Mr. Wilder. Gluck is dead, blown to kingdom come. I won the game, I came out on top like I always knew I would!" he said gleefully. "But one can't be too careful. A joker like that could have arranged some posthumous surprise."

"Do you have a specific surprise in mind?"

"You know, I could lie to you. I could say my astrologer has warned me of danger in my horoscope, or some gibberish like that. But I'm going to level with you because I'd rather have a smart man on my side than against me. I have spies, Mr. Wilder. And I also have cameras all over this mountain. No, not the obvious cameras that the police have been asking about, but my own very special video surveillance. So I know that an attack is about to happen. Any minute now. Does that surprise you?"

"Not especially," said Jack.

"They won't succeed, of course. Because I'm much smarter than they are. I closed down everything. I had the hotel cleared out, the restaurants, the bars. It cost me a lot of money, but I don't mind that. I don't want to have this turn into a massacre, innocent people getting killed, because that wouldn't be good for business. This is just between me and the ghost of Daniel Gluck. Come morning, this will all be over and I'll open up again."

"You seem very sure of yourself."

"You bet I am. I never do anything unless I'm sure. But let's come to the point, Mr. Wilder. What is this so-called information you have that will save my life?"

"I'll get to that. First tell me how you managed to blow up the XR113 rocket. That was quite a feat on your part."

"Oh, no, no, Mr. Wilder. That is for me to know and you to find out. Let me just say that when you have as much money as I do, there are very few things that are impossible."

"So you admit you sabotaged that rocket?"

"I admit nothing. However *if* I did what you're suggesting, I would certainly have good cause. It was Gluck who sabotaged my chairlift, I'm sure you know that. He wished to harm me, to say to the world, the lifts at San Geronimo Peak are not safe to ride. Oh, he knew where to prick me, all right! But I won't let him get away with it. This ski resort may seem unimportant to someone who doesn't know me. This is only my hobby, after all. My fun little toy. But it's a hobby that interests me greatly and I will not—I absolutely will not!—allow that man—that monstrous Gluck!—to spoil my fun!"

Hamm's voice had risen to an angry pitch. He was on the verge of a tantrum, the very edge.

"But it doesn't matter," he continued more quietly, getting hold of himself. "Because I got the better of him in the end. His amateur bit of sabotage was nothing compared to mine. Captain Cosmo, indeed! What a loser! I won!"

"But did you really, Mr. Hamm?"

"Of course, I did. This small skirmish tonight is nothing I can't deal with. I knew this was coming. I have plans in place myself in the case of my death, a small posthumous surprise. People like me think ahead."

Jack listened calmly. He leaned forward and smiled. "What if I were to tell you that Captain Cosmo is alive?"

Hamm laughed. "I'd say you're mad! I followed every millisecond of that launch. I had a live connection to the computer that was monitoring his breathing, his blood pressure, everything. You're probably going to say that Gluck switched places at the last minute, that someone else was on that rocket, not him. But that's not true. Every second of that launch, every angle, was followed by cameras and computers to which I was privy. I know the exact instant that Daniel Gluck ceased to exist."

"No, you only thought you did. Gluck knew what you were up to and he's very good at sleight of hand. You made your fortune by manipulating numbers. Danny made his by manipulating reality. You've been outplayed, Hamm."

Hamm sighed profoundly. He didn't speak for a minute.

"Okay, Mr. Wilder, you have my interest. Tell me exactly what you think you know."

Chapter Twenty-Seven

It took more than half an hour for John Concha, Georgie, and the four tribal cops to clear the tree that was blocking the primitive road up Black Canyon. It was a large fir and it had been necessary to cut it up into a dozen three foot long sections, saw off the lateral branches, and roll the heavy rounds out of the way. Georgie helped haul the branches to the side of the road but she stayed clear of the sawing.

John climbed back into his pickup in a bad mood. Georgie pulled herself up after him into the passenger seat.

"That was a setback," he said. "We're going to have to hurry to catch up."

When the way was clear, the three vehicles continued in a convoy up the switchback. The road had been plowed on the lower part of the mountain but as they drove higher the snow deepened and they soon came to where there had been no plowing at all. From here they followed the tire tracks of a pickup that had come through before them. The tracks continued for only a short way until they came to a white truck with huge tires that was blocking the road. The pickup appeared to be abandoned. An empty flatbed trailer was attached to the rear and there were two snowmobile tracks that continued around a hairpin turn and disappeared up the road. From the tracks, one of the snowmobiles appeared to have pulled a sled. The license plates on the pickup and trailer had been removed and Concha was certain no VIN would be found.

"Looks like Skull and his partner are gone, but let's be careful," he said to Georgie. "Wait here while we check it out."

John took his rifle from the rack and carefully approached the abandoned truck with the four cops following close behind, their guns drawn.

After a few minutes, John returned to Georgie and climbed back into the cab.

"Yep, they're gone," he said. "They got on their snowmobiles and left."

"Can we get around their truck and follow?"

"Nope, the snow's too deep. We'll need snowmobiles to go any further. Mike is on the radio now. The department has two snowmobiles. They're old but they run okay. But it'll take at least forty minutes to get them up to us. I'm not sure we can afford to wait that long."

"So what can we do?"

He looked at her. "I have a pair of snowshoes in back, and Mike has two pairs in his truck. We sometimes need them this time of year just to get around. The ridge isn't too far from here, maybe a twenty minute climb. Three pairs of snowshoes means only three of us can go the rest of the way. I'm afraid I'm going to have to leave you behind, Georgina. You can stay here in the cab with the heater going."

Georgie was about to object. She was good on snowshoes. She and Claire had often gone snowshoeing together in the winter. But she looked at John and realized this would be unfair. He needed two of the tribal police to accompany him. They would be more use to him than she would.

"Okay, John, I understand. I'll be okay here so don't worry about me. Just make sure that you're safe."

"Remember, you have the gun in the glove compartment if you need it. And when the snowmobiles arrive, you can get a ride up the mountain on the back. I'll leave instructions. Okay?"

"Okay," she told him.

He leaned forward, kissed her quickly on the mouth, and then he was gone.

Georgie was disappointed as she sat alone in the cab. But she knew she had done the right thing. She didn't want to lose John by being silly and selfish.

She closed her eyes, realizing suddenly how tired she was. Mike and the other cop who had been left behind were waiting in their pickup, staying warm. She didn't know the second cop's name. Georgie felt very much alone on a winter's night high in the mountains.

She was almost asleep when she heard an odd sound. At first she thought it might be the two police snowmobiles arriving on the road, but the sound was different. It wasn't from a pickup truck or a snowmobile.

Intrigued, Georgie stepped out of the cab into the cold night. The stars overhead were brilliant frozen specks of light. She heard a thwap of something beating the air overhead but could see nothing.

And then she saw, just for an instant, the black shape of a helicopter flying without lights pass between her and the stars. Straining her eyes upward, she watched as it disappeared into the night.

***

Howie watched as the helicopter flashed its spotlight for just a moment to get a better fix on the snow as it descended slowly. It was a tricky landing coming down onto an almost flat ledge a few hundred feet below the ridge that was the dividing line between the ski resort and Pueblo land.

The helicopter was larger than the TV news choppers and medical helicopters that often flew in and out of San Geronimo. It looked military but there were no markings on it to indicate what it was. The engine cut off with a fading whine. The rotor blade slowed to a stop until it hung limp and depleted over the body of the aircraft. The night receded back into silence, with only the sound of the wind.

"What's going on, Sean?" Howie asked.

As Sean watched the helicopter land, he had kept his gun pointed toward Howie's chest.

"Moon Deer, the less you know, the better. Now look, I don't want to hurt you so here's what I'm going to do. I'm going to tie you up inside the Patrol shack. It will be uncomfortable for a few hours, but someone will come in the morning and let you out. It'll be all be over by then."

"What will be over?"

"Howie, don't ask."

"But why are you doing this, Sean?"

"I have my reasons, believe me. Now turn around and walk toward the building. And don't try anything stupid. I don't want to shoot you, but I will if I have to. I'm committed to this, Howie, for better or worse. For me right now, there's no turning back. So just be a friend, okay, and do what I say."

Howie sighed. "You need to tell me what's going on, Sean."

"I will. But now you need to start walking. Move!"

Howie turned reluctantly and walked toward the darkened Patrol building with Sean following close behind. Howie noticed a ski bicycle leaning against the side of the building. These were handmade vehicles that the lift operators liked to use at the end of the day to get down the mountain: a cannibalized bicycle frame with a seat and handlebars welded to a single ski. The lifties loved them, said they were tons of fun, but they weren't very safe. Management had been trying to ban them for years, without success. Lifties were increasingly hard to find, and the bicycle skis were considered a traditional perk of their job. Only lifties were allowed to use them.

Howie had a mad idea. If there was some way he could knock the gun from Sean's hand, he could jump on the ski bike and escape down the mountain. He had never ridden one before, but it couldn't be that difficult.

"Don't even think about it, Howie. Just behave yourself, okay?" Sean said as he prodded Howie into the building and closed the door behind them.

"Right, Sean. I'm not planning to give you any trouble."

"I saw you eyeing that bike! You can kill yourself on those things. Now sit down on the chair by the bulletin board. That's where I'll tie you up. I'll do my best not to make it too uncomfortable, but I'm good with rope and you're not going to get loose."

The white bulletin board had the names of Ski Patrollers written in colored markers with various assignments. Howie's eyes scanned for something, anything he might use to gain an advantage. In the corner below the bulletin board, he saw a fire extinguisher. It was heavy. It would make a good weapon if he could get to it.

Sean looked away for a second to reach for a coil of rope hanging on a peg on the wall. The barrel of his gun moved slightly to the left so that it was no longer pointed directly at Howie.

Howie waited, deciding the odds were against him. But then part of the coil unraveled in Sean's hand. It hadn't been secured properly and Sean fumbled before he got a good grip on it.

Howie knew this was the best chance he was going to get.

In a single motion, he reached for the fire extinguisher, grabbed it by the neck and swung it hard at Sean's head. Sean felt the danger coming and raised his free arm to ward off the blow. But he hadn't expected the attack and he wasn't fast enough. The extinguisher hit his left arm, bounced higher, and struck him under his chin. Sean fell sideways onto the floor with a cry of pain.

Howie moved quickly. He didn't want to hurt Sean any more than necessary, but he was determined to win this fight. He pulled the pin, squeezed the handle, and fired the extinguisher, sending a spray of chemical foam at Sean's head.

Sean screamed, disoriented, covered in foam. Howie grabbed the coil of rope from where it had fallen on the floor and sat on Sean's leg. It took a few seconds to find the end of the rope, roll Sean over on his stomach, and tie his hands behind his back. From there, he uncoiled the rope further so that he could wrap it around Seans ankles, thread the rope back around his arms and leave him hog tied. The initial blow with the fire extinguisher had left Sean in too much pain to fight back.

When he was finished, Howie stood up breathing hard.

"I'm sorry," he said, standing over the tied-up body. "I really hated to do that, Sean. But that chopper didn't come here for a ski holiday. I have to try and stop whatever the hell is going on, I really do."

Howie picked up the gun from the floor and walked to the dispatch office. The room faced a large panoramic window that looked out over the ridge that rose gradually to the Peak itself, the highest point of the mountain, 12,136 feet in altitude, where the revolving restaurant would stand. From the window, the dispatcher had a view of a large portion of the upper mountain, including the steep expert runs that came down from the ridge toward the trails below.

Howie sat in the swivel chair behind an array of radios and telephones, a communication hub from which the dispatcher could contact anyone on the mountain carrying a radio and direct them to accidents and emergencies. None of this equipment was working now without electricity. Through the window Howie was able to see the snow cat sitting a dozen feet from the building and the helicopter in the distance.

He picked up the powerful binoculars on the desk and scanned the ridge, trying to get a better idea of what the helicopter was up to. So far it was doing nothing, just sitting on the snow in the dark, its rotor blade still. There was no sign of any movement from inside.

As Howie watched, he heard the sound of two snowmobiles, the growl of their engines getting gradually louder. He couldn't see them. The binoculars were so powerful they gave only a narrow field of vision. He scanned the ski trails that came down from the ridge, but he couldn't see anything.

He took the binoculars from his eyes to get a wider view, but there was still nothing.

And then he saw them. Two snowmobiles were coming up over the ridge from the Pueblo side of the mountain. One of them was pulling a sled covered with a tarp. Howie trained the binoculars on the sled but couldn't make out what it was carrying.

Just as the snowmobiles came over the ridge, the door of the helicopter opened sending shafts of light onto the snow. Howie moved the binoculars back and forth hoping to see what was happening.

As he watched, an improbable figure came out the door of the helicopter and walked down the retractable steps onto the snow.

It was a man. He was dressed in tight orange pants, red ski boots, a blue long-sleeve shirt, and a red baseball hat. The hat had an emblem of a rocket ship with GALACTIC EXPLORERS CLUB written on the front. Around his shoulders he wore a purple cape. A blue mask came down from the hat, two sharply pointed triangles like tears with oval holes for his eyes. He looked like a character from a Marvel comic book.

Howie had to adjust the focus of the binoculars to make certain what he was seeing was real.

Emblazoned on the front of his uniform in fiery orange letters were the words:

CAPTAIN COSMO.

Chapter Twenty-Eight

State Police Patrolman Ted Hirsch had never been in a spot like this, finding himself in a bunker hundreds of feet below ground with a madman billionaire, a blind ex-police commander, his guide dog, a crass billionaire's wife, and a very sexy Hawaiian girl.

They didn't prepare you for situations like this at the Academy.

Jack was obviously bullshitting, improvising a string of suppositions and lies that had no foundation.

What Jack didn't know was that Leonard Hamm had a huge gun on the desk in front of him, a Smith & Wesson Magnum .357 with a 4-inch barrel. The gun was a revolver, showy but powerful. The long barrel wasn't entirely practical and police departments around the country preferred high-capacity semi-automatics such as the Glock. But Hamm obviously loved his big gun. He fingered it from time to time as he listened to Jack.

What Hamm didn't know was that Ted Hirsch had been a student of taekwondo since the age of twelve. His parents had sent him to martial arts classes so he could discover "the non-duality of body and mind," as they put it. Ted hadn't been the best student in these classes, but he wasn't the worst either. He sat next to Jack in an apparently relaxed manner, but he was prepared to strike the second he had the chance. The Magnum had to be considered, but Ted was certain he could handle an aging billionaire, his overweight wife, and a slight Polynesian girl.

He waited.

Meanwhile, Jack was spinning quite a story.

"You see, I've known Danny Gluck since he was a child, so I know how his mind works," Jack was saying. "I'd describe him as a sick genius."

Hamm snorted. "Don't make me laugh! Sick, certainly. But genius, no."

"As I'm sure you know, Mr. Hamm, I was present at that rocket launch, and I can tell you exactly how he made the substitution after deciding not to go on that rocket. He knew what you were planning and he had no intention of dying. A man who called himself Bill Williamson took his place. Williamson was the head of Gluck's security detail, and he was the one who died in that explosion. Blown to smithereens, as you would put it."

"That's impossible," said Hamm. "As I told you, I was monitoring that launch, every fraction of a second of it. It was Gluck on that rocket, I assure you. Listen to me carefully, Mr. Wilder. Gluck was a guy who grew up on comic books. He had the maturity of a 2 year old. It was his life-long dream to go into space and he wouldn't have missed that trip for anything. Even if a substitution was possible, which it wasn't."

"Patience, Hamm. I'll tell you how it was done, but I need to back up a minute. You see, he came to visit me in the middle of the night before the launch. He knew you were going to try something. He wasn't a fool. He gave me a flash drive that he told me to open in the case of his death. It had some interesting material on it."

"Did it?" said Hamm. "So let's hear it. What was on that flash drive?"

"I'll tell you. But first you have to know that he was gaming me, just as he was playing you. That's all it's ever been for Gluck. Games and play. He was never intending to let you kill him, though he wanted me to think he was."

"Wait a second, Wilder—this is getting a little complicated."

"Yes, of course it is. That's what I'm trying to tell you. Gluck has been playing a game within a game, a play within a play."

"No, no, Wilder. You're losing me. What was on that flash drive?"

"It was a photograph of you having sex with your goddaughter, Leilani, when she was a child, maybe nine or ten years old. I was supposed to take the photo to the cops and have you busted. It would send you to prison for a very long time and this would be Gluck's posthumous revenge."

"That's absurd, Wilder. Absolutely absurd! I don't like sex, I never have. It's unhygienic and a waste of valuable energy. Do you think I would have married Gloria if I liked sex? Making money—now, that's *my* idea of an orgasm!"

"Wait a goddamn minute!" cried his wife.

"This whole thing is phony!" said Hamm.

"Of course, it's phony," said Jack. "That's what I'm trying to tell you. The photo was an AI fake. A rather obvious fake, as a matter of fact. But that was also part of the game, you see. I was supposed to see that it was a fake and follow the clues from there. You and I have been pawns on a game board, Hamm."

"No, no, I don't believe any of this. But let's get back to the explosion. You need to tell me how Gluck made this supposed substitution and wasn't on that flight."

"First, you need to understand that all the crew and passengers wore space suits and helmets that were identical. You couldn't tell one from the other."

"I know that, of course. But I had access to all of Gluck's vitals—his body temperature, pulse, blood pressure, respiration, everything. Plus I use a very advanced A-GPS system that told me to the quarter-inch exactly where Gluck was at every moment. And he was in that capsule, I assure you."

"But that's only what your computer told you. It wasn't what was happening on the ground. Danny was messing with you. He was sending you fake information. A lie."

Hamm was silent. "I don't think that's possible," he said after a moment.

"I keep telling you, Danny knows computers inside out. That's what made him rich. He can fake just about anything."

Hamm sat absorbing this. As Ted watched, he could see that the billionaire was going back and forth with the idea. Could Gluck really have fooled him, he wondered? He couldn't quite believe it. And yet . . .

Suddenly a siren in the bunker began to wail.

Hamm grabbed for his phone. "Yes? What's going on?" he demanded. "A helicopter? They're on the mountain? Well, you know what to do. No excuses! Stop those fuckers at any cost!"

There was a wicked smile on Hamm's face. He was enjoying this. But the distraction was costly. He had looked away for a second too long, his Magnum .357 momentarily forgotten on the desk. Ted was already in motion, leaping from his chair, flinging himself at the billionaire.

***

Leonard Hamm wasn't a problem for an athletic young State Patrolman who had studied martial arts. Ted pummeled Hamm backward onto the floor and quickly had him in a hammerlock. Hamm cried in pain.

"You're under arrest, Leonard Hamm!" said Ted. "You have the right to remain silent. Anything you say can and will be used against you in a court of—"

But he hadn't counted on Gloria Hamm. She jumped on Ted from behind and began pulling his hair violently.

"Don't you dare attack my husband!" she screeched.

Ted managed to rise to his feet with Mrs. Hamm hanging on his back. He spun in a circle and threw her off onto the couch where she had been sitting painting her toenails blue.

"Oomph!" she moaned.

Ted turned back toward Hamm who was on his knees reaching into his drawer for another gun. Ted slammed the drawer shut on his hand and sent his knee sharply under his chin. Hamm flew backward against his desk and slid down onto the floor. He didn't move.

Gypsy was barking with all the excitement. Only Jack remained calm, sitting in his wheelchair with a bemused smile.

"Quiet, girl," he told his dog. "Well, that was amazing, Ted."

Ted was too busy to answer. He gathered up the two guns—the Magnum on the desk and a smaller semi-automatic in the drawer. He turned to Leilani in order to see if she was going to be a problem.

"All right," he said, pointing the .357 at her. "If you don't want to spend the next twenty years in prison, you'll behave yourself and do exactly what I say. Is that clear?"

"Yes, sir," she managed in a barely audible whisper.

"Good. Now we want out of this damn bunker right now and you're going to show us the way."

She nodded. "Yes, of course," she said.

"You're going to go first and we'll follow. If there are any guards out there, you're going to tell them to put down their weapons and let us pass or you will be the first to get shot. You don't want to mess with me in the mood I'm in!"

"Please, I only want to be free," she told him. "I had to do what they told me. I'm innocent, I promise. I haven't done anything wrong. You saw how the Hamms treat me. I'm a victim. They've kept me here as their slave."

She gave Ted her most doe-like expression.

"Well, we will see about that," he said more calmly. "If you've been trafficked, these people are going to go to prison for a very long time. Now, let's all of us get out of this bunker. Show us the way."

Leilani walked to a metal door, pressed a four-digit code into a keypad and the door hissed open. They left the Hamms in the room, Gloria moaning on the couch, Leonard starting to move slowly on the floor. The door hissed closed behind them.

There was no one in the reception area.

"Come quickly," Leilani said.

Leilani led the way across the reception room and down a long underground corridor to the elevator. Ted followed pushing Jack in his wheelchair with Gypsy close behind. She pushed another code into a keypad and the elevator opened.

"Get inside quickly!" she told them, standing by the elevator. "There's one more passcode I need to enter."

As soon as Ted, Jack, and Gypsy were inside the elevator, Leilani raised her middle finger at them in an unmistakable gesture and a smirk on her pretty face. The door closed and the elevator lurched upward leaving her behind.

"My God, girls these days!" Ted bemoaned as they rose upward from the bowels of the earth to the world above. "They just don't behave the way they used to!"

"I wonder why," said Jack.

Chapter Twenty-Nine

Howie watched through binoculars in the darkened dispatch office in Ski Patrol's mountain headquarters as Captain Cosmo, standing alongside the helicopter, used a small flashlight to signal the two snowmobiles that had paused on the ridge high above.

He flashed two times, and from the ridge there came a signal in return, also two quick flashes.

Almost immediately, a dozen uniformed soldiers poured out from the helicopter. To Howie's astonishment, they were all dressed alike in tight orange pants, red ski boots, blue long-sleeve shirts, and red baseball hats. Each hat had the emblem of a rocket ship with GALACTIC EXPLORERS CLUB written on the front. Around their shoulders, every one of them wore a purple cape as well as the blue mask that came down over their foreheads in pointed triangles.

Each soldier had an assault rifle strapped to his back. On every chest, emblazoned in fiery orange letters, were the words: CAPTAIN COSMO. There were thirteen Captain Cosmos in all.

But which of them was the real Captain Cosmo, Daniel Gluck? Or was it none of them at all?

Howie lowered the binoculars momentarily overwhelmed. He raised them again quickly when he saw multiple pairs of skis being handed down onto the snow from the helicopter. As with the uniforms, the skis were identical. Howie recognized the skis as Volkl Mantras. Very good German skis, expensive.

Meanwhile the two snowmobiles were making their way down from the ridge line, the lead snowmobile pulling a sled covered with a tarp. The way down from the ridge was steep, but the snowmobiles appeared to know where to go, traversing the easiest descent, zig-zagging back and forth. An expert skier could come down this way in a few minutes, but it would take the snowmobiles much longer. Howie saw that he had maybe as long as seven or eight minutes to come up with a plan. He knew he had to do something, but he didn't know what.

He scanned back and forth several times with the binoculars from the snowmobiles to the helicopter, panning quickly past the snow cat parked outside that partially obscured the view. Whatever these people were doing, they had to be stopped. Somehow he needed to get down the mountain quickly in order to get help. That wouldn't have been a problem if he had his boots and skis. But he didn't.

Howie swung the binoculars back to the snow cat as an idea began to form in his mind.

He wondered if he could operate the monstrous crab-like machine himself. He had watched Sean drive the cat up the mountain, fascinated by all the levers and pedals. He wasn't sure he could do it, but he didn't see any other choice.

"Okay," he said to himself. "What do I have to lose?"

My life was the answer that came immediately to mind.

***

Howie walked back into the main room where Sean was tied up on the floor. He didn't look either comfortable or happy.

"I need the keys to the snow cat, Sean."

"You're not going to try to drive it, are you?"

"I am," said Howie.

"Are you crazy? You'll kill yourself! There's a lot to learn in order to drive one of those machines."

"I'm going to chance it. I watched you as we were coming up the mountain and it looked fairly straight forward to me, not so different from the backhoe I rented when I was building the cabin for my daughter. I understand the basic idea."

"Yeah, but not going up and down a steep mountain on snow! That's a whole different ballgame. Look, why don't you cut me loose and I'll drive it for you."

"I can't do that, Sean. I'm sorry. Now, where's the key?"

"Howie, you can trust me. I feel terrible about this, I really do. But I had to go along with what these people told me. It's my son, Luke. He's been diagnosed with leukemia. I was desperate for money—you've no idea how expensive his treatment is going to be, hundreds of thousands of dollars. He needs to go to a special clinic in Dallas. Just flying him back and forth to Texas is costing a fortune."

"I'm sorry to hear about Luke. But working up here on the Peak all those years, they must give you good medical insurance."

"Are you kidding? The insurance is lousy and there's a huge deductible. It got even worse when Hamm bought the place—the part I pay every month nearly doubled. And now that I've been fired, I don't know what I'm going to do. So when these guys approached me and said they would pay all the bills, there was no way I could say no. They knew everything about Luke's illness, they knew exactly how to get to me. I hated to go along, but I felt like I didn't have a choice."

Howie believed Sean. He was sympathetic, but only up to a point.

"It all started last summer and it didn't seem such a big deal at first. Right before the start of the season, they asked me to hire Matt Wilson. Matt seemed like he would be a good member of the team, so I thought why not? But then they began pressing me to do more and more stuff."

"So you knew the whole time that Wilson planted that device on Tower 7?"

"No, they kept me in the dark as much as possible. But of course, I suspected it was Matt."

"Was it Matt who fired the dart that killed Tomás?"

"I don't know for certain. For chrissake, I didn't *want* to know! But I don't think it was Matt. I think it was the albino guy who called himself Skull. He's the scariest guy I've ever met! I saw him on skis maybe half an hour before the lift stopped. I think Tomás was on to them somehow. A few days before he was killed, he caught Skull and Matt talking together at Tower 7 making plans. Tomás was up in the nest at Tower 8 and they didn't see him at first, so maybe he heard some of their conversation."

"That's why Tomás was killed? He knew too much?"

"I don't know how much he knew for certain. But I know Skull was worried. He came up to me later that afternoon and asked a lot of questions about Tomás, who he was, if he was married and had kids, stuff like that. It was kind of weird, like he was looking for leverage. Howie, I should have said something, I know that. I deliberately looked the other way. I love this mountain. I liked Tomás. But what could I do?"

What could he do? Howie wondered what *he* would do if Georgie's life was in danger. He could only shake his head and remind himself that Tomás Romero had a family too.

Howie walked back to the window and raised the binoculars to see how things were progressing outside. The two snowmobiles with the sled were making their way slowly down from the ridge, moving very carefully. One wrong move would send them tumbling down the mountain out of control. The thirteen Cosmos were standing by the helicopter watching the descent. Howie sensed their operation was in limbo until the snowmobiles were safely down.

"Look, I'd like to make amends," Sean offered. "I don't know what you're planning, but why don't you untie me and I'll help. I mean, we've known each other for years. You know you can trust me."

Howie turned back to Sean. He could use Sean's help, but trust had vanished when he saw the barrel of Sean's Glock pointed his way.

"I can't take the chance, Sean. I'm sorry. Now tell me where the key is. I don't have time to argue with you."

"It's in my right pocket. But for chrissake, Moon Deer, be careful. If you kill yourself in that machine, I'll feel even worse than I do already!"

"I wouldn't feel so hot myself," Howie agreed.

With the key in hand, Howie returned to the dispatch room, raised the binoculars, and saw that the two snowmobiles had arrived alongside the helicopter. Four of the Captain Cosmos were untying the tarp that covered the sled they had been pulling. When they pulled back the tarp, Howie's breath caught.

His first impression was that the sled was carrying a bazooka or some kind of cannon. But as he adjusted the focus on the binoculars, he realized it wasn't a bazooka, it was a missile launcher. Not the shoulder launched kind, it was bigger than that. It would need to be assembled. It sat in several pieces with a metal tripod folded up alongside it. There was a wood crate next to the tripod that probably contained the missiles.

Howie was shocked. These cartoon characters were about to launch a serious military assault on the ski resort. He knew he needed to get down the mountain to warn the people below. But there wasn't time for that. There was no help here but himself. Somehow he had to stop the attack, and he had to do it now.

***

The night was dark, but not dark enough. The snow had a natural phosphorescence that showed everything in relief. With the moon high in the southwest sky, Howie knew he would be a moving target the moment he stepped out of Patrol headquarters.

But it had to be done.

Staying low, he crept out of the building onto an icy wooden porch, then down onto the snow. From here he lowered himself onto his hands and knees and crawled toward the snow cat. Every muscle in Howie's body was tight with anxiety as he made his way across the open stretch of snow, expecting a bullet at any moment. So far, luck was with him. The Cosmos hadn't seen him. He stood up behind the protective bulk of the cat relieved to find himself still alive.

With no time to lose, he climbed up over the treads onto the back platform and made his way up into the cab. He sat in the driver's seat and studied the pedals and levers trying to remember what Sean had done. The snow cat was a lot more complicated than the backhoe he had rented. At least, some of the levers were clearly labelled. He found the one that raised and lowered the curled front blade. He hoped it was made from good steel, otherwise he was going to be in trouble.

From the cab he saw that the Captain Cosmos were gathered around the sled assembling the missile launcher. He needed to move quickly now if he was going to stop them. His plan was to charge at them with the snow cat, jumping off the cat at the last minute. If he was lucky, he could roll into the trees just below where the helicopter was parked. Howie was counting on the fact that he knew these woods much better than the Cosmos. There was a hidden spot where he had often stopped to pee. Not the most discreet bathroom, perhaps, but real bathrooms were far away.

Howie rested Sean's gun in his lap. It was a Glock and he believed he knew how to use it. He took a deep breath. Now came the dangerous part.

He turned the key, pressed the ignition button, and the snow cat coughed to life with a growl of its diesel engine. He raised the front blade just in time as the first bullet zinged off the steel. There was no time now for second thoughts. He put the cat into its forward gear, worked the foot pedal and the two steering arms and lurched forward, driving blind with the raised snow blade blocking his view. He headed full throttle to where the sled sat on the snow a few feet in front of the helicopter. He hoped he was on course.

The terrain was uneven and it was wild ride. He reeled from side to side as a hail of bullets ricocheted off the front blade, some of them hitting the cab. Howie stayed low in the seat. There was a pop as a bullet passed through the front window. He managed to lay sideways onto the passenger seat with his foot on the pedal as he climbed up a slight incline at the blazing speed of 14 mph, bullets like busy bees zinging into the snow cat.

The crash when it came was jarring. In his blind charge, he missed the sled but had collided with the helicopter instead, sending it rolling onto its side. With its huge treads and powerful engine, the cat had the advantage. But the collision had sent him off course. The cat was lurching downhill at a steep angle. An alarm sounded letting him know that he was in trouble. His only option now was to get out before the cat careened into a tree or over a cliff. He opened the passenger door and leaped over the metal platform onto the snow.

He was lucky to land in soft snow rather than on a rock. But as he stood up sputtering, he saw he was in worse trouble still. There was a single Captain Cosmo standing on the snow twenty feet above him with his rifle raised in Howie's direction.

Howie faced death with incredulity. He had no way to defend himself. He had lost the Glock somewhere in the snow. *This really is it*, he said to himself. The big moment. The end.

It seemed to take a very long time for the rifle that was about to kill him to get a good bead on him. But before the man could fire, there was a loud gunshot from a higher elevation on the ridge. The Cosmo threw his rifle into the air, arched backward, and fell lifeless onto the snow.

Howie looked up and saw three small figures on the ridge high above. He had no idea who they were, but they had arrived just in time. One of them, at least, was a very good shot.

But there was no time to waste. Below him, the twelve surviving Captain Cosmos were already skiing down the mountain in a formation, six on each side of the two snowmobiles that rode between them. The snowmobile on the right pulled the sled that carried the missile launcher. It didn't appear to be fully assembled. Howie's charge had at least done that much. He had slowed them down.

Howie waved to the figures on the ridge to express his thanks and then hurried on foot across the snow, running as fast as he could in the deep snow toward the abandoned snow bike that was leaning against the Patrol building.

The bike offered the last chance he would have to stop the attack.

***

John Concha, the War Chief, stood high on the ridge with a rifle cradled in his arms. He looked down with disbelief at the valley below with the helicopter on its side and the huge snow cat tumbled upside down against a stand of large fir trees.

He shook his head. "This is pretty damn crazy!" he said to the two tribal cops who were standing alongside him. He was still on Pueblo land and wasn't sure he wanted to go any further. Meanwhile, he had backup. Two more snowmobiles were coming up behind him.

"John!" cried Georgie as she ran the final distance to where he stood. The snow was packed from where the snowmobiles had passed earlier, but she lost her footing and fell. It only stopped her for a few seconds. She picked herself up and ran the rest of the way.

"John! I heard shots! What's happening?" she demanded.

He turned to her and resisted the temptation to take her in his arms.

"It's your father," he said. "I was able to get him out of a dicey situation. I wouldn't have done it for anyone else but your dad. But you'll never guess what he's doing now."

"What?" she asked. "Tell me!"

"He got on a bicycle and took off down the mountain."

"A bicycle?" Georgie was bewildered. "You can't ride a bicycle down a ski slope!"

"Well, that's what Moon Deer did. And let me tell you, he was flying!"

Chapter Thirty

Howie tried not to panic as he felt himself accelerating down the mountain on the ski bicycle.

The handlebars didn't turn the way an ordinary bike did. He had to lean one way or the other in order to engage the edge of the mono ski to make a turn. Howie had hopped on the bike without thinking, using his feet to get himself started. He headed down Thunder Road, an intermediate trail with several steep sections that in other resorts would be considered black diamonds. He knew he had to hurry. The convoy of two snowmobiles and twelve Captain Cosmos had already vanished downhill.

Thunder Road was deceptively easy for a hundred yards until it came over a rise and took a steep dive for nearly half a mile before it came to a flat plateau where the trail split in two.

Howie did well at first. He had watched lifties ride these bikes, so he knew to drag his feet in the snow to slow down. If the trail had only continued its gentle descent, he would have been fine. But when the easy stretch of the trail ended and Thunder Road took a steep dive, he quickly found himself flying down the mountain out of control.

He put his heels down into the snow to slough off speed but this threw him off balance. The bike swerved to the right and fell out from under him. With a cry, Howie tumbled onto the snow and slid another dozen feet before he managed to stop. Luckily the bike hadn't gone far. It was lying on its side just below him on the slope.

He had to give it another try, there was no other option. He needed to catch up with the armed convoy and the huge weapon they were carrying. He didn't know what he was going to do when he reached them, but he knew he had to do something. He wished he hadn't lost Sean's Glock.

Howie climbed down to the ski bike, straddled the seat, and set off again.

He adopted a new strategy, traversing across the hill at a slightly downward angle. But now he was going too slowly. He reached the flat plateau where the trails separated, and he stopped to examine the snow. The snowmobile tracks went off to the left onto an intermediate run, Hurricane Harry, named after a legendary ski instructor from the early days of San Geronimo Peak.

"Well, here goes!" he said aloud, a kind of prayer.

Howie headed straight down the fall line, throwing caution aside, knowing he had no more time to lose. He would simply jump off if he found himself heading toward a tree. The snow was still soft from the last storm so probably he would survive.

He was flying down Hurricane Harry, barely hanging on, when he saw the two snowmobiles and the Captain Cosmos several hundred yards below him. They had taken the missile launcher off the sled and were setting it up on its tripod on a flat stretch of snow. One of the Cosmos was carrying a tube-like missile with fins from the wooden crate and sliding it into the barrel of the weapon. From where they were setting up, they would have an unobstructed shot to the base area nearly a mile below where the Hamm House sat prominently at the edge of the snow.

They hadn't seen Howie yet. They were looking the wrong way, downhill rather than up. One of the Cosmos was figuring the angle and the distance to the target on a tablet, tapping the numbers into the instrument panel on the side of the launcher. Two of the men were on their knees in the snow making certain the tripod was stable. The others were entirely focused on the hotel.

Howie came rushing down behind them. If he ever had a plan, it wasn't possible to have one now. Gravity was in command. Leaning slightly to his right, he was able to correct his course so that he and his bike were heading directly toward the rear end of the launcher. At the speed he was going, the collision was only seconds away.

The wind was in his ears. Howie was moving so fast the mono ski barely touched the snow.

The Captain Cosmos had finished their set up, the calculations done. They stepped back a few feet and put their hands over their ears. They saw Howie and his flying bicycle only at the last second, too late to get out of the way.

Howie jumped off the bike when he was less than twenty feet away. The bike continued on its own, smacking hard into the back of the tripod a millisecond before the missile fired.

There was a loud explosion from the weapon but the collision had altered the missile's trajectory. Instead of racing downward toward the hotel, the missile whooshed upward into the sky leaving behind a trail of white smoke. It reached its apex high above the mountain where it slowed, reversed its course, and headed down to where it had come.

As for Howie, he and his bike had been traveling at nearly 50 mph when he jumped off onto the snow, landing on his back. From here, he became a fast-moving human sled. He hit one of the Captain Cosmos from behind, knocking the man's legs out from under him, and continued his slide. The snow was groomed and slippery and his speed kept increasing as he raced down a steep stretch of the trail.

Howie tried to flip over onto his stomach to self-arrest. This was an important move for anyone who skied on steep terrain. Get over onto your stomach, head uphill, legs down, and dig your boots into the snow. But Howie was going too fast. He couldn't do it.

He was aware of gunfire, people shooting at him from above. But the speed he was traveling, flat on the snow, made him an impossible target. That was the good news.

The bad news was he was out of control and there were trees, rocks, and cliffs below where he was sliding.

He hit a bump and suddenly he was airborne.

It seemed to Howie that he flew a very long way. It was a pleasant sensation to be free of gravity, flying through the air with the greatest of ease. He wished he had wings. But he knew that what went up, came down.

With a cry he landed on his back in a soft cloud of snow.

He heard an explosion from behind him, higher up the mountain. The missile, he thought dreamily. It had risen into the air and had come down, he knew not where. He remembered a poem like this from his childhood.

He didn't care, really, one way or the other. It had nothing to do with him anymore. He had done his part, he could do no more. His leg hurt but that didn't matter either.

Nothing mattered. He was exhausted, he was finished, and now he could rest. The snow was soft and wonderful.

He heard an orchestra of sirens coming from somewhere far below. The sirens wailed, rising and falling. Dozens of sirens that grew in volume as they climbed the twisty highway from the desert into the mountains.

Gazing up into the sky Howie saw that dawn had broken. The clouds on the eastern horizon burst into flame, a celestial red that was beyond the imagination of man.

It was morning, a new day.

Chapter Thirty-One

On the last day of February—Leap Year—Jack Wilder sat on the porch in his backyard throwing a slobbery tennis ball for Gypsy to run and fetch, her favorite game.

Spring was still some weeks away and it was a cold grey morning. Jack was bundled up in a bulky goose down jacket over his at-home sweatpants, sweatshirt, and oversized wool sweater that Emma had knitted for him years ago. As Gypsy ran back and forth, he pondered an ethical question that had been worrying him for the past several days.

Two days earlier, a mysterious sum of money, $100,000, had been deposited in his checking account. It was Emma who had noticed the deposit. She handled all their finances. As a general rule, Jack had no idea how much money they had—or didn't have—in their various accounts. He kept a blissful distance from such practical matters.

"Jack, a hundred thousand dollars just popped up in your checking account! Where in God's name did that come from?"

He had shrugged, unconcerned. "I don't know, Emma. Maybe it's a tax return."

"Jack, don't be ridiculous. It's *not* a tax return!"

"Then it's a dividend of some kind. Don't we own some stock somewhere? You know I really don't concern myself about these things. I like to keep my mind focused on more important things."

"Sure, like who murdered whom. But this isn't a dividend! You need to float back down to Earth, Jack, and tell me what's going on. $100,000 is a lot of money."

"It's not as much as it used to be. Why, you can hardly buy a car these days for a hundred grand."

"Oh, Jack! I swear, someday I'm going to strangle you!"

Jack liked it when Emma used words like "whom." She was better educated than he was, with a B.A. from U Cal Berkeley and a masters in library science from San Francisco State. He loved his wife and was amazed—and grateful—that she put up with him.

"Okay, I'll look into it. I'll call the bank."

Jack did look into it. He called his bank, but they could tell him very little, only that the money was in fact real, $100,000 from an unknown source that had been deposited electronically into his account. With a bit of detective work Jack discovered that the money had been sent from a mysterious company that called itself The United Yak Breeders Fund of Nepal, a bank that did not appear to exist on any list of global financial concerns.

Jack couldn't help but smile. He knew, of course, where the money had come from. There was only one individual he knew who could come up with something as crazy as the United Yak Breeders Fund of Nepal. The following day his suspicions were confirmed. A no-reply email arrived without any information concerning its source. Not even Nancy, his super smart computer, could tell him where it had come from.

The email, written in capital letters, was brief: WANTED TO MAKE YOU A MILLIONAIRE BUT KNEW YOU WOULDN'T LIKE THAT. THOUGHT THE LOWER AMOUNT WOULD BE ACCEPTABLE TO YOUR MORAL SCRUPLES. HOPE SO. NOT TOO MUCH, NOT TOO LITTLE, BUT OFFERED WITH LIFELONG GRATITUDE. LONG LIVE JOE MONTANA!

Gratitude for what, he didn't really know. He sensed he should send the money back. But send it where? And to who . . . whom?

The affair between Leonard Hamm and Danny Gluck had left a bad taste in his mouth and remained unresolved. Three men had been killed on San Geronimo Peak in January during the aborted attack: one near the overturned helicopter and two on the ski slope from the missile as it fell back to earth, landing in nearly the same spot it had been launched from. Howie's bizarre efforts to thwart the attack had been successful. Two other Captain Cosmos had been injured, but the rest had somehow vanished.

Meanwhile, when the State Police with help from the FBI raided the underground bunker, they found it empty. In further investigation, a tunnel was discovered, an escape hatch that went from the bunker to the edge of the parking lot. Leonard Hamm, his wife, and Leilani had vanished.

Danny Gluck's fate was also uncertain. He might have been incinerated in the rocket explosion, but perhaps not. No DNA had been recovered from the explosion, there was no evidence either way. Nor was it known if Danny had been present in January among the fighters dressed as Captain Cosmo. After two months of investigation, no criminal charges had been filed against either Gluck or Hamm. Everything they did had been managed indirectly through several layers of intermediaries and nothing could be traced to either of them. When you had enough money, it seemed that you could get away with just about anything.

Jack found this all very unsatisfying. The billionaires had their battle of egos, two dinosaurs thrashing it out, leaving others to pay the price. The criminal investigations would continue, probably for years, but by the end of February only one person had been arrested, Sean Basset, charged with conspiracy to commit homicide. Despite Hamm's absence, the ski resort had reopened under the auspices of his Wall Street company, the Jupiter Group Capital Management.

Though the lifts were running, Howie no longer skied. He had broken his right leg sliding down the mountain and for the past month had been hobbling around on crutches, his leg in a cast.

Meanwhile, Santo was also hobbling about on crutches, his left leg in a cast.

Jack laughed as he took the slobbery ball from Gypsy's mouth. "We're going to outlive them all, aren't we, girl?"

He tried not to rub it in, but he gloated just a little to be the only one of the team who wasn't in a cast. Not counting Georgie, of course. She was doing fine. It worried him a little that she had hooked up with John Concha, but that was her business.

As for Jack, the only question he had was what was he going to do with the $100,000.

After a few more throws, Jack kept hold of the tennis ball and gave Gypsy's furry neck a vigorous rub.

"So what would you say to a nice vacation in Hawaii, my friend? Emma needs some time off, too. It'll be a second honeymoon. We'll stay at a 5-star hotel on the North Shore and have a great time. You'll love the beach, the white sand that goes on forever. You'll be able to run and chase sticks like there's no tomorrow! We'll drink champagne and lie in the sun and spend money like it's water! What do you say?"

Gypsy wagged her tail enthusiastically. Which in doggie language meant: "Sounds good to me, Jack. Can't wait! Let's hop on a jet and go!"

***

In early March, Howie flew to Berlin in order to be with Claire.

He flew business class, so he'd have more room for the colorful cast on his right leg. Georgie had written all over it with magic markers, drawing flowers and hearts and funny sayings. MAKE LOVE NOT WAR was written in large colored letters up and down the front, causing Howie to worry slightly about going through passport control and the looks he might get in the airport. He left Georgie in charge of the office, glad to escape from San Geronimo for a few weeks.

He had been in Berlin before on short visits, always to see Claire, but it wasn't a city he knew well. Berlin wasn't beautiful like Paris or Rome. There was construction everywhere and though there were many pleasant neighborhoods, much of the city was industrial and grim. Yet it was a fascinating place, full of energy and stylish young people, a polyglot metropolis teeming with refugees and artists, entrepreneurs and diplomats from all over the globe. For Claire, Berlin was the music capitol of Europe and she had been spending more and more time there.

In the last month, Howie had taken a long look at himself, and he wasn't pleased with what he saw.

How could he have been so wrong about Leilani? How could he have been so wrong about Sean? Leilani certainly hadn't turned out to be a damsel in distress. He still didn't know if they'd had sex that night she doped him with her "special" mai-tai. All in all, he was left feeling foolish and embarrassed, not the person he wanted to be.

He arrived in Berlin determined to resolve his relationship with Claire. They couldn't go on this way, separated for months at a time. Either he had to break with her, or they needed to be together as a couple. He had resisted coming to this conclusion, but it was clear to him now.

Claire had rented an Airbnb apartment on a quiet street that bordered the Tiergarten, the huge park in central Berlin. It was an expensive neighborhood but Claire could afford it. She was making serious money as a rising classical music star. Unfortunately, that was something else that separated them. In order to do the work she loved, she needed to be in large cities like Berlin. And Howie, for the work he loved—and sometimes hated—he needed to be in San Geronimo.

She didn't meet him at the airport because she had a rehearsal. But she was at the apartment when he walked in the door and greeted him effusively.

She laughed when she saw the artwork on his cast.

"Oh, Howie, I've missed you so much!" she cried, melting into his arms. "I've so much to tell you, but not now. I can't wait a second more. You look good enough to eat and I'm dragging you off to bed!"

Howie was taken aback. "Yes, we do need to talk, Claire."

"We do. And we'll talk our heads off, I promise. But later. You're looking at a sex starved woman."

"Really?"

"Yes, really," she said as she took his hand and led him into the bedroom.

Howie had built a wall in his head between himself and Claire, but—as with Berlin itself—it was astonishing how quickly that wall came down. For the next few days, they did little talking but they laughed and played, went out occasionally for romantic dinners in cozy restaurants, and stayed in bed much of the time. The cast required some creative positioning, but it didn't really get in the way.

Howie had almost forgotten how much he loved Claire, and how he loved being with her. She was so unabashedly alive. She seemed to him the miracle of life itself. The darkness that had enveloped him over the past month evaporated like a mist when the sun came out. When Claire smiled at him, poof! —it was gone.

It wasn't until four days later that they were settled enough to have a real talk. It was a sunny day, blue sky overhead, the first real day of spring, and they took a long walk along the endless gravel paths of the Tiergarten. The whole city seemed to feel the shift of seasons, emerging from winter to get outside and jog, bicycle, walk, sit in outdoor cafés with the sun in their faces.

They needed to walk slowly because Howie was on crutches, but slow was the mood they were in.

"So, how was Jack's vacation in Hawaii?" she asked.

"Oh, he and Emma had a great time. Gypsy too, by the sound of it. They went for two weeks, that's all Emma could take off from the library, and even at a five-star hotel, they only managed to go through $20,000 of the mystery money that was deposited in his account. You heard about that, didn't you?"

"I did. Georgie told me."

"So that left $80,000. And you know what Jack did with that? He gave it away."

"Really? *Jack?*"

"With Emma and Georgie's prodding, of course. Still, I think Jack enjoyed doing it. He looks like Santa Claus, so why not play the part?"

Claire laughed. "This is amazing! So tell me, how did he get rid of $80,000?"

"Well, there were plenty of choices, many good causes. But he decided to go local. He divided it between the three food banks in San Geronimo—St. Cecelia's church that serves free lunches five days a week, the Open Hand that gives out boxes of food once a week, and a new group that gathers food from restaurants and supermarkets that would be thrown away otherwise. They were able to buy a new truck with the money Jack gave them. All these places have long lines of hungry people hoping to be fed."

"Good for Jack! I never really saw him as the philanthropic type."

"Well, it was Georgie who told him the statistics. Rather forcefully, I might add. You know what she's like. While private jets fly in and out of San Geronimo and someone like Leonard Hamm can spend 100 million dollars to build a hotel where the cheapest room is $700 a night, the child poverty rate in the county is 26.6 percent. 15.2 percent of the children in San Geronimo suffer from chronic food insecurity. For many of these kids, the only meal they get once a day is the free lunch at the public schools."

Claire shook her head. "It's horrible to think of children going hungry! I'm so glad Jack could help. Now, tell me about your accident," she said. "When you broke your leg. I didn't want to ask before, I didn't want you to think about it. But, my God, how long did you lie there in the snow before you were rescued?"

"It wasn't that long, really. Georgie found me. Believe it or not, she scooted down from the ridge on her butt in order to get to me. She followed the ruts of the snowmobile tracks which probably saved her from a bad fall. It scares me half to death thinking about it."

"Oh, Georgie! What a wonderful daughter you have! By the way, I had an email from her this morning," Claire said. "I'm so glad for her. It seems she's found herself a new love."

Georgie didn't confide such things to Howie, but of course he knew about John Concha. "I hope it works out for her. John's quite a bit older, you know."

"Oh, I think it's great, Howie. She's very happy. They aren't living together but she sees him nearly every night. Don't you like him?" she asked when she noticed the glum look on his face.

"Like him? I don't know. I respect him, certainly. But he's kind of scary, actually, not the sort of man I thought she'd be attracted to."

"You mean he's not the sensitive intellectual type?"

"No, not exactly that. Sensitive intellectual types can be a real pain in the ass. But John Concha . . . there's something brutal about him. You know, he was in a special ops group in Afghanistan. He's not someone you'd want to mess with."

"Well, that's good, isn't it? Don't you think Georgie can hold her own? She's quite a fierce young woman."

"Yes, I suppose so," said Howie. "Still . . ."

His words trailed off.

"Still what?"

"I don't know, Claire. I'm worried about her, that's all. Sometimes I think I shouldn't have encouraged her to get her private eye license. The whole thing is just too dangerous, and if anything ever happened to her, I don't know what I'd do."

"That isn't entirely up to you, Howie. This is Georgie's choice, what she wants to do. And life involves risk, whatever you do."

"Sure, of course. But sometimes risk gets a little too close for comfort. I didn't tell you, but she came pretty close to getting shot. She was the secretary for a group on the Pueblo that called itself Forest Friends. They were organizing to stop the ski resort from building a restaurant on the top of San Geronimo Peak overlooking Indian land. At their first meeting, an Anglo woman who called herself Julie North came up to Georgie claiming to be a journalist from CNN. She said she wanted to interview Georgie about Forest Friends but when they went outside to talk, she admitted she was a special agent with the FBI. It's all a bit complicated—I'll tell you about it sometime. Basically, the Bureau was investigating a rogue security company in Los Angeles and two of their operatives had been spotted in San Geronimo having conversations with one of the Forest Friends, a guy by the name of Pete Day Rise."

Howie summarized the case as briefly as possible: the feud between two billionaires, and the private armies that had been hired to do each other harm.

"The whole thing was ridiculous, Claire, a gross comedy—these two rich egomaniacs trying to get the better of each other. But it was a deadly game, and it appears that Julie North was starting to be a problem. They didn't want the FBI getting in the way of their fun, so they shot her. Georgie was standing right next to the woman when it happened and it's a miracle she wasn't shot as well. It just about gives me heart failure when I think about it!"

"That's terrible, Howie. Georgie didn't tell me anything like this."

"She wouldn't. She managed to crawl away into the sagebrush and got away. The body disappeared and it still hasn't been found. The killers didn't want to leave behind any trace of what happened, but according to Jack, the FBI has concluded that she's dead. There are millions of places in New Mexico where you can stash a body and it will never be found."

"Howie, I can see why you're worried about Georgie—I mean, I worry about you when you're off on these cases. But both you and Georgie are adults, and I know only you can decide what you're going to do with your one wild and precious life."

"That's a nice way of putting it."

"It's Mary Oliver. My favorite poet at the moment."

"The irony is that the revolving restaurant isn't going to be built after all. The Forest Service has turned down the application for a permit and it doesn't look like the ski resort is going to pursue the matter. Both Hamm and Gluck have vanished, God knows where. They've gotten off scott free, leaving behind some dead bodies and other people to pay the price."

"Surely the police are looking for them."

"Well, they're looking but they probably won't be charged with any crimes. Not unless some new evidence turns up. Believe it or not, there's nothing that connects them directly to any of the crimes. They were each very careful to distance themselves and let others take the blame. And that's what really pisses me off. The world has let itself be taken over by billionaires. If you have enough money you can get away with anything."

"Isn't that the way it's always been? The rich will live, and the poor will die."

"It wasn't that way with my people, Claire. The Lakota. We have our problems, sure. But our lives have never been about power and money. What we seek is harmony between man and the natural world."

"I know you do. Georgie understands that, too. That's why she's in New Mexico finding her Native roots. That's probably why she's with John Concha. Now, let's sit down, Howie. I have something I need to tell you."

***

Howie sat next to Claire on a faded dark green park bench by the side of the gravel path. He felt a wave of apprehension. Claire was about to break up with him, he was sure of it. On the far side of the path, a large black bird sat on the branch of a tree looking down on him with knowing eyes. "You poor human, you can't even fly!" the bird seemed to say.

"Is that a raven?" Howie asked, pointing at the bird.

"It's probably a crow," she told him. "I don't think there are ravens in Berlin."

"It's awfully large to be a crow, Claire."

"Howie, listen to me," she said, taking his hand. "I've decided to make some big changes in my life."

He turned his attention from the black bird to Claire, watching her carefully.

"I haven't been happy in Berlin, Howie. It's taken me some time to really look at my life and understand what's wrong. There are many musicians I know who love trotting around the planet performing for big crowds. If you can manage it, it's a glamorous life full of culture and money and applause. But it's just not me. I get lost so easily in the travel and the exhaustion of being with so many people all the time. It drains me. It's too rich for my soul. I'm just not cut out for it. I need to have my feet on the Earth, not on marble floors."

"But you love music, Claire."

"Yes, I love music. But music for me is something inside that disappears when there's too much noise and confusion. I can only feel music when there's silence in my life. Do you understand?"

"I do. Really, I do. But what are you saying?"

"I'm saying that I've decided to leave Berlin and come back to live with you in New Mexico. Would that be all right, Howie? You have to tell me honestly."

"All right?" he cried. His entire body felt as though he was lit from inside, rising like a hot air balloon. "I'd love to have you back with me on the land!"

She laughed, her smile full of joy. "Oh, yes! I want that too. So, here's what I've done. I've spoken with Sol, and we've agreed that I'll finish my commitments for the next six weeks here in Germany and Amsterdam. But after that, we're going to cancel all the other dates."

Sol Weintraub was Claire's manager in New York. "He can do that?"

"Yes. It's going to cost some money but he's agreed. We're going to say that I'm ill and need a long rest. Which is close to the truth."

"But won't you be bored in San Geronimo without your career?"

"Not at all. Here's what I'm going to do. I'm going to join a string quartet in Santa Fe. I'll be able to commute from San Geronimo. It's only an hour and a half away. There are many very talented musicians in New Mexico, quite a number of us. Sometimes New Mexico doesn't seem entirely real. It sort of shimmers in its enchantment. It's a refuge, a place to hide out while the world goes mad. It's what I need, Howie. And you know what else I'm going to do?"

"What?" he asked breathlessly.

"I'm going to teach music."

"What a good idea! You'll have students lining up to take master classes with you in Santa Fe."

"No, I'm not talking about master classes, Howie. I don't want to teach adults at all. I want to teach music to children."

Howie's mouth fell open with astonishment.

"Why, that's wonderful . . . children! I don't know what to say! I love you so much!"

"And I love you, too. Now there's something else we need to talk about."

Howie knew what that something was, because it had been a bone of contention between them for years. He knew it was his turn to speak.

"Listen, Claire. I'm just an ordinary guy. Sort of bumbling much of the time. Good God, a private detective! It's barely respectable. But would you . . . I mean could you . . ."

Even now he had trouble getting it out. The words, the final commitment, the fear of rejection.

"Here's what I'm trying to say, why don't we get married?"

There were tears in her eyes. "Yes! I will marry you, Howard Moon Deer. I most certainly will!"

"That's an actual yes?" he asked, barely believing his good fortune.

"Yes, it is! Yes!"

They held each other. Their lips met in a long, enduring kiss.

The large black raven looked down on the bench below. He croaked twice, which might have been laughter. Then he stepped off the branch into the empty air, spread his wings, and flew into the pale blue sky.

About the Author

Robert Westbrook is the author of two critically acclaimed mystery series, including *Ancient Enemy,* nominated for a Shamus Award as the Best P.I. Novel of 2002, and *Intimate Lies,* a memoir detailing the relationship between his mother, Hollywood columnist Sheilah Graham and the author F. Scott Fitzgerald, published by HarperCollins in 1995. His first novel, *The Magic Garden of Stanley Sweetheart*, was made into an MGM movie. Robert lives with his wife, Gail, in northern New Mexico. Visit Robert at www.robertwestbrook.com.

Upcoming New Release!

FLOATING MOON
A Howard Moon Deer Mystery
Book 11
by
ROBERT WESTBROOK

They call themselves the Smarties—five upscale trophy wives who meet once a week for lunch in fashionable Santa Fe and decide to start an exclusive escort service. They hope to add spark to their privileged lives, but no one must find out, especially not their wealthy older husbands. It will be most refined, sexual pleasure inspired by the geishas of medieval Japan. Quite Zen, really.

But what begins as a lark quickly turns deadly. When a body is found in a hot tub in San Geronimo, the detective team of Jack Wilder and Howard Moon Deer find themselves embroiled in a dangerous quagmire of murder, blackmail, high fashion, celebrities, politics, and those who will go to any length to keep their dark secrets from the light of exposure.

**For more information
visit: www.SpeakingVolumes.us**

Now Available!
ROBERT WESTBROOK'S
HOWARD MOON DEER MYSTERIES
BOOKS 1 – 9

 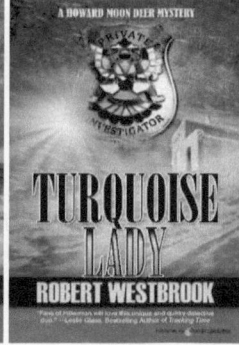 

**For more information
visit:** www.SpeakingVolumes.us

Now Available!
MICAH S. HACKLER'S
SHERIFF LANSING MYSTERIES
BOOKS 1 – 11

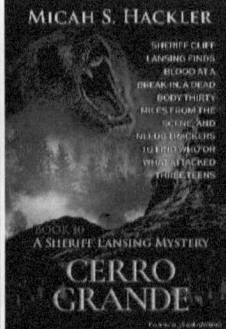

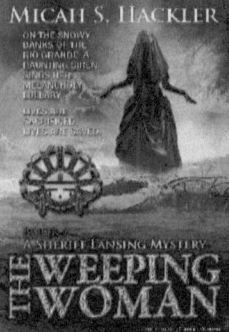

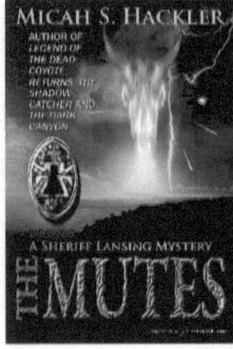

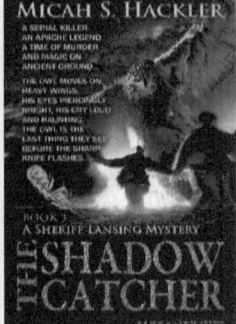

For more information
visit: www.SpeakingVolumes.us

Now Available!

DICK BROWN'S
UNDER THE CANYON SKY SERIES
BOOKS 1 – 3

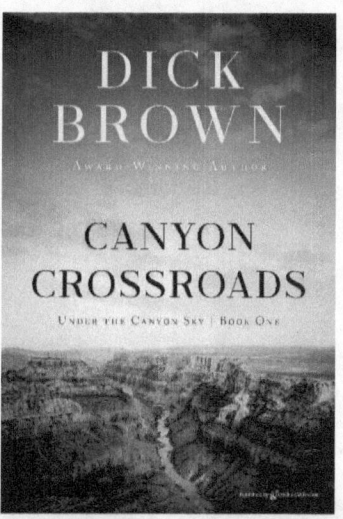
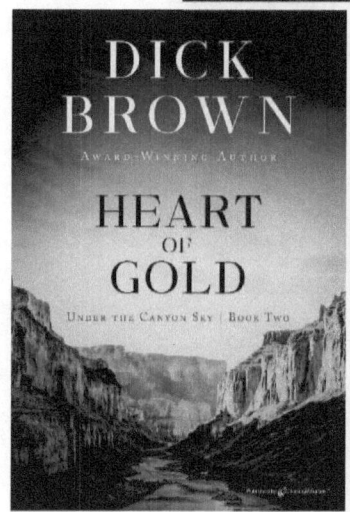
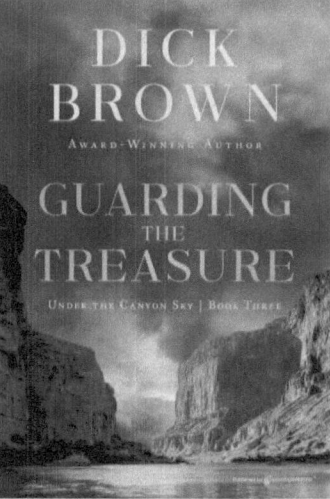

**For more information
visit: www.SpeakingVolumes.us**

Now Available!
AWARD WINNING AUTHOR
MARK WARREN

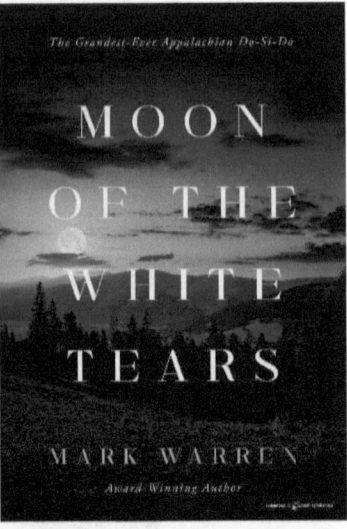

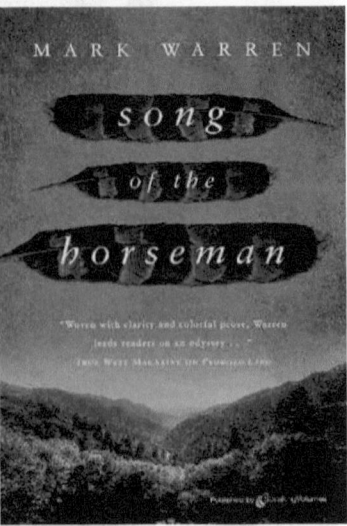

For more information
visit: www.SpeakingVolumes.us

www.ingramcontent.com/pod-product-compliance
Lightning Source LLC
LaVergne TN
LVHW091625070526
838199LV00044B/947